Edmund Bertram's Diary

EDMUND BERTRAM'S DIARY

AMANDA GRANGE

THORNDIKE
CHIVERS

This Large Print edition is published by Thorndike Press, Waterville, Maine, USA and by BBC Audiobooks Ltd, Bath, England.

Thorndike Press, a part of Gale, Cengage Learning.

Copyright © 2007 by Amanda Grange.

The moral right of the author has been asserted.

ALL RIGHTS RESERVED

The text of this Large Print edition is unabridged.

Other aspects of the book may vary from the original edition.

Set in 16 pt. Plantin.

Printed on permanent paper.

LIBRARY OF CONGRESS CATALOGING-IN-PUBLICATION DATA

Grange, Amanda.
    Edmund Bertram's diary / by Amanda Grange.
      p. cm. — (Thorndike Press large print clean reads)
    ISBN-13: 978-1-4104-1300-0 (alk. paper)
    ISBN-10: 1-4104-1300-4 (alk. paper)
    1. Cousins—Fiction. 2. Country homes—Fiction. 3. Social classes—Fiction. 4. Brothers and sisters—Fiction. 5. England—Fiction. 6. Diary fiction. 7. Domestic fiction. 8. Large type books. I. Title.
    PR6107.R35E36 2009
    823'.92—dc22
                                  2009001660

BRITISH LIBRARY CATALOGUING-IN-PUBLICATION DATA AVAILABLE

Published in 2009 in the U.S. by arrangement with The Berkley Publishing Group, a member of Penguin Group (USA) Inc.

Published in 2009 in the U.K. by arrangement with Robert Hale Ltd.

U.K. Hardcover: 978 1 408 43198 6 (Chivers Large Print)
U.K. Softcover: 978 1 408 43199 3 (Camden Large Print)

Printed in the United States of America
1 2 3 4 5 6 7 13 12 11 10 09

EDMUND BERTRAM'S DIARY

■ ■ ■ ■

1800

■ ■ ■ ■

JULY

Tuesday 8 July

Tom was eager to try out his new horse's paces and so we rode out together this morning, jumping walls and hedges, until he was satisfied he had made a good bargain.

'Did you ever see such an animal?' he asked me, as he reined in his horse. 'I would never have been able to get him so cheap if Travis had not lost so heavily at cards. But Travis never learns. A man with such infernal luck should stick to spillikins.' He looked around him, letting his eyes wander over our father's fields, down to the river at the bottom of the hill, and across the water to the woods beyond, but he did not see them as I did, as something to which he belonged. 'I tell you, Edmund, I am longing to be free,' he said. 'I am tired of the country.'

'We will soon be back at Eton.'

'I am tired of Eton, too.'

'It is not long now before we go to Oxford.'

'Ay. Only one year more, and then I will be out in the world, instead of rotting away at school. I mean to have a fine time of it, I can tell you.'

'What do you intend to study?' I asked him, for it was a problem that vexed me, and I wondered if he had found the answer to it.

'Women!' he said, with a laugh. He turned to me. 'But never fear, little brother, I will not seduce them all, I will leave one or two for you.'

And so saying, he wheeled his horse and raced for home.

I found myself thinking about Oxford as I raced after him. It is only two more years until I, too, will leave Eton and go up to university. I have still not thought how to answer Father's question as to what I intend to do with the future. I have no taste for the Army or the Navy, but I must have something to do with my time, I suppose, and I hope the next few years will make my feelings clearer.

Friday 11 July

Aunt Norris was talking about little Fanny Price again this afternoon. Tom stood up as soon as she opened her mouth, for he is sick of hearing about it.

'Let them do good if they must, but let them stop prattling about it beforehand!' he muttered to me as he passed.

As I followed him, I heard Aunt Norris saying, 'We must offer the child a home, for my poor sister has such a large family she cannot afford to look after them all . . .'

And my father saying, 'It is a serious charge, for if we decide to take her in, we must adequately provide for her hereafter, or there will be cruelty instead of kindness in taking her from her family in Portsmouth.'

And Mama saying it was a great shame Mrs Price had married to disoblige her family, settling on an idle fellow who was a lieutenant of marines, instead of looking higher and marrying a man of property. 'For I am sure she was pretty enough to do so.'

I followed Tom as he headed for the stables.

'What a fuss about a ten-year-old brat!' he said. 'Though I wonder my father is deceived by Aunt Norris's profession of a desire to be useful. She will find an excuse not to take the brat when the time comes, you will see, and Mama and Papa will have to do it all.' He looked up at the sky, where

11

black clouds had started to gather. 'It looks like rain. What say you we go into the barn and practise our archery?'

We did as he suggested, and I took pleasure in beating him soundly. He was put out, and blustered that he had not been paying attention.

We emerged from the barn an hour later, better from our exercise, and returned to the house, where we learnt that Tom's prediction had come true. Aunt Norris had said that Uncle Norris was too ill to have a child in the house, and it has been settled that Fanny will come to us.

Saturday 12 July

Maria and Julia did nothing but complain about Fanny's advent this morning as the four of us went riding, until Tom had had enough.

'Why must you be so tiresome?' he asked. 'Can you not talk about anything else? You have done nothing but groan about Fanny since we came out.' And to me he said, 'This is our reward for allowing two silly little girls to accompany us on our morning ride.'

'Julia might be a little girl, but I am almost a woman!' said Maria indignantly. 'It will not be long before I put my hair up and put my skirts down.'

'You are only a year older than me,' retorted Julia.

'But it is an important year. There is a great deal of difference between thirteen and twelve,' said Maria loftily.

'Not so very much, and besides, Mama says I always behave like a lady.'

'She says you *must* always behave like a lady,' returned Maria. 'That is not the same thing at all.'

An argument was brewing, and Tom forestalled it by proposing a race to the old barn. Julia crowed when she beat Maria, and Tom rewarded her by saying that he would dance with her after dinner.

'And you had better dance with Maria,' he said to me. 'If we do not teach our sisters how to go on, they might end up marrying wastrels, and then we shall have to offer them charity and raise their brats in our nurseries.'

Maria declared she would marry a baronet. Julia trumped her by saying she would marry two baronets, at which we all began to tease her, until Julia, determined not to admit her blunder, said she would only marry the second one when the first was dead.

Sunday 20 July

I wish Tom would learn to sit still in church. He was fidgeting again during prayers and I was sure Mr Norris would notice. Mr Norris said nothing, however, and although Aunt Norris saw what was happening, she said nothing, either, for Tom can do no wrong in her eyes. It is a good thing Papa did not see, or he would have taken Tom to task for not setting a better example to the tenants.

AUGUST

Monday 4 August

Nanny set out this morning to fetch Fanny Price. Maria and Julia spent the day wondering about her appearance and her clothes and about her ability to speak French. Tom teased them, saying they were afraid she might be prettier and cleverer than they were, and they could settle to nothing all afternoon, plaguing the life out of Pug, until Mama finally roused herself and sent them up to the nursery.

Tuesday 5 August

Papa spoke to Tom and me at some length this afternoon, telling us that we must make Fanny welcome, but that some distinction of rank must be preserved.

'You will see little of her, being away at school, but I would have you treat her with kindness and respect when you are here. And yet it would be wrong of you, or indeed any of us, to lead her to suppose she will have the same kind of future as Maria and Julia, for they are a baronet's daughters, and will have a handsome dowry when the time comes for them to marry. Encourage Fanny to be useful and respectful. Praise her for her modesty and virtue, and show her by your manner that anything else is unbecoming in a little girl.'

We gave him our word, and Tom began to run as soon as we were out of the study.

'Lord, I thought he would never finish! If we are not quick, the sun will have gone in and we will not get our swim.'

We went into the woods and dived into the pool. The water was bracing and full of weed, but we swam for an hour, for all that.

'When I am Sir Thomas I will have the pool cleaned,' said Tom grandly. 'I will rid it of all this weed so that we may swim without becoming entangled in it.'

'That will not be for many years, God willing,' I said, 'for Papa will have to die before you can become Sir Thomas.'

He laughed at me.

'You are a good fellow, Edmund, but you take the lightest words so seriously. If you want to know what to do with your time when you are a man, you should go into the church. It will suit your serious nature.'

'I might at that.'

'If you do, have pity on me, and keep the prayers short. My knees were aching last Sunday.'

The rain began to fall and we retreated inside. Washed and dressed, I went downstairs. Mama was on the sofa, playing with Pug. Aunt Norris was telling Maria that her new hairstyle was very becoming, and that she would have a string of suitors when she was older; Julia was asking if she would have a string of suitors, too; and Tom was lounging on the chaise longue, laughing at them.

Wednesday 6 August

Our visitor has arrived, and a small, frightened thing she is. I can scarcely believe she is ten years old; she looks closer to seven. Her eyes are large and her face thin; in fact, she is thin altogether. Her mother says she is delicate, and Papa has told us to be gentle with her. I believe such a child would provoke gentleness in anyone. She quaked whenever she was spoken to, and looked as though she wished to be anywhere but in the drawing-room. Papa was very stately in his welcome to her, and I believe his manner frightened her, though his words were kind. Mama's smiles seemed to reassure her, and Maria and Julia, awed into their best behaviour by Papa, added their welcome.

'She is a very lucky girl,' said Aunt Norris. 'What wonderful fortune she has had, to be noticed by her uncle, and brought to Mansfield Park. It is not every child who is so lucky. You will be a good girl, I am sure, Fanny, and will not make us regret the day we brought you here. You must be on your best behaviour, if you please.'

Mama invited her to sit on the sofa next to Pug, and Tom, in an effort to cheer her, good-naturedly gave her a gooseberry tart. She thanked him timidly and tried to eat it through her sobs, until Nanny rescued her, saying she was tired from her long journey, and took her up to the nursery.

Thursday 7 August

Maria and Julia were given a holiday so that they could get to know Fanny better, but they soon tired of her, remarking disdainfully, 'She has but two sashes, and she has never learnt French.'

I saw her standing in the middle of the hall this afternoon looking lost and I asked her what she was doing. She blushed and clasped her hands and said that Aunt Norris had sent her to fetch her shawl from the morning-room, but that she did not know where it was.

I undertook to show her the way, and said kindly, 'What a little thing you are,' but this seemed to make her more anxious so I made no further comments on her size. Once she had found the shawl I watched her until she disappeared safely into the drawing-room.

'She looks at me as though I am a monster,' said Tom when I mentioned it to him later. 'I found her in the drawing-room this morning and asked her how she did. She did not reply, so I told her not to be shy, and she blushed to the roots of her hair.'

He suggested we go fishing, and we took our rods down to the river, where we caught several fish which were served up at dinner with a butter sauce.

Friday 8 August

Aunt Norris is very pleased with her protégée and after dinner, when Fanny had left the drawing-room, Mama and Papa remarked that Fanny seemed a helpful child who was sensible of her good fortune. Maria and Julia pulled faces at each other at the mention of Fanny, but said nothing more than that she seemed very small and always had the sniffles. I could not blame them, for she does always seem to be ill, poor child.

Wednesday 13 August

Tom and I rode out early, basking in the warmth. The dew was on the grass and all nature seemed to be waiting expectantly for the day to begin. Tom laughed when I said as much, and said I should become a poet.

We made a hearty breakfast and then he rode into town whilst I returned to my room. As I did so, I heard a strange sound, and I realized that it was sobbing. I followed it, to find our little newcomer sitting crying on the attic stairs.

'What can be the matter?' I asked her, sitting down next to her and wondering how to comfort her, for she looked very woebegone.

She turned a fiery red at being found in such a condition, but I soothed her and begged her to tell me what was wrong.

'Are you ill?' I asked her, for to tell the truth, she did not look well.

She shook her head.

'Have you quarrelled with Maria or Julia?' I asked, wondering if they had upset her.

'No, no not at all,' she whispered.

'Is there anything I can get you to comfort you?'

She shook her head again. I thought for a

moment and then asked, 'If you were crying at home, what would you do to make yourself feel better?'

At the mention of *home,* her tears broke out anew, and it was easy to see where her sorrow lay.

'You are sorry to leave your mama, my dear little Fanny, which shows you to be a very good girl,' I said kindly. 'But you must remember that you are with relations and friends, who all love you, and wish to make you happy. Let us walk out in the park and you shall tell me all about your brothers and sisters.'

I took her by the hand and led her outside, for the morning was such as to cheer anyone. The sky was blue and soft breezes were blowing across the meadows. I heard about Susan, Tom, Sam and the new baby, but most of all I heard about William.

'How old is William?' I asked her.

'Eleven,' she told me, with the awe that only a ten-year-old can muster for such an advanced age.

It was with William she played, William who was her confidant, William who interceded with her mother on her behalf when needed, for he was clearly a favourite with Mrs Price.

'William did not like I should come away;

he said he should miss me very much indeed,' she said with a sob.

I handed her my handkerchief and persuaded her to take it, for her own was wet through.

'Never fear, he will write to you, I dare say,' I reassured her.

'Yes, he promised he would, but he told me I must write first.'

I soon discovered that this was the cause of her tears, for she had been longing to write to him since her arrival but she had no paper.

I took her into the breakfast-room so that she could send a letter at once, but as soon as I had furnished her with everything necessary, a fresh worry raised its head and she was afraid it might not go to the post.

'Depend upon me it shall: it shall go with the other letters,' I told her, 'and, as your uncle will frank it, it will cost William nothing.'

The idea of my father franking it frightened her, as though such an august personage should not be expected to help her, but I reassured her and at last she was easy.

'Now, let us begin,' I said.

I ruled the lines for her and then sat by her whilst she wrote her letter. I believe that no brother can have ever received a better one, for although it was not always rightly spelt, it was written with great feeling.

When she had finished, I added my best wishes to her letter and enclosed half a guinea under the seal for her brother. The look of gratitude she turned on me was enough to reward me ten times over for my small trouble, and I began to feel that she was a very sweet little thing, with an affectionate heart. I took some trouble to talk to her and discovered that she had a strong desire of doing right, as well as an awe of Maria and Julia.

'You must not be afraid of them,' I said to her. 'They are only further ahead than you because they have had a governess, whilst you have not, but life is not all French and geography, you know. It is fun and games as well. You must remember to play with my sisters, and to enjoy yourself. We all of us want you to be happy, and you will oblige us greatly if you can manage it. Will you try?'

She nodded timidly.

'Good.' I saw my sisters on the lawn. 'Look! They are out in the garden. The sun is shining, it is a beautiful day. You should go out and join them.'

She dried the last of her tears, looked at me for reassurance, then slipped off her chair and went over to the door. She turned back, and when she saw that I was watching her kindly, she smiled and waved, then ran outside. I saw her emerge on to the lawn and approach Maria and Julia. Maria looked about to rebuff her but when she saw me watching she held out her hand to Fanny. Fanny went to her shyly, and before long the three of them were playing together.

I thought she might like some books to read when she returned to her room, so I chose some from the library for her, and then I walked over to John Saddlers to see about some new harness for Oberon.

Friday 15 August

Tom and I went into town this morning. I had some commissions to undertake for Mama and Aunt Norris, and some books to buy for myself, whilst Tom wanted to look at another horse.

'Not to persuade Papa to buy, just to look at,' he told me.

We met at the inn for luncheon and he refused to tell me about his parcels, but when we returned home, all was made clear. After dinner, he gave a new shawl each to Maria, Julia and Fanny, with all the liberality of a future baronet. Maria wished hers had been blue, and Julia coveted Maria's, which, however much she said she disliked it, she would not exchange, whilst Fanny was too overcome to speak. When she could at last thank him, she stumbled over her words and then went bright red, before escaping to the nursery with her treasure.

'She is a funny little thing,' said Tom, as the door closed behind her.

'She seems a pleasant child,' said Mama, stroking Pug behind the ears and adding, 'does she not, Pug?'

'She is prodigiously stupid,' said Maria complacently. 'Only think, she cannot put the map of Europe together. Did you ever hear anything so stupid?'

Aunt Norris shook her head.

'My dear, it is very bad, but you must not expect everybody to be as forward and quick at learning as yourself.'

'Hah!' said Tom, but Maria ignored him.

'I am sure I should be ashamed of myself to know so little,' said Julia. 'I cannot remember the time when I did not know a great deal that she has not the least notion of yet. How long ago it is, Aunt, since we used to repeat the chronological order of the kings of England, with the dates of their accession, and most of the principal events of their reigns!'

'Very true indeed, my dears, but you are

25

blessed with wonderful memories, and your poor cousin has probably none at all.'

'But I must tell you another thing of Fanny, so odd and so stupid,' said Maria. 'Do you know, she says she does not want to learn either music or drawing.'

'To be sure, my dear, that is very stupid indeed, and shows a great want of genius and emulation,' returned Aunt Norris. 'But, all things considered, I do not know whether it is not as well that it should be so, for, though you know (owing to me) your Papa and Mama are so good as to bring her up with you, it is not at all necessary that she should be as accomplished as you are. On the contrary, it is much more desirable that there should be a difference.'

'I believe Fanny will like music and drawing well enough once she knows more about them,' I said, unwilling to have Maria and Julia encouraged to slight her. 'She has not had a chance to study them so far, that is all, and so she does not yet understand their worth. Do you not think so?' I asked Mama.

'You must ask your father, Edmund. He will know. See what Sir Thomas thinks,' returned Mama placidly.

I was disheartened, as I had hoped she would join her voice to mine, but at least my words curbed my sisters' contempt enough to make them conceal it from Fanny. I would not like to find her in tears again, for she is so small and thin she looks as though she could hardly stand it.

Tom was an unexpected ally, for he said he saw no harm in her and he was sure she would grow up to be perfectly charming, then teased Maria and Julia by saying that they should emulate Fanny's gratitude, or he would not bring them any more presents.

Monday 18 August
We heard this morning that the rector of Thornton Lacey had died. Papa called me into his study and gave me the news, then told me that he intended to give the living to Mr Arnold, who will hold it for me until I am of an age to take it myself, if I so wish. He asked me if I had given any more thought to my future, and I confessed that I had not.

'No matter. The living of Thornton Lacey will be held for you anyway and you may take it or not as you please when you are older. It is not the best living in my gift, for that, of course, is Mansfield, but in the fullness of time, that, too, will belong to you. Now, tell me of your studies, and of what you like to do.'

He listened as I told him about my progress at school, and asked me several judicious questions, and then I was free to go.

I went out to the stables and found Tom. Before long, we were riding out towards the woods.

'So Papa was asking you about your choice of profession? I am glad I do not have to make any similar decisions, for I would have no idea what to do if I could not run riot with my friends. I wish Jarvey were here, though perhaps it is better he is not, for he is always wanting to be doing something, and today it is too hot to do anything more than ride in the shade and dream of pretty girls.'

We went home with a hearty appetite and I finished my dinner with three slices of apple tart. Julia called me greedy, but Aunt Norris said that Tom and I were growing boys and that she liked to see a healthy appetite.

Thursday 21 August

I was walking through the park this afternoon when I saw little Fanny returning from the rectory with a large basket. It was far too heavy for a girl of her size and strength, for she was leaning over to one side in an effort to balance the weight, and she was perspiring profusely. Her breathing was shallow as I approached her, and I was concerned for her health.

'Here,' I said, taking her basket, 'you must let me carry that. Whatever possessed you to go out in such heat, without a hat, and to carry such a heavy load?'

'Mrs Norris wanted her work basket and had left it at the rectory,' she said timidly.

'You should not have offered to fetch it for her. You are not strong enough,' I said.

She looked awkward, and I guessed that she had not offered, but that my aunt had sent her.

'Let us sit awhile,' I said. 'It is cool under the trees. You may catch your breath, and then we will return to the house together.'

I spread out my coat for her, and bade her sit down. I was about to ask her about William when she surprised me by reciting:

The poplars are felled, farewell to the
    shade
And the whispering sound of the cool
    colonnade.

'You have read the Cowper I gave you,' I said, much struck, for, although I had defended her at the time, I had been guilty of believing my sisters when they said that she was stupid.

'Yes,' she whispered. 'I read it every night.'

'You seem to be a very devoted student, little Fanny,' I said with a smile.

She gave a tentative smile, too, but this time it was with pleasure.

I talked to her about the things she had read, and found an intelligent mind beneath her timidity.

When she was ready to go on I walked slowly beside her, and took her into the library.

'Aunt Norris . . .' she said.

'A few minutes more will not make any difference.'

I talked to her about what she liked to read and helped her to choose some books, then I accompanied her into the drawing-room, so that I could turn aside the worst of my aunt's ill-humour. I appealed to my mother, who said that Fanny must not be sent out without a hat in such heat again, and received a look of grateful thanks from my little friend.

Tom was lounging on the sofa, and he suggested we go and see Damson's new puppies.

'Though you do not need one,' he remarked, as we left the drawing-room, 'for I am sure it will not follow you around as adoringly as Fanny, nor come so readily when you call.'

I smiled, and he teased me some more, and told me that if I decided against being a clergyman or a poet, I would make a very good governess.

Friday 29 August

The candles were brought in earlier today, and it made me realize that summer is drawing to its end. Soon it will be time to go back to school. I would rather stay here at Mansfield Park.

I confided my feelings to Fanny when we walked together in the grounds, as has become our custom after breakfast, and then I was surprised I had done so. But there is something comfortable about the patter of her little feet next to mine, and something indefinably sweet about her nature that seems to invite confidences. She told me that she would rather I remained at home as well, then looked surprised at her own courage in speaking. I could not help but smile.

'I will miss my shadow when I have gone,' I said.

I asked her about her reading and found that she had read the books I recommended, and that she had committed a surprising amount of verse to heart. She is an apt pupil, and I think it will not be long before she ceases to draw down my sisters' contempt for her lack of learning.

I spoke to both Maria and Julia today, telling them they must be kind to her when I am away, and I have wrung a promise from them that they will protect her from the worst of Aunt Norris's attention. My aunt is very good, but I believe she does not realize how young Fanny is, or how easily wounded. A harsh word, to Fanny, is a terrible thing. And then she is so delicate. She tires quickly and is prone to coughs and colds. I hope the shawl Tom bought her will be enough to protect against winter's draughts.

Tom was morose when I mentioned that we would soon be back at school, but then he brightened.

'Only one more year, Edmund,' he said. 'Only one more, and then I will be up at Oxford. And in two years we will be there together.'

■ ■ ■ ■

1802

■ ■ ■ ■

NOVEMBER

Tuesday 9 November

I wondered what Oxford would be like, and whether I would take to it, but now that I am here I find I am enjoying myself. Tom came to my rooms when I had scarcely arrived and told me he would take care of me. He hosted a dinner for me tonight and it was a convivial evening, though I was surprised to see how much he drank. At home, he takes wine in moderation, but tonight he seemed to know no limit. I held his hand back as he reached for his third bottle, asking him if he did not think he had had enough, and he laughed, and said that he would not listen to a sermon unless it was on a Sunday, and at this his friends laughed, too. I felt uncomfortable but I suppose I must grow used to some wildness now that I am no longer at school.

Wednesday 10 November

Whilst coming back from Owen's rooms in the early hours of this morning I saw a fellow lying across the pavement. I was afraid he was ill, for I saw that he had been sick but, on approaching him, I smelt spirits and realized he was only drunk. I was about to step over him in disgust when I saw that it was Tom. His mouth was slack and his skin was pasty. His clothes were soiled, which distressed me greatly, for he has always been very particular about his dress. Many a time have I seen him berate his valet for leaving a fleck of dust on his coat or a bit of dirt on his boot, and to see him in such a state . . .

I tried to rouse him but it was no good, and so in the end I picked him up: no easy feat, for he is a good deal heavier than he used to be, and carried him back to his rooms.

Thursday 11 November

I called on Tom this afternoon and found him sitting on his bed with the curtains drawn, nursing his head. He said he had had a night of it, and that he could not remember how he got back to his rooms. I told him I had carried him.

'What, so now you are a porter, little brother?' he said, and laughed, but the laugh made his head ache and he clutched it again.

'You should not get in such a state, Tom. What would Mama say?' I asked, hoping that thinking of her would bring him back to his senses.

'She would say, "Tell Sir Thomas. Sir Thomas will know what to do," ' he said, mimicking her.

I did not like to hear him making fun of her, but I knew it would do no good to remonstrate with him. It would only make him laugh at me or, if he was in a bad mood, grow impatient.

'Just try not to drink so much tonight,' I said.

'Always my conscience, eh, Edmund?'

'You need one,' I told him. 'As long as you are all right, I will go. I have some work to do before dinner.'

'You work too hard.'

'And you do not work at all.'

'You sound like Papa,' he said testily.

'You make me feel like him,' I returned, and then I felt dissatisfied, for Tom and I have always been friends.

I tried to say something softer but he only cursed me. I saw that there was no talking to him whilst his head was so sore, and so I left him to himself and sought out Laycock instead.

Tom called on me this afternoon and my spirits sank, for he only ever comes to my room now to ask for money. He told me that he had lost heavily at cards last night and had exhausted his allowance.

'It is a debt of honour and I must pay it,' he said. 'I need twenty pounds.'

I gave it to him, but I told him that it was the last time I would help him.

'You might have money to lose, but I do not,' I said.

'Why worry? You are already provided for. You will have the Mansfield living when you take orders, and the living of Thornton Lacey as well. You will not be poor.'

'If I go into the church. I might not.'

'Oh, what else are you thinking of doing?' he asked curiously, as he sat down on the sofa and crossed one leg over his knee.

'That is the problem, I do not know,' I said with a sigh as I sat down next to him.

'You take everything too seriously, Edmund.'

'And you do not take things seriously enough.'

'Then we make a good pair, for we balance each other's faults. But do not go into the church if you do not like the idea.'

'I have not said that I will not, only that I

am not sure. There is a lot of good I could do —'

'You sound like Aunt Norris!'

I shuddered at the notion, and said quickly, 'Perhaps I may go into the law instead.'

'A good alternative, for there is decidedly *no* chance of you doing good there. Papa would find it harder to help you, though,' he said more seriously.

'Then I will have to do what everyone else does, and manage on my own.'

'In that case, you must have your fun now,' he said, standing up. 'Come, I insist. Kreegs is having a party at his rooms this afternoon — a sedate party,' he said, seeing my look. 'No drinking, no gambling, no women — unless you count his mother and sister. He is entertaining them to tea.'

'Well . . .'

'Miss Kreegs is very pretty,' he said temptingly. 'You should marry, Edmund, you are the type. Marry someone as sensible as yourself, then you and your wife can sit at home in the evenings in your slippers, with your noses in a couple of books!'

I punched him playfully and he responded in kind, and before long we were wrestling as we used to when we were at school.

'Do you ever wish we were boys again?'

he asked.

'Never,' I said.

But it was not quite true. Sometimes I wish that life could be as simple as it was when I was at school, when I did not have to decide on anything more important than whether to have an extra slice of pie for dinner, and my problems were no deeper than the difficulties of learning Latin verbs.

'No!' he said, but he did not sound convinced. 'Neither do I.'

Wednesday 17 November

I wrote to Mama and told her how I was going on, adding my love for my sisters and for Fanny. I wrote separately to my father and gave him news of my studies, whilst thanking him for my allowance. I wondered whether to say something about Tom, for he was drunk all day yesterday and could not crawl out of bed, but I decided that loyalty outweighed every other feeling.

I often wonder, if Tom had been the younger and I the elder, would I have been more high-spirited and would he have been more studious? Or is the difference between us in our characters, and would he have been wild and I serious whatever the case?

Friday 19 November

Owen has invited me to spend some time with his family near Peterborough when we break up for the Christmas holidays, and I have accepted.

DECEMBER

Monday 20 December

It is good to be home. I was met by kindness from Mama, enquiries about my health from Mrs Norris, judicious interest from Papa, squeals from Maria and Julia, a shamefaced anxiety from Tom — which, however, evaporated when it became clear that I did not mean to mention any of his university exploits — and unabashed happiness from Fanny. The way her face lit up when she saw me lifted my spirits, and it was not long before we were outside.

'Are you sure you are warm enough?' I asked her, for the air was cold even though the sun was shining.

'Yes,' she said.

'Let me look at you to be sure.'

I cast my eyes over her cloak, which she wore over her pelisse, and saw that her bonnet was pulled down over her ears, and that her hands were gloved as well as being hidden in her muff.

'Yes, I think you are.'

As we began our walk I asked her what she had been reading. She had read the Goldsmith I recommended, and we were soon so engrossed in the conversation that we lost track of the time, being taken by surprise when we discovered that dusk was falling.

We returned to the house. Just before we went in I took the opportunity of quizzing her on the constellations, which were beginning to appear in the sky, and I found she had memorized all that we could see.

We went inside and I returned to my room to find Tom lolling there, bored. He sat and talked whilst I dressed for dinner and then we went downstairs. After dinner I called Fanny to me, for I saw my aunt's eyes on her and suspected Fanny would soon be sent on an errand through the cold corridors if I did not keep her by my side. She repaid me by telling me all about the letter she had had from her family, and regaling me with stories about Susan and William.

Tuesday 21 December

Tom thanked me for not mentioning his conduct to Papa. I told him I would never betray him, and said how glad I was to see him looking better for being at home. He told me it was just high spirits that made him wild at Oxford, and I should join him in his pleasures.

'There will be time enough to be sober when you are older,' he told me.

'After seeing you lying facedown in the quad, I would rather be sober now,' I said.

I think that is why I have never succumbed to the worst temptations university life has to offer. Tom has always been there before me, and shown me the evil of excess by his example. If he could only see himself when he is drunk I am sure he would be as disgusted with it as I am.

He looked annoyed, but his face soon cleared and he challenged me to a race over to Hampton's Cross. I accepted the challenge, and I would have beaten him if my horse had not thrown a shoe. He laughed at me when I said as much, saying he had been letting me edge into the lead to humour me, and that he would have overtaken me before we reached the cross. We were still arguing the point when we returned to the house. We had hearty appetites and begged some food from Mrs Hannah in the kitchen, knowing it was still some hours until dinner. She gave us a hunk of roast beef and a loaf to share between us, and we ate it hungrily before returning to our rooms.

After dinner we had an impromptu ball and Tom taught us all a new dance. He could not remember half the steps, but the girls enjoyed it. Aunt Norris said she had never seen finer dancing, remarking that Maria would have many admirers when she came out. Julia went into a pet, and Tom teased her out of it, saying she would no doubt marry a prince, and we ended the evening very merrily.

■ ■ ■ ■

1803

■ ■ ■

APRIL

Thursday 7 April

The weather is remarkably fine and I am enjoying my holiday. I decided to ask Fanny if she would like to go for a ride with me this morning, but when I went into the drawing-room I found her opening a letter from Portsmouth. I did not like to disturb her so I sat down for a few minutes and let her read in comfort, whilst Aunt Norris busied herself about her sewing and Mama played with Pug.

I was surprised to hear a choked sob from Fanny and, looking up, I saw that she was crying. I went over to her at once.

'Fanny, my dear, whatever is wrong?'

I took the letter from her hand, as she could not speak, and read the sad news, that her sister Mary had died.

'What is it? What is wrong?' asked Aunt Norris.

'Fanny's sister has died,' I told her.

49

Mama murmured kind words of sympathy, and offered Fanny Pug to play with. It was a kind offer, but Fanny declined it, being too distressed for Pug to cheer, whilst Aunt Norris said only, 'A blessing for my sister, for she has so many children, she will not miss one.'

I gave her an angry look and took Fanny into the library, where I took her head on my shoulder and let her cry.

'She was such a pretty little thing,' said Fanny, clutching her handkerchief. 'I believe I loved her even more than I loved Susan. She was only five years old. If only I had known! I should have been with her. I could have nursed her. I could have helped Mama to take care of her.'

'Your mother and Susan looked after her,' I soothed her. 'They did all they could. No one could have done more, not even you, my dear. Now dry your eyes, Fanny, do, for I cannot bear to see you so distressed. Your sister is with God now.'

She took comfort from this and her tears changed to healthy tears. I comforted her until her sobbing ceased.

I took pains to cheer her this evening, and, having told Maria and Julia what had happened, and begged their kindness for her, I found them very affectionate. Maria asked Fanny if she would like to help her trim a bonnet and Julia gave her a silver thimble.

As I watched them I thought again about making the church my career. I know Papa would like it, for he could give me the family livings, but it is not something I could do without a vocation. And yet I am beginning to think I have one. I found it natural to help Fanny in her time of grief, and though I have a great affection for her that I do not have for other people, I think I could help them, too.

It has also been growing on me that I have a desire to live a good life, and though I would not say so to Tom, for fear of being laughed at, I think it is no bad thing. My father lives a good life and he is respected by everyone around him. I would like to be respected by those around me, too, for if I am respected I can set a good example and help others escape the miseries I see: the drink that has contributed to the poverty of Fanny's family, so that they cannot afford to keep her, and the idleness and profligacy that are blighting Tom's life.

Wednesday 13 April

My father is delighted with my thoughts about the future, and he has promised me he will do everything he can to assist me with a career in the church.

■ ■ ■ ■

1805

■ ■ ■ ■

MARCH

Tuesday 26 March

We are all in turmoil. Uncle Norris has died. I cannot believe it. He seemed so well, and he was so young. He ate too much, to be sure, and drank perhaps too freely, but none of us expected this. My aunt has been bearing up bravely; Tom has spent the afternoon standing about looking grave and Papa has given his attention to all the business naturally following on from the calamity. It has come as another burden to him at a time when he is already burdened with worries about his business affairs, and I am sorry I cannot do more to help him.

APRIL

Wednesday 3 April

Papa called Tom into his study this morning, and Tom emerged an hour later looking sick and ill. I was about to ask him what was wrong when I was summoned, and found myself closeted with Papa.

He looked very serious, and hummed and hawed as though he did not know how to begin.

'This is a sad business, Edmund, a very sad business.'

'Yes, sir.' Then, as he did not seem to know how to continue, I added, 'Mr Norris always seemed so hearty. Apart from his gout, he was in good health. It has come as a shock to us all.'

'Indeed, indeed.' He collected himself. 'And it could not have come at a worse time. I had expected to give the living of Mansfield to you upon Mr Norris's death, for I was sure he would not die until you were old enough to be in holy orders, but this has put a new complexion on matters. I should, by rights, be giving the living to a friend to hold for you until you are old enough to claim it for yourself but, as you know, things have been going badly for me in Antigua and, as you perhaps do not know, Tom came home a few weeks ago with very heavy debts. I have settled them, of course, but his excesses have left me in difficulties. I blush for the expedient which I am driven on, but I am forced to sell the living of Mansfield. I only hope this might curb your brother at last, for he has robbed you for ten, twenty, thirty years, perhaps for life, of more than half the income which ought to be yours, and I am extremely sorry for it.'

'It is no matter,' I said, though in truth it was a blow. I had expected the living of Mansfield, and I had wanted it, for it was the very living to which I belonged.

'You have taken it like a gentleman. You make me proud,' he said with a grave smile. 'I promise I will do everything I can to make it up to you in the future if possible.'

We talked for some little time more and then he said I might go.

I went out to the stables, thinking a ride would clear my head, and found Tom there, preparing to mount.

He was awkward, as well he might be, and stammered out an apology, but he was soon making light of it.

'It was not so very much money after all,' he said. 'I was not half so much in debt as some of my friends. And besides, I am sure you will not have to wait long for the living. As soon as the new incumbent dies the living will revert to you, and he cannot live for ever.'

He suggested we ride together but I had no taste for his company and, without realizing what I was doing, I found myself walking up to the attic to see Fanny.

I found her in the schoolroom with a book. She looked up as I entered, and smiled, and made me welcome, like a hostess receiving a friend, and we were soon discussing the books she has read. And then, I do not know how it happened, I was telling her about the living of Mansfield and my disappointment at finding it had been sold.

'It is a bad thing,' she said, entering into my feelings and shaking her head, 'a very bad thing. But you do not need Mansfield, Edmund. You have yourself, and that is all you need to do good in the world.'

I smiled, cheered by her attitude.

'And you will still have Thornton Lacey. It

is not such a large parish as Mansfield, to be sure, or such a prosperous living, but it is still yours.'

She so comforted me that by the time dinner was served I was able to greet Tom with civility, and I believe I am reconciled to the loss of the Mansfield living.

■ ■ ■ ■

1806

■ ■ ■ ■

AUGUST

Tuesday 12 August

I cannot believe it! My father is to leave us and go to Antigua for a year. I knew his affairs were not prospering as he had hoped, but I had no idea things had come to such a pass.

'You will have to look after my affairs here at home whilst I am gone, and the family, too,' he told me. 'It is a heavy responsibility for a young man of two-and-twenty years, but I have confidence in you, Edmund. Take your tone of conduct from me. If you are in difficulties then ask yourself what I would do in the same circumstances and act accordingly.'

I said I would do my best.

'I will be taking Tom with me,' he said. 'I had hoped he would grow more settled, but he appears to be getting worse instead of better. His friends are badly chosen and lead him astray, and Tom, alas, does not have the character to resist them. If I leave him behind, I fear he will squander what remains of our fortune whilst I am away.'

He told me what he expected of me, and then I was free to go.

'He cannot do this to me,' said Tom angrily, coming into my room as I dressed for dinner. 'He cannot take me out of England at such a time — and to the Indies, for God's sake! What the devil am I to do in Antigua?'

'Learn about his business affairs?' I asked.

'Like some moneygrubbing shopkeeper, or a mill owner? I am not an estate manager, I am a baronet's son!'

'The baronet does it,' I pointed out.

'More fool him. Why does he not leave it to his men of business?'

'Because his affairs have not prospered in their hands.'

'Then he should get rid of them, and hire new men.'

'There is no one he can trust so well as himself.'

'Antigua!' said Tom with a groan, flinging himself down across a chair. 'The heat . . . the people . . . it will be abominable. I cannot stand it. I will not go.'

'Then tell him so.'

He shuffled uncomfortably.

'I have already tried. He told me plainly that if I refuse, he will not honour my gambling debts.'

'What, none of them?'

'None of them,' he said morosely. He broke out passionately. 'It was not my fault. I had an unbeatable hand! The only thing I had to fear was an ace. And then Watkins turned his card over, and there it was. The ace of hearts. It was damnable luck. Quite damnable. So of course I had to keep playing, to win back what I had lost. Except I had a run of bad luck that led me to such ruin I had to apply to Papa.' He shook his head. 'It was not my fault. The cards were against me, that is all.'

'You might like the Indies,' I said.

'Hah!' He swung his leg over the arm of the chair. 'A likely tale. And whilst I am sweltering in all that heat, with no one to talk to and nothing to do, you will be here enjoying yourself.'

'I will be here looking after the estate,' I said, shrugging on my coat.

'Which no doubt you will relish.'

'At the moment, I am terrified. What if we have a poor harvest, or there is a French invasion, or Maria and Julia elope, or are preyed upon by fortune hunters? I tell you plainly, Tom, I am dreading it.'

He was cheered by thoughts of my responsibilities, and by the idea that I would not be enjoying myself at home.

We went down to dinner, and had a sorry evening. Mama was out of spirits, too, and lamenting the fact that Papa will soon be far away, whilst Aunt Norris was elated by the thought of everything she would have to do. I glanced at Tom, and he laughed to think of Aunt Norris organizing us all with no one to check her officiousness, for I am sure my father is the only one who has the slightest influence over her.

'You may rely on me, Sir Thomas,' she said. 'Young ladies of eighteen and nineteen years of age need a great deal of care, but it will not be lacking, I assure you. I will see to it that they do you credit whilst you are away.'

My father thanked her, and told Maria, Julia and Fanny to mind their mother and their aunt whilst he is away.

My sisters seemed relieved at the news of his departure.

'Papa is always so grave,' said Maria, as she walked over to the pianoforte with Julia. 'I feel quite cast down whilst he is by.'

Julia agreed, saying there was something stately in his manner that put her high spirits to flight.

Fanny said nothing, and yet even she seemed to feel his coming absence as a relief.

As for me, I will be glad when he is safely home again.

September

Wednesday 3 September

And so my father has gone, and I am in charge of his affairs. I rose early, conscious of how much there was to do, and after spending the morning with the steward, so that I could refresh my mind as to my duties for the coming month, this afternoon I began on them in earnest. Dinner-time came quickly and I hesitated before taking my father's place. It seemed strange to sit in his chair and carve the meat, providing a focus at the head of the table. And afterwards, when the ladies withdrew, I was conscious of how alone I was, for without Tom and my father to talk to I sat in state by myself. I quickly repaired to the drawing-room where the others were gathered.

'Well, Edmund, and so we are alone, and must get used to being alone, for who knows when we may see Sir Thomas again?' said my aunt with a sigh.

'He has gone for a year, not for ever,' I said.

'I only hope it may be so,' she said, relishing the new situation and determined to make a drama of it. 'But who knows what may happen to a man, once he leaves his own fireside? There are villains everywhere. At this very minute, Sir Thomas may be in the power of pirates.'

'Sir Thomas will not have been caught by pirates, will he?' asked Mama, stirring.

'I hardly think so,' I told her.

'Who can say?' countered Aunt Norris. 'The sea is a very unsafe place. And if he has not been captured by pirates, then what other dangers might he not be facing? There are typhoons and tidal waves . . . I shall not be surprised if Sir Thomas is shipwrecked, only to return to us after fifteen years with long white hair and a beard.'

Mama was alarmed.

'Do not say so! I have never been able to abide a beard,' she said.

'Depend upon it, he will have fine weather and make the crossing in a month,' I told her.

'If he is not set upon by an enemy vessel,' said my aunt, 'for then he will be thrown into the sea, as like as not, and eaten by a whale.'

Fanny heroically distracted my aunt's attention, allowing us to pass the rest of the evening without any further visions fit for one of Mrs Radcliffe's novels.

DECEMBER

Wednesday 31 December

The last day of the year, and nothing terrible has happened. Papa has not been shipwrecked, nor has he drowned in a storm, nor been eaten by a whale. And I have managed to maintain the estate and family without them suffering any calamities either, for which I am truly thankful. I was able to write to Papa today and tell him that the estate is flourishing; that Maria and Julia are fast becoming the belles of the neighbourhood; and that Fanny's strength is improving by virtue of her daily rides. I gave him news of Mama and Aunt Norris, and sent him my best wishes for his affairs in Antigua.

I have survived the year, and I only hope I can survive the next one, so that I can hand both estate and family back to my father and turn my attention to my own life again.

■ ■ ■ ■

1807

■ ■ ■ ■

MAY

Wednesday 27 May

I am beset with problems on every side. Having just returned from my dealings with the bank in London I found that Fanny's grey pony had died, and that neither Mama nor Aunt Norris had thought of buying her another one. I said at once that I meant to rectify the situation, only to find myself blocked at every turn.

'There is no need to buy a pony just for Fanny. I am sure she does not expect it,' said my aunt, as though that justified the omission.

Mama said she might borrow Maria's horse, or Julia's, but on enquiring, I found out that my sisters' horses were never free in fine weather, and of what use would it be for Fanny to ride in the rain?

'That is true,' said Mama.

'But there is no need to buy something especially,' said my aunt. 'There must be an old thing among the horses belonging to the Park that would do. Why, I am sure Fanny could borrow one from the steward whenever she wanted one. That would be a much better solution.'

'No young lady of Mansfield Park will ride a steward's horse,' I told her.

She switched to another tack, saying my father would not want her to have one.

'Indeed, it would be improper for Fanny, situated as she is, to have a young lady's horse, quite as though she were a daughter of the house,' said my aunt. 'The distinctions of rank must be preserved. Sir Thomas himself said so. It would not do to let Fanny get above herself.'

'Fanny is the last person in the world who would ever get above herself. Besides, she must have a horse. Do you not agree?' I appealed to Mama.

'Oh, yes, to be sure, she must have a horse. As soon as Sir Thomas comes home she must have one. Only leave it to him, Edmund. Your father will know what to do, and it is not so very long until September, when he returns.'

'It is four months, and Fanny cannot go without her exercise for so long, particularly in the summer months.'

'Your father would not agree with the

idea, I am sure,' said my aunt, shaking her head, 'and to be making such a purchase, with his money, in his absence, when his affairs are unsettled seems to me to be a very wrong thing. It is not only the expense of the purchase, but the expense of keeping the animal.'

Against my will, I found myself agreeing with her. My father's last letter spoke of ever dwindling profits, and I could tell how worried he was.

I was at a stand, and I walked over to the window, displeased. I was determined to secure to Fanny the pleasure of regular outings, but I could not see how to do it, until, glancing across the park, I saw my own horses being given their exercise. I immediately saw a way round the problem.

'I must give Fanny one of my horses,' I said.

'There is no need for you to inconvenience yourself, that would be quite wrong. You, a Bertram, and a son of the house, to give up one of your horses? I am sure Fanny would be the first to protest against it. Besides, your horses are not fit for a woman to ride. Two of them are hunters and the third is a road horse. They are all of them far too strong and spirited. Fanny would fall and break her neck, most likely,' said

Aunt Norris.

Knowing she was right, I decided to exchange one of my horses for an animal that Fanny can ride. I know where one is to be met with, and I mean to look it over tomorrow.

JUNE

Monday 8 June

I have been rewarded for my small trouble by seeing Fanny so happy. The new mare suits her very well.

'I never thought anything could replace the old grey pony in my affections, but my delight in the mare is so far beyond my former pleasure . . . It is so good of you . . . I cannot express my gratitude.'

'There is no need for gratitude between friends,' I said, smiling. 'It is enough for me to see you happy and well. Shall we ride to the stone cross? Then we can discuss Shakespeare on the way. I have barely seen you since I returned from London, and I have had no one to discuss poetry with whilst I was away.'

The summer afternoon was such as to encourage our taste for poetry and we returned in a happy mood, to while away the evening in the same manner.

September

Saturday 12 September

It is a good thing I did not wait for my father to come home before providing Fanny with a horse, for I had a letter from him this morning saying that his affairs are still in such a state that he cannot come home until next year. I was not as alarmed by this as I would have been a few months ago, for I have learnt how to manage the estate and I believe it to be prospering.

Friday 25 September

We have all been thrown into an uproar, for Tom is home! He arrived late this afternoon, as careless and laughing as ever, but as brown as a nut, and with hair so bleached by the sun it resembled a piece of driftwood. He was barely recognizable, being slimmer and fitter than when he went away, with his eyes looking so green in the brown of his face that my aunt was moved to say that they looked like a pair of emeralds.

'All the better for wooing,' said Tom merrily, catching her round the waist and spinning her round before putting her down, breathless.

Mama bestirred herself so far as to leave the sofa and kiss him, and he repaid her with a kiss on the cheek. He delighted her by asking after Pug, who sat like a fat potentate on the sofa, and then turned his attention to Maria and Julia. They were pleased to see him, and eager to discover what was in the packages that had followed him into the room.

He had brought presents for us all: exotic material for Mama and my aunt — 'To make you some splendid new gowns. You will be the talk of the neighbourhood' — fans and shoes for Maria and Julia, a pair of shoes for Fanny and a compass for me.

'How is Sir Thomas?' asked Mama, when she had seated herself once more on the sofa with Pug on her lap.

'Very well.'

'It is a terrible thing for him to be so far from home. I wished he would not go, but he said he must, and there was an end of it. I do not like to think of him in all that heat, on his own. He will miss us all dreadfully.'

'He scarcely has time. There is plenty to

do, and he is busy from morning 'til night.'

'How are his affairs?' I asked.

'Lord knows. I could not make head nor tail of them. Sugar plantations are a mystery to me. Now horses . . .'

'You have not been gambling again, Tom?' asked Aunt Norris.

'No. I have promised my father not to bet on another card or horse — at least until his affairs are settled!' he added.

'Impudent boy!' said Aunt Norris indulgently. 'But, were it not for the joy you bring us by returning like this, I cannot help thinking that it must bode ill for Sir Thomas,' she went on, shaking her head. 'Indeed, it is a singularly bad portent. It is so like Sir Thomas to send you home if he had a foreboding of evil. I have a terrible presentiment that something dreadful is about to occur.'

Mama was beginning to look worried, and stir anxiously on the sofa, so Fanny put an end to my aunt's woeful imaginings by saying to Tom, 'Tell us about Antigua.'

Tom was only too happy to talk, for he was full of energy and liveliness.

'It was hot,' he began. 'Very hot. You would not believe the heat, little Fanny. Not all your hats and fans and parasols would keep you cool. I believe the ladies there were made from less pliable material than those at home, for they bore it well, and managed to walk around with only a little droop, instead of melting like candles.'

'And were there any balls?' asked Maria.

'Not in all that heat,' said Mama.

'Nothing would stop me dancing,' said Julia. 'Tell us about them, Tom.'

'Oh, they were the usual sort of thing, you know,' he said carelessly.

'You have been breaking hearts, I warrant,' said my aunt, putting her presentiments aside for the moment and joining in with the more agreeable conversation.

'There were so many to break, it would have been ungentlemanly not to.'

'Tom!' protested Mama.

'There is nothing the young ladies like better than the son of an English planter, and I could not disappoint them by refusing to flirt with them.'

'Especially not as you are such a fine young man,' said my aunt.

Maria and Julia pulled faces behind Tom's back at this, whilst Fanny looked at her new shoes; a fine pair, but two sizes too small.

'The men were gentlemen, I hope?' asked my aunt.

'Lord, yes.'

'Though not what we are used to over

here, I suppose. Maria and Julia have been attracting a great deal of attention whilst you have been away. They are the belles of the neighbourhood. All the young men are eager to dance with them, and if Mr Rushworth does not propose to Maria by Christmas I will be very much surprised.'

Maria looked conscious, and Julia retaliated by saying that the young men round about were dull.

'He is very taken with your sister,' went on my aunt, as though Julia had not spoken. 'And what a fine man he is, with a good face and figure, charming manners and a house in town. His fortune is sizeable, too, for he has twelve thousand a year.'

'Then it is no wonder that Maria likes him,' said Tom with a sly look.

Maria blushed.

'I am sure Mr Rushworth has no thought of proposing,' she said, tossing her head.

'And I am sure he has,' was my aunt's rejoinder.

I could get nothing more out of Tom about Antigua for he said he must dance, and before long we were all doing some of the steps he had learnt in the Indies. Even Mama was persuaded to dance, whilst my aunt played, and Pug sat on the sofa and watched us all.

OCTOBER

Thursday 22 October

The winter evenings have had enough balls even to satisfy my sisters, and Aunt Norris is now determined to see them well married.

'Maria is twenty now, and of an age to be married,' she said to me as we sat in the drawing-room this evening. 'And Julia, too, is not far behind. What a thing it would be if we could find suitable matches for them both before your father returns. I am sure Mr Rushworth wants only a little encouragement to offer for Maria, and there are several young men who seem remarkably fond of Julia. And if poor Sir Thomas fails to return,' she added, for she has still not despaired of him being shipwrecked, or lost overboard, 'it will be a consolation to see Maria married, and to know that he would have approved.'

But no young men offered for my sisters

tonight, despite my aunt's hopes. We returned to find Fanny sitting peacefully with Mama. She looked up as I entered the room, an eager smile on her face, for though she is too young for balls, she loves to hear of them. I sat by her for half an hour and told her all about our evening. She wanted to know every dance I had danced, and with whom; and when I had done, I told her I was looking forward to standing up with her at her first ball, as soon as Mama thought she was old enough to attend. She looked at the floor, reminding me how young she was, for even the smallest compliment discomposes her. Perhaps it is a good thing she does not go into company, after all.

■ ■ ■ ■

1808

■ ■ ■ ■

January

Monday 11 January

It seems my aunt's fondest wishes are about to be fulfilled, for Maria has received an offer of marriage from Mr Rushworth.

'Such a nice man,' said my aunt. 'He has such a way with him; such manners, and such —'

'— a large property,' finished Tom.

My aunt perceived no irony in Tom's comment, but replied with, 'Very true, it is a fine property. One of the best in the country, and then there is his house in town as well. Maria is a very lucky girl to have attracted such a man, with everything in his favour: his home, his fortune and his person. I only hope the rest of you will marry as well. Julia, we will have to look about us and find another such a one for you.' She turned to Maria. 'We must have an early wedding.'

'Sir Thomas's permission must first be sought,' said Mama, rousing herself a little as she lay on the chaise longue.

'He will be very pleased, mark my words. What, to find his daughter affianced to such a man as Mr Rushworth? To be sure, he will be delighted. A spring wedding would be very fine,' said my aunt. 'Dr Grant must perform the ceremony, for I am sure he does little enough since he bought the Mansfield living. And if you have an early wedding, you will be able to go to London for the Season, Maria. With such a fine house in town, it would be a pity not to make use of it this year.'

Maria was soon making plans with my aunt, and saying that she would invite Julia to spend the Season with her, so that she, too, could find a husband.

'You must invite Fanny,' I said. 'She would enjoy the theatres and the galleries. Would you not, Fanny?'

'I am sure it is more than she looks for,' said my aunt ungraciously, before Fanny had time to reply. 'There is no need to invite her.'

'I have no objection to it,' said Maria. 'Fanny will be very welcome, only she is too young this year. But next year, Fanny, you must come and stay. You will be eighteen then, and of an age to enjoy everything.'

Fanny was all gratitude, and I liked to

think of her having her share of the pleasure.

'And Tom, you must visit your sister, too,' said my aunt. 'I am sure she will find you an heiress, someone with twenty or thirty thousand pounds, and a beauty besides.'

Tom laughed, and said he had no intention of marrying for at least another twenty years, whereupon my aunt remarked that it must be up to me, then, to make an advantageous marriage.

As the conversation continued I could not help but be grateful that it was not up to me to give or withhold my consent to Maria's marriage. I have little liking for Rushworth. Indeed, if he did not have twelve thousand a year I would think him a very stupid fellow.

'Maria,' I said to her, calling her aside this evening. 'Are you sure you wish to marry Rushworth? Just because he has asked for your hand, does not mean you have to give it, you know. I am not happy about the match, I must confess. Rushworth seems to be a very dull fellow. Are you sure you have not been blinded to his faults by his fortune and his house in town? They are very desirable, I am sure, but is marriage to Rushworth a price worth paying for them? Do anything rather than marry without love, for that way great unhappiness lies.'

'Oh, Edmund, you do prose on. Of course I love him.'

'But you have seen very little of him, except at balls.'

'I have seen quite enough of him, I assure you.'

I was not convinced I liked this answer, and told her so.

'I want you to be happy,' I said.

'And I will be.'

'If I could be sure —'

'You must own me to be the best judge of my happiness,' she said impatiently, 'and I tell you I will be.'

With this I had to be content.

'Very well. Then I will write to Papa tomorrow,' I told her, but I did so with a heavy heart.

It lightened somewhat when I talked the matter over with Fanny, for, as she reminded me, my father will no doubt say the marriage cannot take place without him. And that when he returns, he will be able to decide whether Maria is truly attached to Mr Rushworth or not.

July

Friday 1 July

I wrote to my father this morning and I was just sending the letter when my aunt entered the drawing-room. She had visited the Grants to give them a hint of Maria's nuptials and had returned from the Parsonage with some news.

'One wedding brings on another. It seems you will not have to go to London in search of an heiress after all,' she said portentously to Tom. 'We are to have an addition to the neighbourhood, or rather, two additions. Mrs Grant's brother and sister — her mother's children by a second marriage — will soon be joining her. It is a sad tale. Their parents died some time ago, whereupon they went to live with an aunt and uncle, but now their aunt has died, too, and as their uncle proposes to move his mistress into the house, they do not feel they can stay with him any longer, and so they are to come here.'

'Shocking,' said Mama placidly, as she played with Pug. 'I am sure Sir Thomas would never approve of such a thing.'

'But although it may be unfortunate for Mr and Miss Crawford, it is likely to be a good thing for us,' said my aunt. 'Miss Crawford is a considerable heiress, with twenty thousand pounds, and Mrs Grant assures me she is as elegant as she is accomplished, being a beauty besides.'

'How is that good for us?' Tom teased my aunt.

'Why, because you can marry her,' she replied.

Tom was still laughing at the notion as we went out for a ride this afternoon.

'I think *you* should marry Miss Crawford,' he said to me, 'in fact I have a mind to promote the match. I promised Papa that I would make it up to you for losing you the Mansfield living; and as the new incumbent, Dr Grant, is refusing to die of an apoplexy as I hoped he would, so that the living would revert to you, then a good marriage is the quickest way to ensure your prosperity.'

I begged him to be serious but he said that he was.

'She is just the wife for you. Her fortune

will allow you to enlarge the rectory at Thornton Lacey and keep a carriage.'

'If she is to be rich and beautiful I am surprised you do not want to marry her yourself,' I said.

'God forbid! The last thing I want is a wife.'

But I find myself hoping he might take a liking to her, for a wife would be the very thing to steady him, and perhaps marriage would make him take a pride in his inheritance and give him a desire to work to preserve it.

Monday 11 July

I scarcely know what I am writing, for I have had such a jolt to my feelings that I am quite dazed.

I returned from estate business this afternoon to find a beautiful young woman in the drawing-room. I caught a glimpse of her profile first and felt my pulse quicken, and when she turned her face towards mine, the hope flashed through my mind that Tom would not care for her after all, for she was the most charming young woman I had ever seen. She had bright, dark eyes and dark hair, with a clear brown complexion and a smiling mouth, whilst her figure was small and dainty. She was a complete contrast to

Maria and Julia, whose tall fairness, as they sat next to her, set off her dark loveliness like two willowy reeds setting off a forest pool.

But as I took my seat I found that Tom seemed to have abandoned his intention of remaining a bachelor, for he was at his liveliest. He was entertaining Miss Crawford with tales of his trip to Antigua and she was smiling and laughing. She seemed delighted with him. And how could she not be? For when Tom puts himself out to please, he never fails. And were he not half so amusing, his position as a baronet's heir, with the added advantages of person and conversation, could hardly fail to please any young woman.

Tom at last turned his attention to Mr Crawford, who happened to mention his horse, and the two of them began a lengthy conversation about the merits of their hunters. Miss Crawford turned her attention to me and to my surprise I found myself tongue-tied, but luckily her conversation was lively enough for two.

When I had command of myself once more I asked her about her journey into Northamptonshire and she answered me civilly, making the commonplace remarks about the roads and the carriage seem interesting and amusing. I was about to ask her what she thought of Mansfield when Tom caught her attention and she was soon laughing with him again.

I ought to be pleased that he has taken a liking to her, and she to him, but instead I find myself hoping that Tom will soon grow tired of her, and that I might see a great deal more of her in the coming weeks.

Tuesday 12 July

Tom was full of admiration for Miss Crawford this morning, saying that she was a very elegant young woman, and Maria and Julia seemed equally struck with Henry Crawford.

Wednesday 13 July

We dined at the Parsonage this evening. Fanny was very quiet, but nevertheless I believe she enjoyed herself, for she does not go out so often that it is a commonplace to her. Miss Crawford was very lively, and matched Tom's wit with her own. I managed to speak to her, too, and found her as agreeable to listen to as to look at. The Crawfords are an addition to our circle, and their presence bodes well for the summer.

Thursday 14 July

We have seen the Crawfords twice now, and on both occasions Miss Crawford has delighted me. She has such a lively way of talking and such dancing dark eyes that I can think of nothing else.

Mama and Aunt Norris are pleased with the Crawfords, too.

'I knew how it would be,' said my aunt. 'Miss Crawford is as elegant and charming a young woman as you could wish to meet, and with her fortune, Tom, she would make you an excellent wife. Her brother, too, is quite the gentleman. I thought him plain at first —'

'Plain?' cried Maria and Julia together in astonishment.

'At first,' said my aunt. 'But after the second meeting I thought him not so very plain, and after dining at the Parsonage yesterday, I find I consider him to be one of the handsomest men of my acquaintance. He has so much countenance, and his teeth are so good, and he is so well made, that he is a great addition to our circle.'

'Indeed,' said Maria, 'he is the most agreeable man I ever met.'

'But not so agreeable as Mr Rushworth?' I asked.

'Of course our dear Maria favours Mr

Rushworth,' put in my aunt. 'He is everything that is amiable and amusing. Such manners, such an air . . .'

'He is not half so agreeable as Mr Crawford,' said Julia, with far more truth.

'And if I do not mistake the matter — which I am sure I do not — he finds you extremely agreeable, too, Julia,' said my aunt, keen to promote this preference on the part of Julia. 'A double wedding would be a very pleasant thing, with Tom marrying Mary Crawford, and Julia marrying Mr Crawford. I am persuaded Sir Thomas would be very pleased.'

'As to that, it would be a triple wedding, for I am already engaged,' said Maria. 'But for all that, there really is no harm in my paying attention to an agreeable man. Everybody knows my situation, and Mr Crawford must take care of himself.'

This speech did nothing to reassure me, but when I spoke to my aunt about it, she said, 'Depend upon it, Maria is only paying attention to Mr Crawford because she is cross with Mr Rushworth for leaving her in order to visit a friend. He cannot expect Maria to stay indoors until he returns. I believe it will be no bad thing if Mr Crawford pays some attention to Maria, for it will teach Mr Rushworth a lesson, and when he returns he will see that he must guard his treasures if he is not to lose them.'

'Do you think he may lose them?' I asked. 'Do you think Maria is not really in love with him? If that is the case, I should not have allowed things to go this far. Long engagements are never a good thing, and this engagement of Maria's, unsanctioned by my father and not likely to be sanctioned for many weeks, is worse than most. It puts everyone in a false position.'

'You misunderstand me. I am sure Maria loves him but a woman does not like to be ignored, and it will do Mr Rushworth no harm to learn this fact. We all want Maria to be happy when she becomes Mrs Rushworth, and not to find herself left behind whilst her husband goes roaming about the country.'

Rushworth's going to stay with a friend for a fortnight did not seem like roaming about the country to me, but my aunt knows far more about women than I do, and no doubt she is right. Even so, I wish Papa might come home soon, for I am sure he will be better at looking after his daughters than I can ever be.

Besides, I feel in need of some advice myself. I can think of nothing but Miss Crawford — but it seems Miss Crawford can think of nothing but Tom.

Friday 15 July

The Crawfords called again today. Crawford
had been intending to bring his sister to
stay with the Grants and then leave the
neighbourhood, but he seems to find it
agreeable here, for he said it was now his
intention to stay awhile.

The day was fine and we were soon walking together.

'You have an excellent property here, Mr
Bertram,' Miss Crawford said as she strolled
along next to Tom. 'It has a real park, some
five miles round, my sister tells me?'

'That is so, five miles exactly,' said Tom.

'I must congratulate you on it. There are
not many so fine. Why, a mile or two seems
to be enough for some people to proclaim
they have a park, when really it is nothing
of the kind. The house, too, is remarkable.
It is very spacious, and I like a house that is
modern built, with none of the small windows that make older houses so dark. The
ceilings are so high, and the rooms so large,
that it is a pleasure to sit in them.'

'Then we must hope you will grace it with
your presence for a long time to come!' said
Tom courteously.

She inclined her head and smiled bewitchingly, and made me long to offer her my arm, which, however, I could not do, as she was clearly not at all fatigued and was instead very lively. She moved her hands expressively when she talked, and everything about her spoke of health and life.

'You should have an engraving made of the house,' she said. 'I always say that a well-built house should be honoured with an engraving. I am sure I have seen many smaller houses treated in this way, and Mansfield Park would grace any collection in which it was included.'

'I have always thought it a very fine house,' said Mama. 'Sir Thomas is very proud of it.'

'And with good reason. It is one of the finest baronet's seats in the land,' said my aunt.

'My brother tells me you have a horse running in a race soon?' Miss Crawford asked Tom.

My aunt smiled at this, and exchanged a glance with Mama, who, however, did not appear to notice. But the meaning of my aunt's smile was clear: Miss Crawford's interest was not in a horse race, but in my brother.

'Indeed I do! It is running at Brighton, a very fine animal and sure to win. Have you ever been to the Brighton races?'

'No, I must confess I have not.'

'Then we must correct that.'

'Are they not a little wild?' she asked.

'Nonsense. All the best people go. Why, the Prince of Wales himself goes. I saw him there myself, the first time I attended. It was when I was with my friend Frobisher. Do you know Frobisher?'

'I do not believe I have had the pleasure.'

'You would like him. He makes us roar with laughter. When we were in Brighton last we decided to go sea bathing and Frobisher swam off by himself. Then he gave a strangled cry, to make us all look at him, flailed his arms wildly and disappeared under the waves. We all swam over there and searched for him frantically. Then up he popped behind us, laughing fit to burst at the expressions on our faces! You really must come. I cannot promise you Frobisher, for his father has sent him out of the country, but I can show you the sights and take you to the races. You would enjoy it, I have no doubt. We could make a party of it. We could all go. What do you say to that, Mama? Would you like to go to Brighton?'

'It is a very long way,' said Mama.

'Nonsense!'

The subject was discussed back and forth,

but nothing was decided on by the end of the visit, and Miss Crawford promised to think of it more overnight so that we could resume the discussion tomorrow.

Saturday 16 July
The weather being fine we walked out this morning and the subject of making a party to attend the races was again raised, but the difficulties of finding enough carriages and arranging accommodation made it clear that the matter would only do to be talked of, for realizing it was beyond our reach.

Fanny was soon tired and I offered her my arm, but Crawford was too quick for me, saying that he would escort her back to the house. Maria and Julia went with them, though I believe Julia would have stayed if Maria had not made a very pointed remark about needing her, leaving Tom, Miss Crawford and me to continue our walk.

'I begin now to understand you all, except Miss Price,' said Miss Crawford to me, as we wandered through the shrubbery. 'Pray, is she out, or is she not? I am puzzled. She dined at the Parsonage, with the rest of you, which seemed like being *out;* and yet she says so little, that I can hardly suppose she *is.*'

'I believe I know what you mean, but I

104

will not undertake to answer the question. My cousin is grown-up. She has the age and sense of a woman, but the outs and not outs are beyond me,' I replied.

'And yet, in general, nothing can be more easily ascertained. The distinction is so broad. Manners as well as appearance are, generally speaking, so totally different. Till now, I could not have supposed it possible to be mistaken as to a girl's being out or not. A girl not out has always the same sort of dress: a close bonnet, for instance; looks very demure, and never says a word. You may smile, but it is so, I assure you; and except that it is sometimes carried a little too far, it is all very proper. Girls should be quiet and modest. The most objectionable part is, that the alteration of manners on being introduced into company is frequently too sudden. They sometimes pass in such very little time from reserve to quite the opposite — to confidence! *That* is the faulty part of the present system. One does not like to see a girl of eighteen or nineteen so immediately up to every thing — and perhaps when one has seen her hardly able to speak the year before. Mr Bertram, I dare say *you* have sometimes met with such changes.'

'I believe I have, but this is hardly fair; I

see what you are at. You are quizzing me about Miss Anderson,' said Tom.

'No, indeed. Miss Anderson! I do not know who or what you mean. I am quite in the dark. But I *will* quiz you with a great deal of pleasure, if you will tell me what about.'

'Ah! you carry it off very well, but I cannot be quite so far imposed on. You must have had Miss Anderson in your eye, in describing an altered young lady. You paint too accurately for mistake. It was exactly so. The Andersons of *Baker Street.* We were speaking of them the other day, you know. Edmund, you have heard me mention Charles Anderson. The circumstance was precisely as this lady has represented it. When Anderson first introduced me to his family, about two years ago, his sister was not *out,* and I could not get her to speak to me. I sat there an hour one morning waiting for Anderson, with only her and a little girl or two in the room, the governess being sick or run away, and the mother in and out every moment with letters of business, and I could hardly get a word or a look from the young lady — nothing like a civil answer — she screwed up her mouth, and turned from me with such an air! I did not see her again for a twelvemonth. She was then *out.* I met her at Mrs Holford's, and did not recollect her. She came up to me, claimed me as an acquaintance, stared me out of countenance; and talked and laughed till I did not know which way to look. I felt that I must be the jest of the room at the time, and Miss Crawford, it is plain, has heard the story.'

'And a very pretty story it is, and with more truth in it, I dare say, than does credit to Miss Anderson. It is too common a fault. Mothers certainly have not yet got quite the right way of managing their daughters. I do not know where the error lies. I do not pretend to set people right, but I do see that they are often wrong.'

'Those who are showing the world what female manners *should* be, are doing a great deal to set them right,' said Tom gallantly.

'The error is plain enough, such girls are ill brought up. They are given wrong notions from the beginning. They are always acting upon motives of vanity, and there is no more real modesty in their behaviour *before* they appear in public than afterwards,' I said, for the business seemed clear to me.

'I do not know, I cannot agree with you there,' said Miss Crawford. Turning back to Tom, she said, 'It is much worse to have girls not out give themselves the same airs and take the same liberties as if they were, which I have seen done. That is worse than anything — quite disgusting!'

'Yes, *that* is very inconvenient indeed,' agreed Tom. 'It leads one astray; one does not know what to do. The close bonnet and demure air you describe so well (and nothing was ever juster) tell one what is expected; but I got into a dreadful scrape last year from the want of them. I went down to Ramsgate for a week with a friend . . .'

And he embarked on another anecdote, which entertained Miss Crawford no less than the first.

I searched my memory for something light and amusing with which to entertain her, but my years spent looking after the estate had given me no such diverting moments, and I was pleased when at last the conversation returned to Fanny.

'But now I must be satisfied about Miss Price,' said Miss Crawford. 'Does she go to balls? Does she dine out everywhere, as well as at my sister's?'

'I do not think she has ever been to a ball,' I said.

'Oh, then the point is clear. Miss Price is *not* out.'

I could not help thinking about the matter further, though, when Miss Crawford left us. Fanny is eighteen, and my sisters were both attending balls by that age, schooled in what was expected of them by Mama and my aunt. But for some reason Fanny had been overlooked.

I raised the point with my aunt, who said only that she was sure Fanny had no notion of being brought out, and Mama, who said that Fanny was too young, for she was not strong and so it was unsuitable for her to be brought out as early as my sisters.

'Besides,' she said, 'I need Fanny to stay with me when you all go to a ball. I could not do without Fanny.'

I think, for the time being, I will say no more, but I will not have her neglected, and once my father returns I mean to broach the subject with him. Fanny must have her share of the pleasures as well as everyone else, and as Mama will no longer be lonely when Papa returns it will then be the time for Fanny to start going into society.

Monday 18 July

Tom left for Brighton this morning. He went early, saying to me, 'Never fear, I have promised Papa not to gamble, and I mean to keep my word. I am a reformed character!'

I gave him a look, but he only laughed,

and then he was on his way.

He showed no regret at leaving Miss Crawford, and as he had never once talked of abandoning his trip so that he might spend more time with her, I believe he is not serious in his feelings for her.

To my relief, Miss Crawford does not seem to be serious in her feelings for him, either. I thought she would be in low spirits at his departure, but when she and her brother called on us this afternoon she was *bright as the day, and like the morning, fair*.

'And are you missing your brother?' Miss Crawford asked Julia, as we walked out in the grounds.

'Not in the least,' said Julia.

'And you, Mr Bertram?' she asked me. 'How well that sounds,' she mused, 'for now that your brother is away, you are no longer Mr Edmund Bertram, but Mr Bertram. Will you miss your brother?'

'I will not have time, for he will be home again in a few weeks,' I said.

'Very true. I should not miss *my* brother if he were to go away, as he talks of doing, to look after his estate, but perhaps others here would.'

Maria said politely that of course he must be missed if he went, whereupon Crawford said that his going was by no means certain, and that as he had only himself to please, and as Mrs Grant pressed him to stay, he believed his estate could do without him a little longer.

I was pleased for Miss Crawford's sake. She and her brother are close, and I know she enjoys his company, for all her teasing: small wonder, when she has neither mother nor father, and only a half sister in Mrs Grant.

We soon parted company, too soon for my liking, but we are to meet again tomorrow. Miss Crawford's person and appearance grow on me daily and I find myself thinking that any day in which I do not see her is a day ill spent.

Thursday 21 July

We were joined for dinner by Rushworth, for he had returned from visiting his friend. Maria seemed pleased to see him and introduced him proudly, which did much to allay my fears about her feelings for him, and Rushworth seemed very pleased to be with us.

Before long he began talking about the improvements his friend was making to his estate.

'I mean to improve my own place in the same way,' he said as we went into dinner.

'Smith's place is the admiration of all the country; and it was a mere nothing before Repton took it in hand. I think I shall have Repton.'

'If I were you, I would have a very pretty shrubbery. One likes to get out into a shrubbery in fine weather,' said Mama.

'Smith has not much above a hundred acres altogether in his grounds, which is little enough, and makes it more surprising that the place can have been so improved. Now, at Sotherton we have a good seven hundred, without reckoning the water meadows; so that I think, if so much could be done at Compton, we need not despair.'

I saw Miss Crawford glance at Maria, and Maria looked pleased at this talk of her future home.

'There have been two or three fine old trees cut down, that grew too near the house,' went on Rushworth, 'and it opens the prospect amazingly, which makes me think that Repton, or anybody of that sort, would certainly have the avenue at Sotherton down: the avenue that leads from the west front to the top of the hill, you know,' he said.

Fanny and I exchanged startled glances.

'Cut down an avenue!' said Fanny to me in an aside. 'What a pity! Does it not make you think of Cowper? *Ye fallen avenues, once more I mourn your fate unmerited.*'

'I am afraid the avenue stands a bad chance, Fanny,' I said.

The conversation turned to talk of alterations in general and Miss Crawford began to speak of her uncle's cottage at Twickenham, but as she did so I was surprised to find that she seemed to blame him for the dirt and inconvenience of the alterations he was making. Her liveliness seemed out of place and her droll comments, instead of lifting my spirits, dampened them, for it was disagreeable to hear her speak so slightingly of the man who had taken her in when her parents had died.

I was glad when the conversation moved on to her harp.

'I am assured that it is safe at Northampton; and there it has probably been these ten days, in spite of the solemn assurances we have so often received to the contrary,' she said. 'I am to have it tomorrow; but how do you think it is to be conveyed? Not by a wagon or cart: oh no! nothing of that kind could be hired in the village. I might as well have asked for porters and a handbarrow.'

I smiled at her naïveté, for she was surprised that it should be difficult to hire a horse and cart at this time of year! What did she expect, when the grass had to be got in?

'I shall understand all your ways in time; but, coming down with the true London maxim, that everything is to be got with money, I was a little embarrassed at first by the sturdy independence of your country customs,' she said. 'However, I am to have my harp fetched tomorrow. Henry, who is good-nature itself, has offered to fetch it in his barouche. Will it not be honourably conveyed?'

Her humour was infectious, and I found myself looking forward to the morrow, for if there is one instrument I like above all others, it is the harp. Fanny expressed a wish to hear it, too.

'I shall be most happy to play to you both,' said Miss Crawford. 'Now, Mr Bertram, if you write to your brother, I entreat you to tell him that my harp is come. And you may say, if you please, that I shall prepare my most plaintive airs against his return, in compassion to his feelings, as I know his horse will lose.'

'If I write, I will say whatever you wish me,' I replied, rather more reluctantly than I had intended, for I was dismayed to know that she still thought of Tom, even though he was no longer with us. 'But I do not, at present, foresee any occasion for writing.'

'What strange creatures brothers are! You would not write to each other but upon the most urgent necessity in the world. Henry, who is in every other respect exactly what a brother should be, who loves me, consults me, confides in me, and will talk to me by the hour together, has never yet turned the page in a letter; and very often it is nothing more than, "Dear Mary, I am just arrived. Bath seems full, and everything as usual. Yours sincerely." That is the true manly style; that is a complete brother's letter,' she said comically.

Fanny, however, saw nothing amusing in it, and was indignant on behalf of her own brother, her much-loved William. She could not help saying boldly, 'When they are at a distance from all their family, they can write long letters.'

I was glad that love had driven her to do what encouragement had not; for it did me good to hear her join in the conversation and express her views, rather than sit quietly by.

'Miss Price has a brother at sea, whose excellence as a correspondent makes her think you too severe upon us,' I explained, as Miss Crawford looked startled.

'Ah. I understand. He is at sea, is he? In

the King's service, of course?'

Fanny had by that time blushed for her own forwardness, but as it was an excellent opportunity for her to speak, I remained resolutely silent, so that she had to continue. As she began to talk of William she lost her shyness, and her voice became animated as she spoke of the foreign stations he had been on; but such was her tenderness that she could not mention the number of years he had been absent without tears in her eyes.

Miss Crawford civilly wished him an early promotion, and a thought occurred to me.

'Do you know anything of my cousin's captain? Captain Marshall? You have a large acquaintance in the Navy, I conclude?' I asked her, thinking that perhaps something might be done to help William.

'Among admirals, large enough, for my uncle, as you know, is Admiral Crawford; but we know very little of the inferior ranks,' she said. 'Of various admirals I could tell you a great deal: of them and their flags, and the gradation of their pay, and their bickerings and jealousies. But, in general, I can assure you that they are all passed over, and all very ill used.'

Again I was surprised and unsettled by her lack of respect for her uncle and his friends, and I replied with something or nothing, saying, 'It is a noble profession,' and the subject soon dropped.

A happier one ensued, and before long we were talking of the improvements to Sotherton again. Crawford's opinion was sought, as he has done much to improve his own estate, and the long and the short of it is that we are all to make a trip to Sotherton, so that we can give our opinions as to what should be done with the park.

Friday 22 July

I found that Miss Crawford's remarks about her uncle preyed on my mind and I decided to consult Fanny, for I knew I could rely on her judgement. I repaired to her sitting-room at the top of the house and tapped on the door. A gentle 'Come in' bid me enter, and I was soon inside the room. I felt better the moment I stepped over the threshold. Everything about the room spoke of Fanny's personality: the three transparencies glowing in the window, showing the unlikely juxtaposition of Tintern Abbey, a cave in Italy and a moonlight lake in Cumberland; the family profiles hanging over the mantelpiece; the geraniums and the books; the writing desk; the works of charity; and the sketch of HMS *Antwerp,* done for her by

William, pinned against the wall. I believe there is scarcely a room in the house with so much character or so much warmth.

'Well, Fanny, and how do you like Miss Crawford now?' I asked her as I took a seat.

'Very well,' she said with a smile. 'Very much. I like to hear her talk. She entertains me; and she is so extremely pretty, that I have great pleasure in looking at her.'

'She has a wonderful play of feature!' I agreed, lost, for the moment, in remembrance of her beauty. But then I returned to my reason for coming. 'Was there nothing in her conversation that struck you, Fanny, as not quite right?'

'Oh yes!' she said at once, as though reading my mind. 'She ought not to have spoken of her uncle as she did.'

I knew she would see it and I let out a sigh as I was reassured that I had not been wrong. But when Fanny went on to speak of Miss Crawford as ungrateful I had to defend her, saying, 'Ungrateful is a strong word. She is awkwardly circumstanced. With such warm feelings and lively spirits it must be difficult to do justice to her affection for her departed aunt, without throwing a shade on the admiral.'

'Do not you think,' said Fanny, after a little consideration, 'that this impropriety is a reflection upon that aunt, as her niece has been entirely brought up by her?'

At this, I was struck anew by Fanny's intelligence, for that was undoubtedly the case: Miss Crawford's faults were not her own, they were the faults of her upbringing.

'Her present home must do her good,' I said, much relieved. 'Mrs Grant's manners are just what they ought to be. I am glad you saw it all as I did, Fanny. No doubt, before long, Miss Crawford will see it all as we do, too.'

Having eased my feelings, I spent the afternoon seeing to estate business, but I could not keep my mind on my work, for it kept drifting back to Mary Crawford. She is the kind of woman I most admire, with a slight figure, dainty and elegant, and just the sort of features I love to look at. She has sense and cleverness and quickness of spirits. She is in every way an addition to Mansfield Park.

Saturday 23 July
The harp has arrived, and after dinner at the rectory, Miss Crawford took her place at the instrument. Beyond her was the window, cut down to the ground, and through it I could see the little lawn surrounded by shrubs. Clad in the rich foliage

of summer the garden made a striking contrast with her white silk gown and set her off to great advantage.

I was surprised at Crawford, who whispered to my sister Maria throughout the recital, for the music was excellent, and I could scarce take my eyes away from Miss Crawford as she played.

'You are an avid listener, Mr Bertram,' she said, as she stood up at last. 'I do not believe I have ever had a more attentive audience.'

I thought fleetingly of Tom's ease with women and the kind of clever reply he would have made, but I was not adept at teasing phrases and I could only assure her of my great pleasure in listening to her. It seemed to satisfy her, however, for she smiled at me, and I felt myself drawn to her even more.

The sandwich tray was brought in and Dr Grant did the honours. Even this simple activity seemed full of interest tonight and the time passed so quickly that I could scarcely believe it when it was time to leave.

I thanked Miss Crawford and she said that I must come again. Mrs Grant echoed her invitation and I accepted with pleasure.

What a summer this is turning out to be!

Monday 25 July

It has always been Miss Crawford's habit to take a stroll in the evenings and it has now become a regular thing that we all walk out together. My work about the estate is being left to others, and I am spending less time with my family, but I cannot help myself. Miss Crawford is so agreeable that I cannot tear myself away.

Saturday 30 July

'I saw you ride past my window this morning,' said Miss Crawford to my sisters as she and her family joined us at the Park for dinner. 'How I envied you your exercise.'

'You must come with us,' said Maria.

'It would do no good, for I cannot ride.'

'Cannot ride?'

The idea was startling.

'Then you must learn,' said Maria.

'Alas, I have no horse,' she said ruefully.

'Then you must borrow one of ours.'

'Indeed you must,' I pressed her. 'I have just the animal, a quiet mare who is perfect for beginners.'

'What if I am frightened?' she asked, glancing at me teasingly, so that I could not tell whether she meant it or not, for her temperament is so different from my own that half the time I do not know how to understand her.

'There is no need,' I said, taking her at her word. 'She is the quietest creature imaginable. I bought her for Fanny when the grey pony died.'

'In that case I must decline,' she protested. 'I cannot think of taking Miss Price's mare from her. It would be very wrong.'

'There would be no question of that. If Fanny does not object, it would only mean taking the mare down to the Parsonage half an hour before your ride, well before Fanny usually goes out, and you may both have your exercise.'

Fanny said at once that she did not mind at all.

'Then I will bring the mare down to the Parsonage tomorrow,' I said.

'And will you instruct me?' Miss Crawford asked me.

'If you wish.'

'I do wish. I will feel safer with you there, for I am sure you will be able to teach me how to go on, you are such an experienced horseman. I should have learned before this; Henry was always trying to teach me; but somehow I never had the urge before now.'

'Then we must not disappoint you. I will be at the Parsonage early with the groom.'

Her face fell.

'I have no habit,' she said.

'That is nothing,' said Mrs Grant, 'you may borrow one of mine until you can have one made. You will want something in a newer style eventually, but mine will serve you for the present.'

As the ladies continued to talk of their habits, I found myself looking forward to the morrow with an eagerness I have not felt since I was a boy.

Sunday 31 July

I set out after church for the Parsonage, rejoicing in the day. It was calm and serene, with just enough cloud to prevent it being too hot, and a welcome breeze. Miss Crawford was waiting for me, attired in Mrs Grant's habit.

'You must excuse my dress,' she said drolly, glancing at the yards of material that trailed on the floor behind her. 'My sister is inches taller than I am.'

Tom would have thought of a compliment, but such things do not spring easily to my mind. Instead I told her that her habit would do very well and helped her to mount. She was almost as light as Fanny, and with my hands round her waist she was soon sitting on the mare. She looked nervous to find herself so far off the ground, but I reassured her, and she laughed at her fears and was soon restored to her usual humour. I gave her instructions on how to sit, and how to hold the reins, and everything else necessary for her to begin, and then told her how to walk forwards, which she did with surprising grace.

'If I had known it was so enjoyable I would have learnt to ride long ago,' she said, as her confidence grew, 'though I suppose with riding, as with everything else, it is the company that determines the enjoyment.'

She cast me a smiling glance and I felt that she had read my mind, for it was her company that was making the day so enjoyable for me.

After half an hour I felt she had had enough and she reluctantly dismounted.

'You seem formed for a horsewoman,' I said to her as I escorted her back into the Parsonage.

'And for a musician,' she said, glancing at the harp. 'If you will but give me a moment to change out of my habit, I will play for you.'

'I should be getting back to the house. Fanny will be wanting her mare.'

'Cannot the groom take her back? I feel I cannot let you go without a reward for your efforts. Do not make me shame myself by taking so much from you without giving you something in return.'

I could not resist her and, having instructed the groom to take the mare back to the Park, I awaited her in the sitting-room. Mrs Grant sat with me whilst I waited, telling me how pleased she was with her brother and sister, and before long Miss Crawford returned, to entertain me with her playing. I do not know whether it was the liquid notes of the harp or the graceful movement of her white arms across the strings that enthralled me most but I was held captive, and I felt that I had never spent a pleasanter morning in my life.

AUGUST

Monday 1 August

Miss Crawford made even better progress this morning than she did on Friday, and delighted me with her daring.

'This is wonderful!' she said, as she walked the mare about the stable yard. 'Why have I never done this before?'

'Because you have lived in town, and there it is not so easy to learn.'

'But here, with you, it is simple,' she said, giving me a smile. 'I am beginning to think a country life is the life for me after all. To spend my time in the open air, in country pursuits, is becoming the ideal for me, whereas a few months ago the thought of it filled me with horror. What, to live amongst green fields with no shops or theatres to entertain me? But then I did not know what pure entertainment could come from simply living.'

I felt she had been in the saddle long

enough, and was about to help her dismount when she said she wanted to try her skills beyond the stable yard. She was playful yet determined, and at last I gave in. Mrs Grant, coming into the stables at that moment, proposed that we made a party of it, and before long Dr and Mrs Grant, Crawford, Miss Crawford and I ventured into the meadow, escorted by our grooms.

We were about to walk round the meadow when Crawford suggested that, if I would escort his sister, the rest of the party would watch her and see how she did.

'We can observe her much better if we are not too close to her,' he said.

The others were agreeable and Miss Crawford and I set off round the meadow together. To begin with we went at a walking pace but then she said, 'This is so tame! Why do we not go faster?'

And with that she began to canter. She had a good seat and sat with her back straight and her head held high. Her veil was blowing behind her in the wind and a lock of her hair fell clear of its pins and blew about her face. It drew my eye, and I was not sorry when I had to call her to a halt and show her how to manage the bridle.

'But there is Miss Price,' she said, with an effort glancing towards the Park. 'I have been very remiss. I have enjoyed myself so much I had quite forgotten her. Take me to her, if you please, so that I can apologize to her for keeping her from her exercise.'

I walked beside her, through the gate and into the lane, and we saw Fanny coming to meet us. I felt I had not behaved as I ought, for I had forgotten Fanny entirely whilst I had been with Miss Crawford, but Miss Crawford apologized so prettily that Fanny could not help but be satisfied.

'I give way to you with a very bad grace,' said Miss Crawford. 'But I sincerely hope you will have a pleasant ride, and that I may have nothing but good to hear of this dear delightful animal.'

I helped her to spring down and then the old coachman lifted Fanny up on to the horse and they set off together.

Maria and Julia were delighted to discover that their new friend showed such a natural ability.

'I was sure she would ride well,' said Julia, 'she has the make for it. Her figure is as neat as her brother's.'

'Yes,' added Maria, 'and her spirits are as good, and she has the same energy of character. I cannot but think that good horsemanship has a great deal to do with the mind.'

I could not help but agree.

When we parted at night, I asked Fanny whether she meant to ride the next day.

'No, I do not know — not if you want the mare,' she said kindly.

'I do not want her at all for myself, but whenever you are next inclined to stay at home, I think Miss Crawford would be glad to have her a longer time — for a whole morning, in short. She has a great desire to get as far as Mansfield Common: Mrs Grant has been telling her of its fine views, and I have no doubt of her being perfectly equal to it. But any morning will do for this. She would be extremely sorry to interfere with you. It would be very wrong if she did. *She* rides only for pleasure; *you* for health.'

'I shall not ride tomorrow, certainly. I have been out very often lately, and would rather stay at home. You know I am strong enough now to walk very well.'

She is right in this, but I cannot help protecting her for I have done so almost half my life, and indeed I do not think I could stop now even if I wanted to.

Tuesday 2 August

We rode out to the common this morning and I was astounded by Miss Crawford's rapid progress.

'You did not think I could do it,' she said to me teasingly. 'Come, admit it.'

'On the contrary, I never had a doubt of it,' I told her. 'I have seldom seen anyone take to horseback as rapidly as you have done.'

'We must go out again tomorrow,' she said. 'I am sure there must be some other fine rides hereabouts, and we ought to make the most of the weather whilst it is so fine.'

'Oh, yes, there are many pleasant rides,' said Maria, 'and there are an abundance of shady lanes, so that we may take our exercise even if the day is hot.'

'Then I am at your disposal,' said Miss Crawford.

Crawford was included in the invitation and we have arranged to meet again early tomorrow morning.

Wednesday 3 August

Three times now we have ridden around the country and Miss Crawford has never once complained of the heat, though it has been very hot. Today was no exception and we were all glad to arrive back at the Parsonage, where we sat in the shade and drank lemonade.

'You must dine with us this evening,' said Mrs Grant. She turned to Maria. 'We cannot prevail upon you to stay with us, of course, Miss Bertram, as rumour has it a certain person might be calling at the Park this evening, and we must not suppose any entertainment we can offer you will be equal to his. But I hope we may prevail upon you, Mr Bertram, and you, Miss Julia, to join us.'

Maria returned to the Park and Julia and I spent a very agreeable evening at the Parsonage, with a fine dinner and Miss Crawford's excellent harp to entertain us. Crawford joined her in a song and persuaded Julia to join in, too. Usually reluctant to sing, she yielded to Crawford's entreaties and we were all very well entertained.

Julia and I walked home through the warm summer evening, glowing and cheerful, but when we returned to the Park we found that Maria, Mama and Aunt Norris were very much the reverse. Maria would scarcely raise her eyes from her book and wore a scowl; Mama was half asleep and even Aunt Norris was silent. Fanny was nowhere to be seen, but when I asked if she had gone to bed, her own gentle voice spoke from the other end of the room and she said she was on the sofa.

'That is a very foolish trick, Fanny, to be idling away all the evening upon a sofa,' my aunt scolded her. 'Why cannot you come and sit here, and employ yourself as *we* do? If you have no work of your own, I can supply you from the poor-basket. You should learn to think of other people; and take my word for it, it is a shocking trick for a young person to be always lolling upon a sofa.'

'I must say, ma'am, that Fanny is as little upon the sofa as anybody in the house,' remarked Julia.

Fanny by this time had joined my aunt at the table, and I saw that she was looking far from well. When I questioned her, she admitted she had a headache, and that she had had one since before dinner. It was not hard to find out why, for my aunt had sent her out into the garden to cut roses.

'It was very hot,' said Mama, 'though it was shady enough in the alcove where I was sitting.'

I was vexed that Fanny had been so ill used, and further vexed to discover that she had not only been standing and stooping in the hot sun, but that she had been sent across the park to my aunt's house twice, the first time to take the roses and the second time to lock the door.

'For she forgot to lock it the first time, so she was obliged to go again,' said my aunt.

'This should never have happened,' I said,

as I put my hand sympathetically on Fanny's head. 'It was too hot for anyone to walk much in the sun today, and certainly too hot for Fanny.'

'If Fanny would be more regular in her exercise, she would not be knocked up so soon,' said my aunt. 'She has not been out on horseback now this long while, and I am persuaded that when she does not ride she ought to walk.'

I said no more, but took a glass of Madeira to Fanny and made her drink it.

Vexed as I was with Mama and Aunt Norris for keeping her out so long in the sun, I was more vexed with myself, for it was I who had deprived her of her exercise by encouraging Miss Crawford to ride the mare. And it was I who had left her without any choice of companionship whilst we were away.

However unwilling I was to check a pleasure of Miss Crawford's, I resolved that Fanny must have the mare whenever she wanted, for I would not see her ill again.

Thursday 4 August

I made good my resolve and took Fanny out for a ride this morning. I found that I had missed her company. The pleasant, fresh-feeling morning inspired us to travel farther afield than usual and we rode to Bridge's farm. We called in to see Mrs Bridge, for Fanny had heard that she was not well, and found her in bed with the new baby beside her. The other children were running wild, for although the eldest girl did her best, the younger ones would not mind her. Fanny set about seeing to Mrs Bridge's comfort and helping her with the baby whilst I called the children to order, and soon they were usefully occupied. When we left the house there were fresh flowers in an earthenware jar on the windowsill, the floor had been swept, Mrs Bridge was easy, the baby was sleeping, and the other children were playing outside in the sunshine.

We returned to the house. Having seen Fanny safely indoors, I went round to the stables to speak to the coachman, and when I went into the house at last I found that Rushworth and his mother were there. They had revived the plan of a visit to Sotherton and it had been decided that we would all go on Wednesday; all except Fanny, who was to stay at home with Mama.

'I am sure Fanny would like the visit,' I said. 'I know she particularly wants to see the avenue. She may take my place and I will stay at home with you, Mama.'

There were the usual protests but at last I

had my way.

Monday 8 August

There was a change of plan this morning, for Mrs Grant offered to stay behind with Mama, and so I am to go with the others to Sotherton. I could not help my spirits rising at the thought of spending a day with Miss Crawford.

Wednesday 10 August

It was a perfect morning for our journey to Sotherton. Crawford arrived early with his sisters and Mrs Grant alighted from the carriage, saying, 'As there are five of you, it will be better that one should sit with Henry, and as you were saying lately, that you wished you could drive, Julia, I think this will be a good opportunity for you to take a lesson.'

Julia mounted the box and sat next to Crawford whilst Maria took her seat within. Fanny and Miss Crawford joined her and I mounted my horse. Mrs Grant and Mama waved us off, with Pug barking in Mama's arms, and we were away.

As I rode behind the barouche I could not help but observe Fanny, and take satisfaction from her expression, which spoke of her delight at everything she saw. The road to Sotherton was new to her and her face lit up at each new view. The landscape was pretty with the harvest and there was plenty to see, with the cottages, the cattle and the children all adding to the colour.

'These woods belong to Sotherton,' said Maria as we reached Rushworth land, and she was rewarded by a look of admiration from Fanny, for indeed, the woods were majestic, and in the heat of the day they delighted us not only with their grandeur but with their ability to provide us with welcome shade. 'I believe it is all now Mr Rushworth's property, on either side of the road.'

The mansion soon came in view. Miss Crawford looked curious, Fanny interested, and Maria proud, and small wonder, for it is a fine property. Julia paid it no heed, for she was attending to Crawford, and he was equally absorbed in teaching her.

We arrived at last and found Rushworth at the door to receive us. Maria blossomed under his attentions, and the attentions of his mother, and she pointed out all the attractions of the house to Mary Crawford with the consciousness of a young woman who would soon be calling it home.

'This is very elegant,' said Miss Crawford as we went into the dining-parlour, where a collation was laid out.

'It is one of the newer additions to the house,' said Mrs Rushworth.

She was an attentive hostess and, as we ate, Rushworth returned to the subject of the improvements to the estate. He proposed driving Crawford round it in his curricle when he should have finished his repast, the better to give his opinion.

'But that would be to deprive ourselves of other eyes and other judgements. Would it not be better to find some carriage that could accommodate us all?' Crawford asked.

The point was still being discussed by the time we finished our repast, and the matter was delayed by Mrs Rushworth offering to show us around the house before we set out.

Fanny was fascinated by the furniture and the rugs; the marble and the damask; and the family portraits which lined the walls. Miss Crawford, though, was restless, and confided in me that she had seen many such houses.

We went into the chapel, and here Fanny was disappointed.

'This is not my idea of a chapel. There is nothing awful here, nothing melancholy, nothing grand, no fleur-de-lys, or quatregeuille, or garlands.'

'You have been influenced too much by

Scott. This is no Melrose Abbey,' I said with a smile, for Fanny's reading had prepared her for something far more Gothic.

'Perhaps I have,' she returned, and I knew that, in her imagination, she was seeing the Abbey Scott had described, in the eerie light of moonlight. She began to murmur:

'The darken'd roof rose high aloof
On pillars lofty and light and small;
The key-stone, that lock'd each ribbed
    aisle,
Was a fleur-de-lys, or a quatre-geuille,
The corbells were carved grotesque and
    grim;
And the pillars, with cluster'd shafts so
    trim,
With base and with capital flourish'd
    around,
Seem'd bundles of lances which garlands
    had bound.'

I continued:

'Full many a scutcheon and banner riven,
Shook to the cold night-wind of heaven,
Around the screenëd altar's pale;
And there the dying lamps did burn,
Before thy low and lonely urn,
O gallant Chief of Otterburne.'

'But here are no pillars, no lamps, no inscriptions,' she said, disappointed.

'You forget, Fanny, how lately all this has been built, and for how confined a purpose, compared with the old chapels of castles and monasteries. It was only for the private use of the family. They have been buried, I suppose, in the parish church. *There* you must look for the banners and the achievements.'

'It was foolish of me not to think of all that; but I am disappointed all the same. I hoped to find banners being blown *by the night wind of heaven.* Or even,' she added with a smile, *'rustling with the current of air, foretelling woe and destruction.'*

'Now *that* I know,' said Miss Crawford. 'It is from Charlotte Smith's *The Old Manor House.'*

'You have read it?' I asked.

'Indeed, I am fond of Gothic romances — particularly on long winter evenings when there is nothing better to do. Henry read it to me last year. And to be sure, this chapel needs a current of air foretelling woe, for it is very dull.'

Mrs Rushworth, ahead with the others, was explaining that, although the house had its own chapel, it was no longer used for family prayers.

'Every generation has its improvements,' said Miss Crawford in a droll voice.

And, just as I felt I was getting to know her, I realized I did not know her at all.

I was dismayed by her attitude, for I have always felt there was something fine about a family assembling for prayers, all together, turning their thoughts into the same path before they separate for the day.

Fanny voiced my thoughts, but Miss Crawford was not to be persuaded, saying satirically, 'Very fine indeed! It must do the heads of the family a great deal of good to force all the poor housemaids and footmen to leave business and pleasure, and say their prayers here twice a day, while they are inventing excuses themselves for staying away.'

'*That* is hardly Fanny's idea of a family assembling,' I told her.

But she would not be serious, saying, 'Cannot you imagine with what unwilling feelings the former belles of the house of Rushworth did many a time repair to this chapel? The young Mrs Eleanors and Mrs Bridgets — starched up into seeming piety, but with heads full of something very different — especially if the poor chaplain were not worth looking at — and, in those days, I fancy parsons were very inferior even to what they are now.'

Fanny coloured, for she felt all the un-luckiness of this remark as it reflected on my chosen profession. But although I was dismayed at Miss Crawford's attitude, I took heart from the fact that she was surely capable of thinking seriously on serious subjects if only she was given encourage-ment to do so. She could not have reached womanhood without realizing that not everything in life could be turned into a jest.

I was hoping to discuss it with her, but barely had we begun when Julia distracted our attention by saying, 'Do look at Mr Rushworth and Maria, standing side by side, exactly as if the ceremony were going to be performed. Have not they completely the air of it? Upon my word, it is really a pity that it should not take place directly, if we had but a proper licence, for here we are altogether, and nothing in the world could be more snug and pleasant.'

'It will be a most happy event to me, whenever it takes place,' said Mrs Rush-worth.

'My dear Edmund, if you were but in orders now, you might perform the cer-emony directly. How unlucky that you are not yet ordained. Mr Rushworth and Maria are quite ready.'

Miss Crawford looked stunned.

'Ordained!' she said, turning to me and looking aghast. 'What, are you to be a clergyman?'

'Yes, I shall take orders soon after my father's return — probably at Christmas,' I told her.

She regained her colour quickly, saying, 'If I had known this before, I would have spoken of the cloth with more respect.'

I smiled, for it showed that, as I suspected, she had a good heart, and had simply been carried away by playfulness. As we left the chapel I walked beside her to show I was not offended by her unfortunate remarks.

We soon afterwards came to a door leading outside. We took it, and found ourselves amidst lawns and shrubs, where pheasants roamed at will. There was also a bowling-green and a long terrace walk, backed by iron palisades, beyond which lay a wilderness.

Crawford spotted the capabilities of the area and was soon deep in conversation with Maria and Rushworth, whilst Fanny, Miss Crawford and I went on. The day was hot and after a walk along the terrace, Miss Crawford expressed a wish to go into the wilderness, where we would be cool beneath the trees. We went in, going down a long flight of steps, and found ourselves in darkness and shade.

'This is better,' said Miss Crawford. 'Give me a wilderness and I am happy, rather than a straight path which is hard beneath the feet. Here is nature untrammelled, not bent into shapes which do not suit her, but allowed to roam free. It is a much happier place. Do you not think so, Mr Bertram?'

'For my own part I prefer a path, but the wilderness has a certain allure,' I conceded.

'There is too much regularity in the planting, but otherwise a pretty wilderness, very pretty indeed,' said Miss Crawford.

'Too much regularity! Not at all,' said Fanny. 'Nature must have some order, or we would lose our way.'

Miss Crawford was soon speaking again of my plans to become a clergyman.

'Why should it surprise you?' I asked her. 'You must suppose me designed for some profession, and might perceive that I am neither a lawyer, nor a soldier, nor a sailor.'

'Very true; but, in short, it had not occurred to me. And you know there is generally an uncle or a grandfather to leave a fortune to the second son.'

'A very praiseworthy practice, but not quite universal!'

'But why are you to be a clergyman?' she

said, puzzling over it. 'I thought *that* was always the lot of the youngest, where there were many to choose before him.'

'Do you think the church itself never chosen?' I asked, amused at her ignorance.

'Men love to distinguish themselves, and a clergyman is nothing.'

I was only too happy to prove her wrong, and Fanny ventured her own opinions, which were in support of mine.

'You have quite convinced Miss Price already,' said Miss Crawford satirically.

'I wish I could convince Miss Crawford, too,' I returned.

She laughed and said, 'I do not think you ever will. You really are fit for something better. Come, do change your mind. It is not too late. Go into the law,' she offered.

'Go into the law! With as much ease as I was told to go into this wilderness!' I said, torn between exasperation and amusement.

'Now you are going to say something about the law being the worst wilderness of the two,' she said with an arch smile, 'but I forestall you.'

'You need not hurry when the object is to prevent me from saying a bon mot, for there is not the least wit in my nature,' I said, for I was frustrated by her determination to turn everything into a joke.

A general silence fell, and I regretted my ill-humoured words, but they were said and could not be recalled. It was broken only when Fanny said she was tired and that, when we came to a seat, she would like to rest for a while.

I immediately drew her arm through mine, to give her my support, and after a moment's hesitation I offered my other arm to Miss Crawford. To my relief she took it and we walked on.

The gloom did not last long, and I blessed Miss Crawford's wit and good humour just as much as, a few minutes before, I had been condemning them, for she bore no grudge for my sharpness and was soon teasing me again.

'We have walked a very great distance,' she said airily. 'It must have been at least a mile.'

'Not half a mile!' I protested.

'Oh! you do not consider how much we have wound about. We have taken such a very serpentine course, and the wood itself must be half a mile long in a straight line, for we have never seen the end of it yet since we left the first great path.'

'But if you remember, before we left that first great path, we saw directly to the end of it. We looked down the whole vista, and saw it closed by iron gates, and it could not have been more than a furlong in length.'

'Oh! I know nothing of your furlongs,' she said, 'but I am sure it is a very long wood.'

'We have been exactly a quarter of an hour here,' I teased her, taking out my watch. 'Do you think we are walking four miles an hour?'

'Oh! do not attack me with your watch. A watch is always too fast or too slow. I cannot be dictated to by a watch!'

Perfect good humour was restored by the time we came to the bottom of the wood, where there was a seat, and we all sat down.

'To sit in the shade on a fine day, and look upon verdure, is the most perfect refreshment,' said Fanny.

Miss Crawford, however, was of a livelier disposition and was soon eager to be walking again. There was a straight green running along the side of the ha-ha, and she proposed walking along it, to better determine the dimensions of the wood. I fell in with her wishes and, leaving Fanny sitting on the bench to rest, we walked on together.

'Now, Miss Crawford, if you will look up the walk, you will convince yourself that it cannot be half a mile long, or half half a mile,' I said.

She smiled saucily. 'It is an immense

distance. I see *that* with a glance.'

We were still laughing and arguing the point when we came to a side gate which led into the Park. To my surprise and pleasure — for I was growing tired of the wilderness, despite its beauty — Miss Crawford expressed a wish to go into the Park. I tried the gate; it was not locked; and we went through.

We came at last to the avenue.

'So these are the trees Mr Rushworth thinks his landscaper will cut down,' mused Miss Crawford.

'Indeed.'

'It would look better, I agree, for it would open the prospect wonderfully, but I am glad the avenue is here today. It is much pleasanter beneath the trees.'

We sat beneath them and talked of many things, Miss Crawford charming me as she so easily does, and I began to think that, if only she could be brought to think seriously from time to time, she would be my idea of a perfect woman.

We soon resumed our walk and found Fanny much rested on our return. I gave her my arm and we walked back to the house, where soon the whole party assembled for dinner. The talk was all of the projected improvements to the estate and we set out for home in great good humour.

It was a beautiful evening, mild and still, and I could not help wishing for more such days, and such evenings, in the future.

Monday 15 August

The mail brought a letter from my father, saying he intended to take his passage in the September packet, and that he would be with us in November.

The Crawfords dined with us this evening and Miss Crawford looked lovelier than ever in a simple muslin gown. After tea, as we stood by the window looking out into the twilight, the pearls in her dusky hair glowed like the moon in the darkening sky and I had an urge to lift my hand to her head. It was only with difficulty that I resisted.

'Your father's return will be an interesting event,' she said, turning towards me.

'It will indeed, after such an absence; an absence not only long, but including so many dangers,' I agreed.

'It will be the forerunner also of other interesting events; your sister's marriage, and your taking orders,' she said pensively.

'Yes.'

'Don't be affronted,' she said, with an air both humorous and restless, 'but it does put me in mind of some of the old heathen heroes, who after performing great exploits in a foreign land, offered sacrifices to the gods on their safe return.'

'There is no sacrifice in the case,' I said, glancing at Maria, who sat at the pianoforte with Rushworth, 'it is entirely her own doing.'

'Oh yes I know it is. I was merely joking. She has done no more than what every young woman would do; and I have no doubt of her being extremely happy. My other sacrifice, of course, you do not understand.'

But she was wrong; I did understand; and I assured her that my taking orders was also voluntary.

'It is fortunate that your inclination and your father's convenience should accord so well,' she said. 'There is a very good living kept for you, I understand, hereabouts.'

'Which you suppose has biased me? It has, but not in any blameworthy way: I do not see why a man should make a worse clergyman because he knows he will have a competence early in life.'

Fanny had joined us and she added her agreement, saying, 'It is the same sort of thing as for the son of an admiral to go into the Navy, or the son of a general to be in the Army, and nobody sees anything wrong in that. Nobody wonders that they should prefer the line where their friends can serve them best, or suspects them to be less in earnest in it than they appear.'

'No, my dear Miss Price, and for reasons good,' said Miss Crawford. 'The profession, either Navy or Army, is its own justification. It has everything in its favour: heroism, danger, bustle, fashion. Soldiers and sailors are always acceptable in society. Nobody can wonder that men are soldiers and sailors.'

'But the motives of a man who takes orders with the certainty of preferment may be fairly suspected, you think?' I asked. 'To be justified in your eyes, he must do it in the most complete uncertainty of any provision.'

'What! take orders without a living! No; that is madness indeed; absolute madness.'

'Shall I ask you how the church is to be filled, if a man is neither to take orders with a living nor without?' I asked her in amusement. 'No; for you certainly would not know what to say.'

At this she smiled, acknowledging the point.

'But I must beg some advantage to the clergyman from your own argument,' I went on. 'As he cannot be influenced by those feelings which you rank highly as temptations to the soldier and sailor in their choice of a profession; as heroism, and noise, and fashion, are all against him, he ought to be less liable to the suspicion of wanting sincerity or good intentions in the choice of his.'

'Oh! no doubt he is very sincere in preferring an income ready made, to the trouble of working for one; and has the best intentions of doing nothing all the rest of his days but eat, drink, and grow fat,' she said airily. 'It is indolence, Mr Bertram, indeed; indolence and love of ease; a want of all laudable ambition, of taste for good company, or of inclination to take the trouble of being agreeable, which make men clergymen. A clergyman has nothing to do but be slovenly and selfish — read the newspaper, watch the weather, and quarrel with his wife. His curate does all the work, and the business of his own life is to dine.'

'You can have been personally acquainted with very few of a set of men you condemn so conclusively,' I said, thinking, as before, that her thoughts came from others and not herself, for she had not enough experience to draw such conclusions from the few opportunities she had had to mix with clergymen. 'You are speaking what you have been told at your uncle's table.'

But she immediately contradicted me.

'I have been so little addicted to take my opinions from my uncle that I can hardly suppose — and since you push me so hard, I must observe, that I am not entirely without the means of seeing what clergymen are, being at this present time the guest of my own brother, Dr Grant. And though Dr Grant is most kind and obliging to me, and though he is really a gentleman, and, I dare say, a good scholar and clever, and often preaches good sermons, and is very respectable, *I* see him to be an indolent, selfish bon vivant, who must have his palate consulted in everything; who will not stir a finger for the convenience of any one; and who, moreover, if the cook makes a blunder, is out of humour with his excellent wife. To own the truth, Henry and I were partly driven out this very evening by a disappointment about a green goose, which he could not get the better of. My poor sister was forced to stay and bear it.'

My suspicions were every moment being confirmed. She had only had bad examples before her and so it was not to be wondered at that she should feel as she did. But I hoped that when she had seen more she would change her mind; and I knew her to be so reasonable that I did not have a doubt of it.

'It is a great defect of temper, and to see your sister suffering from it must be exceedingly painful to such feelings as yours,' I acknowledged. 'Fanny, it goes against us. We cannot attempt to defend Dr Grant.'

'No, but we need not give up his profession for all that,' said Fanny. 'Besides, a sensible man like Dr Grant cannot go to church twice every Sunday, and preach such very good sermons, without being the better for it himself. It must make him think; and I have no doubt that he oftener endeavours to restrain himself than he would if he had been anything but a clergyman.'

'We cannot prove to the contrary, to be sure; but I wish you a better fate, Miss Price, than to be the wife of a man whose amiableness depends upon his own sermons,' said Miss Crawford satirically. 'For though he may preach himself into a good humour every Sunday, it will be bad enough to have him quarrelling about green geese from Monday morning till Saturday night.'

'I think the man who could often quarrel with Fanny must be beyond the reach of any sermons,' I said affectionately.

Fanny smiled, and turned her face to the

window so that I should not see how much my words had pleased her. I thought how pretty she was looking, and I was glad that my father was returning, so that she would soon be able to take part in all the pleasures of life to which her growing maturity entitled her.

'I fancy Miss Price has been more used to deserve praise than to hear it,' said Miss Crawford, seeing how shyly she received the compliment.

I was about to say that that would change when Fanny went more into society, but I was forestalled by Maria calling for Miss Crawford from the pianoforte, and inviting her to join them in a glee.

Miss Crawford agreed at once, tripping off to the instrument. I looked after her, thinking what a wonderful woman she was, from her obliging manners down to her light and graceful tread.

'There goes good humour, I am sure,' I said. 'How well she walks! and how readily she falls in with the inclination of others! joining them the moment she is asked. What a pity that she should have been in such hands!'

Fanny agreed, for if Miss Crawford had had better friends and relatives, it was clear to both of us that her opinions would have matched our own.

We remained by the window and looked out into the darkening night. All that was solemn and soothing and lovely appeared in the brilliancy of the unclouded sky, and the contrast of the deep shade of the woods.

'Here's harmony!' said Fanny softly. 'Here's repose! Here's what may leave all painting and all music behind, and what poetry only can attempt to describe! Here's what may tranquillize every care, and lift the heart to rapture! When I look out on such a night as this, I feel as if there could be neither wickedness nor sorrow in the world.'

She spoke with great feeling, and I said it was a great pity that not everyone had been given a taste of nature, for they lost a great deal by it.

'*You* taught me to think and feel on the subject,' she said with a warm smile.

'I had a very apt scholar,' I replied. I turned my head to look up at the star-speckled sky. 'There's Arcturus looking very bright.'

'Yes, and the Bear,' mused Fanny. 'I wish I could see Cassiopeia.'

'We must go out on the lawn for that. Should you be afraid?'

'Not in the least. It is a great while since

we have had any stargazing.'

'I do not know how it has happened,' I said.

I was about to give her my arm and suggest we supply our recent lack, when the bustle around the pianoforte died down and the music began.

'We will stay till this is finished, Fanny,' I said.

I walked over to the instrument and as I did so Miss Crawford began to sing. I was enchanted by her voice which flowed, silvery, into the warm night; and I was enraptured by the sight of her standing with her hands clasped in front of her, showing the delicacy of her white arms and the grace of her carriage. I was so enchanted by the whole that, when it was over, I asked to hear it again.

The evening at last broke up and I walked Miss Crawford's party back to the rectory.

It was only when I returned to the Park that I realized that Fanny and I had not had our stargazing, after all.

Saturday 27 August

Tom has returned and has regaled us all with stories of Brighton and Weymouth, of parties and friends, and all his doings of the last six weeks. I watched Miss Crawford, fearing to see signs of her earlier liking for him returning but, although she listened politely to everything he had to say, she seemed more interested in talking to me. It relieved me more than I can say.

Her face, her voice, her carriage, her air, all delight me. Indeed, I find myself thinking that, if I had anything to offer her, I would be in some danger, for she is the most bewitching woman I have ever met.

Monday 29 August
Henry Crawford has returned to his own estate in Norfolk, for he cannot afford to be absent in September when there is so much to be done. My sisters seem listless without him, for they have both greatly enjoyed his company, but Miss Crawford and Fanny are the same as ever and their spirits carry us through.

Tuesday 30 August
Owen wrote to me this morning inviting me to stay with his family again at Christmas. He suggested I make it a longer visit than previously, as we are going to be ordained together, and I have accepted.

September

Monday 12 September

After a fortnight's absence, Henry Crawford is with us once more. He made a welcome addition to our party this evening, for I fear we were all tired of hearing Rushworth's commentary on his day's sport, his boasts of his dogs, his jealousies of his neighbours and his zeal after poachers. Indeed, he seems to have no other conversation.

Fanny was surprised at Crawford's return, for he had told us often that he was fond of change and moving about and she had thought he would have gone on to somewhere gayer than Mansfield. But I was pleased he had come back, for I was sure his presence gave his sister pleasure.

'What a favourite he is with my cousins!' Fanny remarked.

I agreed that his manners to women were such as must please and I was heartened to find that Mrs Grant suspected him of a preference for Julia.

'I have never seen much symptom of it,' I confessed to Fanny, 'but I wish it may be so. He has no faults but what a serious attachment would remove, and I think he would make her a good husband.'

Fanny was silent and looked at the floor. After a minute she said cautiously, 'If Miss Bertram were not engaged, I could sometimes almost think that he admired her more than Julia.'

'Which is, perhaps, more in favour of his liking Julia best, than you, Fanny, may be aware,' I told her kindly, for she has seen very little of the world. 'I believe it often happens that a man, before he has quite made up his own mind, will distinguish the sister or intimate friend of the woman he is really thinking of more than the woman herself. Crawford has too much sense to stay here if he found himself in any danger from Maria, engaged as she is to Rushworth.'

I found myself wishing Mary Crawford had a friend or unmarried sister here, so that I could distinguish her, for I am afraid of showing Miss Crawford too much attention, and yet I cannot help myself.

I believe I am worrying unnecessarily, though. Even if she suspects a preference on my part, she will not want an offer from a man in my position, and so I need have no fear of raising expectations which I am not in a position to fulfil.

Wednesday 21 September
One of Tom's friends arrived today. Tom was surprised to see him, for he had issued no more than a casual invitation, but nevertheless he made Yates welcome. Yates's unexpected arrival was soon explained. He had come from Cornwall where he had been at a house party, but it had been cut short by the sudden death of a relative of those with whom he was staying. He had had no choice but to leave, and remembering Tom's invitation, he had come to us. He arrived with an air of one whose enjoyment had been curtailed, and on learning we had a violin player in the servants' hall, he suggested a ball.

Julia and Maria agreed eagerly, whilst Miss Crawford turned a dazzling countenance on him and told him it was an excellent idea. I was in favour of it, too. Fanny had never been to a ball, and I was pleased that her first experience of such an entertainment would take place at Mansfield, where her shyness would be no handicap and where she would be sure of partners. I secured her hand for the first two dances and made sure Tom would ask her later on. I knew I could rely on Crawford to act the gentleman and ask her as well, and so he did.

Miss Crawford and I danced together, and though we danced 'til late, I would have been happy for the ball to have gone on 'til dawn.

Thursday 22 September

'By Jove! we are a happy party,' said Yates at breakfast. 'Even happier than the party in Cornwall, or at least happier than we were before Ravenshaw suggested we all perform a play. Ecclesford is one of the best houses in England for doing such a thing. What a time we had of it! The rehearsals were going along splendidly . . .' he said, with a sigh and a shake of the head.

'It was a hard case, upon my word,' said Tom.

'I do think you are very much to be pitied,' said Maria.

'The play we were to have performed was *Lovers' Vows,* and I was to have been Count Cassel. A trifling part, and not at all to my taste, and such a one as I certainly would not accept again; but I was determined to make no difficulties. Lord Ravenshaw and the duke had appropriated the only two characters worth playing before I reached Ecclesford; and though Lord Ravenshaw offered to resign his to me, it was impossible to take it, you know. Our Agatha was inimitable, and the duke was thought very great by many. And upon the whole, it would certainly have gone off wonderfully. It is not worth complaining about; but to be sure the poor old dowager could not have died at a worse time; and it is impossible to help wishing that the news could have been suppressed for just the three days we wanted. It was but three days; and being only a grandmother, and all happening two hundred miles off, I think there would have been no great harm, and it was suggested, I know; but Lord Ravenshaw, who I suppose is one of the most correct men in England, would not hear of it.'

'An afterpiece instead of a comedy,' said Tom. '*Lovers' Vows* were at an end, and Lord and Lady Ravenshaw left to act *My Grandmother* by themselves. To make *you* amends, Yates, I think we must raise a little theatre at Mansfield, and ask you to be our manager.'

The idea seized the party.

'Let us be doing something,' said Crawford. 'Be it only half a play, an act, a scene;

what should prevent us? And for a theatre, what signifies a theatre? We shall be only amusing ourselves. Any room in this house might suffice.'

'We must have a curtain,' said Tom. 'A few yards of green baize for a curtain, and perhaps that may be enough.'

'Oh, quite enough,' cried Yates, 'with only just a side wing or two run up, doors in flat, and three or four scenes to be let down; nothing more would be necessary on such a plan as this. For mere amusement among ourselves we should want nothing more.'

I was startled, for such an undertaking would involve a great deal of expense at a time when the estate could little afford it, besides taking the carpenter from his regular duties at a time when he could not be spared. But Tom waved my doubts aside and was soon pressing the merits of a comedy, whilst my sisters and Crawford preferred a tragedy.

There was so much argument I began to breathe easily again, for I thought they would argue so much over the play that nothing would come of it after all. But in this I was mistaken, for when we were in the billiard room this evening, Tom declared it to be the very size and shape for a theatre.

'If we move the bookcase away from the

door in my father's room, it can be made to open, and as it will then communicate with our theatre in the billiard room we can use it as a greenroom.'

'You are not serious?' I asked him.

'Not serious! Never more so, I assure you. What is there to surprise you in it?'

'We cannot make free with my father's room,' I objected.

'Why not? What does it matter, when he is not here to see it?'

My thoughts ran to wine stains on the carpet, white rings on the desk — for I believed Yates to be capable of putting a hot cup down on the polished wood — and all the attendant evils of carelessness, but Tom would not listen.

I spoke to him of our reputation and our father's absence but he only said, 'Pooh! You take everything too seriously, Edmund. Anyone would think we were going to act three times a week till my father's return, and invite all the country! And as to my father's being absent, it is so far from an objection, that I consider it rather as a motive; for the expectation of his return must be a very anxious period to my mother; and if we can be the means of amusing that anxiety, and keeping up her spirits for the next few weeks, I shall think our time very well spent, and so, I am sure, will he. It is a *very* anxious period for her.'

As he said this, we looked towards our mother who, sunk back in one corner of the sofa, the picture of health, ease, and tranquillity, was just falling into a gentle doze.

I could not help giving a wry smile, and Tom had the grace to laugh.

'By Jove! this won't do,' he cried, throwing himself into a chair. 'To be sure, my dear mother, your anxiety — I was unlucky there.'

'What is the matter?' she asked, half-roused. 'I was not asleep.'

'Oh dear, no, ma'am, nobody suspected you! Well, Edmund,' he continued, 'but *this* I *will* maintain, that we shall be doing no harm.'

Nothing I could say would sway him; no concern for Maria and Julia's reputations, for if word of it got out they would be regarded as fast; nor considerations of our father's wishes, for he would surely not wish us to take such liberties with his house whilst he was away; nor thoughts of the upheaval and expense.

'I know my father as well as you do; and I'll take care that his daughters do nothing to distress him. Manage your own concerns, Edmund, and I'll take care of the rest of the family,' he said. 'Don't imagine that nobody in this house can see or judge but yourself. Don't act yourself, if you do not like it, but don't expect to govern everybody else.'

He walked out of the room and I sat down by the fire, feeling exceedingly low, for I was sure one thing would lead to another and I feared that, before long, we would find ourselves embroiled in a major undertaking. And I was responsible, for I had promised my father I would look after affairs in his absence. What would he feel if he returned to find the profits of the estate spent on something so frivolous, when he had just spent two years in Antigua in an effort to mend the family fortunes?

Fanny followed me and sat down beside me.

'Perhaps they may not be able to find any play to suit them. Your brother's taste and your sisters' seem very different,' she said.

'I have no hope there, Fanny,' I said with a sigh. 'If they persist in the scheme, they will find something. I shall speak to my sisters and try to dissuade *them,* and that is all I can do.'

She agreed that this would be my best choice of conduct. Tomorrow, then, I must try to dissuade my sisters from acting, and hope it puts an end to the scheme.

I did my best to dissuade Maria and Julia from putting on a play this morning, but they would not listen to me.

'Of course the estate can bear the expense,' said Maria.

'I am persuaded Rushworth would not like you to act,' I said, trying to sway her.

'He must learn I have a mind of my own,' she returned.

Julia was no easier to persuade, for although she thought Maria had better not act, as for herself, there could be no objection to it.

At that very moment Henry Crawford entered the room, fresh from the Parsonage, calling out, 'No want of hands in our theatre, Miss Bertram. No want of understrappers: my sister desires her love, and hopes to be admitted into the company, and will be happy to take the part of any old duenna or tame confidante, that you may not like to do yourselves.'

Maria looked at me as much as to say, 'Can we be wrong if Mary Crawford sees no harm in it?'

I was obliged to acknowledge that the charm of acting might well carry fascination to the mind of genius; and to think that Miss Crawford, as ever, was the most obliging young woman. She, at least, was blameless, for she did not know how my father's affairs stood, and could not be expected to know that any additional expense, coming at such a time, was very undesirable.

My aunt expressed a few reservations when Tom told her of the scheme and I hoped, briefly, that this would dampen his enthusiasm, but he and Maria joined forces and soon talked Aunt Norris out of her objections, and the play became a settled thing.

I must now make it my concern to limit the scope of the production so that it does as little harm as possible.

Saturday 24 September

Tom lost no time in calling the estate carpenter to the house, despite the fact that Jackson was needed to finish mending the fences blown down in last week's strong winds. Tom told him to take measurements for a stage.

'And when you have done, there is a bookcase in my father's room that needs moving,' he said.

I reminded Jackson about the fence, and bid him see to it as soon as he was free, but if Tom is to continue as he has begun, he is going to make my life very difficult over the weeks to come.

'And now for the baize. Where are we to get it, Aunt?' asked Tom.

'Had you better not wait until you have decided on a play?' I asked him.

'Details,' he said, with a wave of his hand.

'You must send to Northampton,' said Aunt Norris. 'They have quite the finest baize in the county, I saw it there the last time I went. It was of a superior quality, and they had just the shade we are looking for.'

Friday 30 September

The green baize has arrived, my aunt has cut out the curtains and the housemaids are busy sewing them, but no play has as yet been decided upon. At least I have had the fences repaired, for I forbade Christopher Jackson the house until the work was done.

OCTOBER

Monday 3 October

A play has been decided on at last, the worst play imaginable. If I had been there I would have spoken against it, but I was out for the day, and knew nothing about it until I returned just before dinner, when Rushworth told me the news.

'It is to be *Lovers' Vows.* I am to be Count Cassel, and am to come in first with a blue dress and a pink satin cloak,' he said. 'And afterwards I am to have another fine fancy suit, by way of a shooting-dress. I do not know how I shall like it. Bertram is to be Butler, a trifling part, but a comic one, and it is comedy he wants to play. And Crawford is to be Frederick.'

I was dumbstruck. *Lovers' Vows*! With all its embracing and clasping to bosoms! The last play my father would want in his house!

'But what do you do for women?' I asked, knowing that my sisters could not play the parts, for Agatha was a fallen woman and Amelia was a shameless one.

Maria blushed in spite of herself as she answered, 'I take the part which Lady Ravenshaw was to have done, and . . .' she lifted her eyes to mine instead of letting them drop to the floor. 'Miss Crawford is to be Amelia.'

I could not believe it. To condemn Miss Crawford to such a part! It was not worthy of her. And for Maria to play Agatha!

'I come in three times, and have two-and-forty speeches,' said Rushworth. 'That's something, is not it? But I do not much like the idea of being so fine. I shall hardly know myself in a blue dress and a pink satin cloak.'

I could not think how Tom had allowed it. I could say nothing in front of Yates, as his friends had been about to perform it at Ecclesford, but later I remonstrated with Maria.

'My dear Maria, *Lovers' Vows* is exceedingly unfit for private representation, and I hope you will give it up. I cannot but suppose you *will* when you have read it carefully over. Read only the first act aloud to either your mother or aunt, and see how you can approve it. Agatha is a fallen woman. She is seduced by her lover and left with child. You cannot play such a part. You cannot pretend to have been seduced, you cannot speak of fervent caresses, or embrace the man who plays your son, pressing him to your breast. You would not want to do such a thing, especially not now you are engaged. Only read the play, and it will not be necessary to send you to your *father's* judgement, I am convinced.'

'We see things very differently,' said Maria uncomfortably. 'I am perfectly acquainted with the play, I assure you; and with a very few omissions, and so forth, which will be made, of course, I can see nothing objectionable in it; and *I* am not the *only* young woman you find who thinks it very fit for private representation.'

'You are Miss Bertram. It is *you* who are to lead. *You* must set the example.'

I thought her pride would sway her, for she looked as though she was about to give way, but then her face closed and she said, 'I am much obliged to you, Edmund; you mean very well, I am sure: but I still think you see things too strongly; and I really cannot undertake to harangue all the rest upon a subject of this kind. *There* would be the greatest indecorum, I think.'

'Do not act anything improper, my dear,' said Mama, overhearing a part of our conversation, and rousing herself momentarily. 'Sir Thomas would not like it.' But her concern was short-lived, for a moment later she was saying, 'Fanny, ring the bell; I must have my dinner.'

'I am convinced, madam,' I said to my mother, pressing what small advantage I had gained from her contribution to the conversation, 'that Sir Thomas would not like it.'

'There, my dear, do you hear what Edmund says?' said Mama to Maria.

'If I were to decline the part,' said Maria, 'Julia would certainly take it.'

'Not if she knew your reasons!' I said.

'Oh! she might think the difference between us — the difference in our situations — that *she* need not be so scrupulous as *I* might feel necessary. I am sure she would argue so. No; you must excuse me; I cannot retract my consent; it is too far settled, everybody would be so disappointed, Tom would be quite angry; and if we are so very nice, we shall never act anything.'

'I was just going to say the very same thing,' said my aunt. 'If every play is to be objected to, you will act nothing, and the preparations will be all so much money thrown away, and I am sure *that* would be a discredit to us all. I do not know the play; but, as Maria says, if there is anything a little too warm (and it is so with most of them) it can be easily left out. We must not be over-precise, Edmund. As Mr Rushworth is to act too, there can be no harm. I only wish Tom had known his own mind when the carpenters began, for there was the loss of half a day's work about those side-doors. The curtain will be a good job, however. The maids do their work very well, and I think we shall be able to send back some dozens of the rings. There is no occasion to put them so very close together. I *am* of some use, I hope, in preventing waste and making the most of things.'

And off she went, delighted at having saved the estate half a crown by her careful use of curtain rings, when she had cost it pounds by her excessive use of baize.

Dinner passed heavily. The only thing that heartened me was the discovery that Julia had refused to act.

As soon as we returned to the drawing-room, discussion of the play began again. Whilst the others were engaged, I took the opportunity of drawing Tom to one side.

'I cannot believe you mean to perform *Lovers' Vows*,' I said to him.

'Why ever not?' he said. 'There is nothing wrong with it.'

'Nothing wrong with having Maria act out

the part of a woman who is seduced and left with an illegitimate child? Especially situated as she is, in a long engagement with Rushworth —'

'And you think it will give him ideas? You need not have any fear that he will seduce her. I doubt if he has it in him,' said Tom.

'I wish you would be serious, Tom.'

'I am perfectly serious.'

'Very well then, what will Rushworth think of seeing his fiancée perform the speeches and acquire the mannerisms of such a woman?'

'He will not pull back, if that is what you are worried about. Listen to him! He is too busy thinking about his pink satin cloak to notice what Maria does. I verily believe it has taken the place of his dogs in his affections, for I have not heard him mention the animals once all day.'

'If Julia knows it is wrong, and has refused to act —'

Tom laughed. 'The only reason she refused to act is that she wanted the part of Agatha, and once it went to Maria she refused to take any other. It was ill-humour, and not scruples, that prevented her taking part.'

I was dismayed. I felt I had let my father down. He had entrusted his daughters to my care, and what had become of them? Had they turned into the young women he would like them to be? No, they had turned into creatures who fought over the dubious pleasure of portraying a fallen woman.

'Besides, Miss Crawford has agreed to it, so how can it be wrong?' continued Tom.

'She is a very obliging woman who would agree to anything if it would increase the pleasure of others,' I said.

But he only laughed and went off to join the others, saying, 'We must have three scene changes. No, four. . . .'

I retired to the side of the room, where I sat beside Mama and listened to her tales of Pug.

By and by, I walked over to the table, where I saw a copy of *Lovers' Vows* lying open. I picked it up, hoping I might have misremembered it, but my fears increased as soon as I opened it and read what was written there.

Agatha. I cannot speak, dear son! [*Rising and embracing him*] My dear Frederick! The joy is too great . . . I was not prepared . . .

Frederick. Dear mother, compose yourself: [*leans her against his breast*] now, then, be comforted. How she trembles!

She is fainting.

I could not think of Maria embracing Crawford, or he leaning her against his breast, without fearing for my sister's reputation; to say nothing of her future, for her eagerness to play such a part left me with the disquieting belief that her feelings for Rushworth were far from fixed.

My only consolation was that the performance was to be a private one, and that no one beyond our family circle would ever know of it.

I put the book down and returned to Mama, who had been joined by Fanny.

'This is a bad business, Fanny,' I said.

She shared my feelings, and it was a relief to me to be able to talk of them with someone who felt the same.

We were soon joined by the Crawfords, who had walked over from the Parsonage.

Miss Crawford, ever solicitous for the feelings of others, spoke at once to Mama.

'I must really congratulate your ladyship,' said she, 'on the play being chosen; for though you have borne it with exemplary patience, I am sure you must be sick of all our noise and difficulties. The actors may be glad, but the bystanders must be infinitely more thankful for a decision; and I do sincerely give you joy, madam, as well as Mrs Norris, and everybody else who is in the same predicament,' she said, glancing towards Fanny and me.

'I am glad it is settled on at last,' said Mama.

Miss Crawford joined the others, but I could tell she had no real taste for the endeavour, and who could blame her, being asked to play the part of such a pert, forward young woman as Amelia?

I could tell there was something on her mind and at last it came out when she asked, 'Who is to play Anhalt?'

'I should be but too happy in taking the part, if it were possible,' cried Tom; 'but, unluckily, the Butler and Anhalt are in together. I will not entirely give it up, however; I will try what can be done — I will look it over again.'

Yates suggested I do it, but I could not in all conscience take the part, for that would be to condone the folly. My father left his daughters and his estate in my care, and I have no intention of handing them back to him ruined when he returns in two months' time.

Miss Crawford soon left the others and joined Fanny and me.

'They do not want me at all,' said she,

seating herself. 'Mr Edmund Bertram, as you do not act yourself, you will be a disinterested adviser; and, therefore, I apply to *you*. What shall we do for an Anhalt? Is it practicable for any of the others to double it? What is your advice?'

'My advice is that you change the play,' I said.

'*I* should have no objection, for though I should not particularly dislike the part of Amelia if well supported, that is, if everything went well, I shall be sorry to be an inconvenience; but as they do not choose to hear your advice at *that table,* it certainly will not be taken.' She fell silent for a moment and then said, 'If *any* part could tempt *you* to act, I suppose it would be Anhalt, for he is a clergyman, you know.'

'*That* circumstance would by no means tempt me,' I said ungraciously, remembering how she had ridiculed my calling. 'It must be very difficult to keep Anhalt from appearing a formal, solemn lecturer; and the man who chooses the profession itself is, perhaps, one of the last who would wish to represent it on the stage.'

She fell silent and then moved her chair away.

I was instantly sorry for my ill-humour, and feared I had not been polite. Besides, I could not help wondering if her words had been meant as an olive branch. By asking me to play Anhalt, was she not telling me that she no longer found the clergy objectionable?

I was about to speak to her when Tom began to urge Fanny to take the part of Cottager's wife.

'Me!' cried Fanny, with a most frightened look. 'Indeed you must excuse me. I could not act anything if you were to give me the world. No, indeed, I cannot act.'

This provoked such an unkind torrent of words from my aunt, saying that Fanny was ungrateful and other such nonsense, that I would have spoken, except that I was for the moment too angry to do so. But I found there was no need, for Miss Crawford glanced at her brother to prevent any further urging from the actors and then pulled her chair close to Fanny's so that she could comfort her in the most charming way.

'You work very neatly,' she said, looking at Fanny's needlework. 'I wish I could work as well. And it is an excellent pattern. You would oblige me very much if you would lend it to me.'

Fanny's tears were blinked back from her eyes and soon turned to smiles when Miss Crawford asked about William.

'You are lucky to have such a brother, but I am sure you deserve him. I have quite a curiosity to see him. I imagine him a very fine young man. If you will take my advice, Miss Price, you will get his picture drawn before he goes to sea again, it will be something good for you to keep by you.'

Such kindness could not help but provoke affectionate feelings from me, and, Miss Crawford happening to look up at that moment, her eyes met mine. We smiled.

And then Tom called out, 'I have just been looking at my part again, and can see no way of taking Anhalt as well as the Butler. I had thought, if I left out a few words here and there, I could make it do, but it is impossible. But there will not be the smallest difficulty in filling it. I could name at this moment at least six young men within six miles of us, who are wild to be admitted into our company, and there are one or two that would not disgrace us. I should not be afraid to trust Charles Maddox. I will take my horse early tomorrow morning and ride over to Stoke and settle with him.'

Miss Crawford was too well-mannered to make a complaint but she looked perturbed, and remarked to Fanny, 'I am not very sanguine as to our play, and I can tell Mr Maddox that I shall shorten some of his speeches, and a great many of my own, before we rehearse together.'

I felt all the wrongness of it, that a lovely young woman like Miss Crawford should be obliged to act such a part, and, even worse, to act it with a stranger. I began to feel that anything would be better than to leave her to such a fate, and to wonder whether I should agree to play the part of Anhalt, after all.

Tuesday 4 October

I could not sleep, and turned the idea of the play over and over in my mind as I lay awake in my bed. Was it best to resist every effort to persuade me to take part in the play and expose Miss Crawford to the indignity of acting with a man she did not know; especially in such a part, where the scenes were so warm; or should I save her from such a fate by taking the part myself? I was faced with a choice of two evils; and whilst it was the act of a responsible son to do the former, it was the act of a gentleman to do the latter.

I rose early, too restless to lie abed, and went out for a ride, but I was no nearer deciding what to do when I returned, and so I repaired to Fanny's sitting-room at the top of the house. A tap on the door, a gentle

'Come in,' and I was inside the room, feeling better the moment I stepped over the threshold. The geraniums were still in bloom, their red heads looking bright and cheerful against the white windows, and the transparencies were glowing as the autumn sun shone through them, casting coloured light on to the floor. And there was Fanny herself, the best sight of all, looking up from her book with her welcoming smile.

'Can I speak with you, Fanny, for a few minutes?' I asked.

'Yes, certainly.'

'I want to consult. I want your opinion.'

'My opinion?' she asked in surprise.

'I do not know what to do.'

I sat down and then stood up again, walking about the room as I laid the matter before her.

'I know no harm of Charles Maddox; but the excessive intimacy which must spring from his being admitted among us in this manner is highly objectionable, the *more* than intimacy — the familiarity. I cannot think of it with any patience; and it does appear to me an evil of such magnitude as must, *if possible,* be prevented. Do not you see it in the same light?'

'Yes; but what can be done? Your brother is so determined.'

'There is but *one* thing to be done, Fanny. I must take Anhalt myself. I am well aware that nothing else will quiet Tom.'

Fanny did not answer me. I knew exactly what she was feeling, for I was feeling it myself.

'After being known to oppose the scheme from the beginning, there is absurdity in the face of my joining them now, when they are exceeding their first plan in every respect,' I said, 'but I can think of no other alternative. Can you, Fanny?'

'No,' she admitted. 'I am sorry for Miss Crawford. But I am more sorry to see you drawn in to do what you had resolved against.'

I did not like it myself, but I felt it must be.

'As I am now, I have no influence, I can do nothing,' I said. 'I have offended them, and they will not hear me; but when I have put them in good-humour by this concession, I am not without hopes of persuading them to confine the representation within a much smaller circle than they are now in the high road for.'

I could tell she did not like it.

'Give me your approbation, Fanny. I am not comfortable without it. If you are against me, I ought to distrust myself —

and yet — but it is impossible to let Tom go on in this way, riding about the country in quest of anybody who can be persuaded to act. I thought *you* would have entered more into Miss Crawford's feelings. She never appeared more amiable than in her behaviour to you last night. It gave her a very strong claim on my goodwill.'

'She *was* very kind, indeed, and I am glad to have her spared,' said Fanny.

'I knew you would think so,' I said, much relieved to find she thought as I did. 'And now, dear Fanny, I will not interrupt you any longer. You want to be reading. But I could not be easy till I had spoken to you, and come to a decision. Sleeping or waking, my head has been full of this matter all night. It is an evil, but I am certainly making it less than it might be. If Tom is up, I shall go to him directly and get it over, and when we meet at breakfast we shall be all in high good-humour at the prospect of acting the fool together with such unanimity.'

I left her to her books and went down to breakfast, where I had the unpleasant task of telling Tom and Maria that I would take the part of Anhalt after all. They did not crow too loud, and, as I had hoped, were so pleased at my actions, that they agreed to limit the audience to Mrs Rushworth and the Grants.

After breakfast I walked down to the Parsonage and gave the news there as well. Miss Crawford's smiles rewarded me for my troubles and I felt that, after all, I had done the best I could in a difficult situation.

There was one other consolation. Miss Crawford, in the goodness of her heart, persuaded her sister to take the part of Cottager's Wife, so that Fanny would not be entreated to perform again.

My joy was short-lived, for when I returned to the Park I found Maria and Crawford rehearsing their parts so avidly I thought they could not forget their lines if they lived to be ninety. Every time I came upon them, Maria was either embracing Crawford or laying her head on his breast, so that I began to think I should have forbidden the play, sent Yates about his business, and locked Maria in her room until my father returned.

Wednesday 5 October
The house was in chaos this morning. I could not move without falling over someone. If it was not Tom, prancing around and saying:

'There lived a lady in this land,

186

Whose charms the heart made tingle;
At church she had not given her hand,
And therefore still was single.'

it was Yates, telling Julia she should not have been allowed to sit out, but should have been persuaded to take the part of Amelia, which would have suited her talents admirably; or my aunt, telling us she had managed to save half a crown here and half a crown there; or Rushworth, attempting to learn his forty-two speeches and failing miserably to learn even one.

Fanny was dragooned by my aunt, who, seeing her with a moment to herself between prompting Rushworth and condoling with Tom over the shortcomings of the scene painter, said, 'Come, Fanny, these are fine times for you, but you must not be always walking from one room to the other, and doing the lookings-on at your ease, in this way; I want you here. I have been slaving myself till I can hardly stand, to contrive Mr Rushworth's cloak without sending for any more satin; and now I think you may give me your help in putting it together. There are but three seams; you may do them in a trice. It would be lucky for me if I had nothing but the executive part to do. *You* are best off, I can tell you: but if nobody did more than *you,* we should not get on very fast.'

I was about to speak up for Fanny when Mama pleased me greatly by saying, 'One cannot wonder, sister, that Fanny *should* be delighted: it is all new to her, you know.'

I blessed her silently and went into the billiard room to find my script, for I had a great deal to learn.

As soon as I entered I heard Maria and Crawford rehearsing their lines.

Maria said, in languishing tones: *'He talked of love, and promised me marriage. He was the first man who ever spoke to me on such a subject. His flattery made me vain, and his repeated vows — Oh! oh! I was intoxicated by the fervent caresses of a young, inexperienced, capricious man, and did not recover from the delirium till it was too late.'*

I was horrified. Fervent caresses! Delirium! And Tom was standing there, listening to them from the side of the room, and encouraging them!

'Tom, I thought those lines had been cut,' I said.

'Why should they be cut?' he asked, whilst singing:

'Count Cassel wooed this maid so rare,
And in her eye found grace;

And if his purpose was not fair,
It probably was base.'

under his breath all the while.

'They are far too warm,' I said.

'Too warm? Nonsense.'

Maria, meanwhile, was declaiming: *'His leave of absence expired, he returned to his regiment, depending on my promise, and well assured of my esteem. As soon as my situation became known —'*

'Her *situation!*' I exploded.

'— I was questioned, and received many severe reproaches: But I refused to confess who was my undoer; and for that obstinacy was turned from the castle.'

'Be quick with your narrative, or you'll break my heart,' said Crawford, pressing her hand to his lips in a way I was sure was not in the script.

'I will say something if you will not,' I said to Tom.

'Oh, very well, I suppose those lines could be cut. Maria!' he called. 'There is no need to say that about fervent caresses.'

'But it is one of the most touching lines in the play!' protested Crawford.

'It shall not be said in this house,' I replied, and carried my way.

'Ah! Count!' said Tom, as Rushworth

entered the room. 'Just the fellow I was looking for. Give me my line.'

'Line? What line?' said Rushworth.

'The line that leads into my verses:

'For ah! the very night before,
No prudent guard upon her,
The Count he gave her oaths a score,
And took in change her honour.'

'You are out there, Bertram,' said Rushworth. 'That comes before the Count enters, and not afterwards.'

'No, no, before the Count enters I say:

'Then you, who now lead single lives,
From this sad tale beware;
And do not act as you were wives,
Before you really are.'

I found my script and left them to their arguing, glad to escape to the garden. It was refreshing to be outside, where I was not surrounded by fallen women, seducers and libertines.

I got my part by heart, and though it was not perfectly learnt, at least it was learnt after a fashion.

I returned to the house, where I found my aunt still at work on the curtains.

'And when you have finished there, you will oblige me by running across to my house and fetching my scissors,' said my aunt to Fanny, as I entered the drawing-room.

'Send someone else,' I said. 'I need Fanny.'

And so saying, I rescued her from her needlework and took her into the library, where we had a sensible conversation until dinner-time.

Even our meal could not be eaten in peace, for hardly had we all entered the dining-room than the others began reciting their parts.

'I'll not keep you in doubt a moment,' boomed Yates, as we all sat down. *'You are accused, young man, of being engaged to another woman while you offer marriage to my child.'*

'To only one other woman?' Rushworth replied.

'What do you mean?' Yates declaimed.

'My meaning is, that when a man is young and rich, has travelled, and is no personal object of disapprobation, to have made vows but to one woman is an absolute slight upon the rest of the sex.'

I was astonished at his remembering such a long speech, until I noticed he had a copy of the script hidden under the table.

'Please, let us have no more until we have eaten our dinner,' I begged, as the soup was brought in, but I was talking to myself.

'*He talked of love, and promised me marriage,*' said Maria in sepulchral tones.

'*Why should I tremble thus?*' asked Crawford.

It was a very Bedlam.

Mary caught my eye and gave me an understanding smile. Then she said, 'But we must forgive them, you know, the performance is now so very near. You and I must practise our scenes together tomorrow. We must have them right before we perform.'

I agreed, but only with a nod; for when I thought of the words I must say to her, and she to me, I found I could not speak.

Thursday 13 October

I rose early and went downstairs, where I found Christopher Jackson putting the finishing touches to the stage. It stretched from one end of the room to the other, and was set to rival the stage at Drury Lane.

'Master Thomas's orders,' said Jackson, when I protested. 'When I've finished with the stage, I'm to see about building the wings.'

I countermanded Tom's orders and then, over breakfast, I finished learning my lines.

I found I was dreading saying them to Mary, and so I repaired to Fanny's sitting-room, there to gain courage by reading them through with her first. But when I tapped on the door and went in I found, to my surprise, that Mary was already there, bent on the same task. There was surprise; a little awkwardness; then I said, 'As we are both here, we must rehearse together,' for it seemed easier to think of reciting our parts if there was a third person present.

She was at first reluctant but soon gave way to my entreaties. I handed my script to Fanny, begging her to help us, and to tell us when we went wrong.

Mary began nervously, for the part of Agatha was not an easy one for her: to pretend to be a young girl who was being persuaded into marrying a man she did not love by her father, when all the time her heart belonged to my character, a lowly clergyman.

'Ah! good morning, my dear Sir; Mr Anhalt, I meant to say; I beg pardon,' said Mary to me.

'Never mind, Miss Wildenhaim; I don't dislike to hear you call me as you did,' I said, rather stiffly.

'In earnest?' she asked, looking up at me.

'Really,' I said, more tenderly. *'You have been crying. May I know the reason? The loss*

of your mother, still?'

'*No,*' she said, with a heartrending sigh. '*I have left off crying for her.*'

'*I beg pardon if I have come at an improper hour; but I wait upon you by the commands of your father.*'

'*You are welcome at all hours,*' she said. '*My father has more than once told me that he who forms my mind I should always consider as my greatest benefactor.*' She looked down shyly. '*And my heart tells me the same.*'

Was there more to her words than a performance of the play? Did she think I was the man who could form her mind? And did she want me to be that man? Did her heart tell her that it was so?

'*I think myself amply rewarded by the good opinion you have of me,*' I said, and to my surprise, I found myself wanting to take her hand.

'*When I remember what trouble I have sometimes given you, I cannot be too grateful,*' she said, with a speaking look.

I thought of the trouble she had given me, and thought how well our lives matched the play; and how strange it was that Tom should have chosen it; and that it was perhaps not such a bad thing that he had.

'*Oh! Heavens!*' I said.

Fanny said gently, 'That bit is to yourself.'

'Oh? Is it? Thank you, Fanny.' I turned aside, and said the words as she directed.

'I — I come from your father with a commission,' I said. *'If you please, we will sit down.'* I looked about me for a chair. I found one and Mary found another. We both sat down, I nervously, and Mary very elegantly, arranging her skirts gracefully about her. *'Count Cassel is arrived.'*

'Yes, I know,' she said.

'And do you know for what reason?'

She looked at me with liquid eyes; eyes that were as transparent as the sunlight.

'He wishes to marry me,' she said.

I could not blame him. At that moment, I believe any man alive would have wished to marry her.

'Does he?' Fanny prompted me, when I did not speak.

'Does he?' I asked hastily. *'But believe me, your father . . . the Baron will not persuade you. No, I am sure he will not.'*

'I know that,' she said, with downcast eyes.

'He wishes that I should ascertain whether you have an inclination —'

'For the Count, or for matrimony do you mean?'

'For matrimony,' I said, finding myself growing hot, and, glancing at the grate, being surprised to see that there was no fire.

'All things . . .' whispered Fanny.

'Thank you, Fanny,' said Mary, then continued with her lines. *'All things that I don't know, and don't understand, are quite indifferent to me.'*

'For that very reason I am sent to you to explain the good and the bad of which matrimony is composed.'

As I said it, I found my eyes meeting hers, and something passed between us.

'Then . . . then I beg first to be acquainted with the good,' she said.

'When two sympathetic hearts . . .' I swallowed. *'When two sympathetic hearts meet in the marriage state, matrimony may be called a happy life. When such a wedded pair find thorns in their path, each will be eager, for the sake of the other, to tear them from the root. Where they have to mount hills, or wind a labyrinth, the most experienced will lead the way, and be a guide to his companion. Patience and love will accompany them in their journey, while melancholy and discord they leave far behind. Hand in hand they pass on from morning till evening, through their summer's day, till the night of age draws on, and the sleep of death overtakes the one. The other, weeping and mourning, yet looks forward to the bright region where he shall meet his still surviving partner, among trees and flowers which them-*

selves have planted, in fields of eternal verdure.'

She looked deep into my eyes and said, *'You may tell my father — I'll marry.'*

She rose from her chair and I wondered if her look, her tone and her meaning could be for me. Would she marry me?

I wished there was no more to be said, but Fanny, faithful prompter that she was, reminded me of my next line.

'This picture is pleasing,' I said, *'but I must beg you not to forget that there is another on the same subject. When convenience, and fair appearance joined to folly and ill-humour, forge the fetters of matrimony, they gall with their weight the married pair.'*

'Discontented . . .' said Fanny.

'Discontented with each other,' I went on, *'at variance in opinions — their mutual aversion increases with the years they live together. They contend most, where they should most unite; torment, where they should most soothe. In this rugged way, choked with the weeds of suspicion, jealousy, anger, and hatred, they take their daily journey, till one of these also sleep in death. The other then lifts up his dejected head, and calls out in acclamations of joy — Oh, liberty! dear liberty!'*

Mary's face had fallen, and there seemed something more in her look than could be explained by the play. There was something in her eye that reminded me of a caged bird.

'I will not marry,' she said.

'You mean to say, you will not fall in love,' I said, moving closer to her.

'Oh no!' She looked abashed, then said with great sweetness and simplicity, *'I am in love.'*

'Are in love!' How I wished it could be so.

'And with . . .' Fanny said.

'And with the Count?' I asked.

'I wish I was.'

'Why so?' I asked her tenderly.

'*Because* he *would, perhaps, love me again.*'

'Who is there that would not?' I asked, bending closer.

She leaned in towards me and said, *'Would you?'*

I forgot my lines, and fell silent.

'Ay, I see how it is,' she went on. *'You have no inclination to experience with me "the good part of matrimony": I am not the female with whom you would like to go "hand in hand up hills, and through labyrinths"; with whom you would like to "root up thorns; and with whom you would delight to plant lilies and roses." No, you had rather call out, "O liberty, dear liberty." '*

'*Why do you force from me, what it is villain-ous to own?*' I cried. '*I love you more than life. Oh, Amelia! had we lived in those golden times, which the poet's picture, no one but you.*'

No one but you. That is what I thought as I looked at her, with her eyes so bright. No one but you.

She seemed to feel it, too, for she could not go on until Fanny prompted her, and then made but an indifferent effort at the rest of the scene. My own efforts were no better, for I could think only, *No one but you.*

Fanny was kind. She said that, although we had missed some lines, our performance did us credit, and I found myself looking forward to a repetition of it when we should rehearse with the others in the evening.

The evening, however, brought a blow. Dr Grant was ill. It was not serious, but Mrs Grant had to remain at home, which left us without a Cottager's Wife. Everyone looked to Fanny, for we could not rehearse without Cottager's Wife.

'If Miss Price would read the part?' said Yates.

'Certainly, you would only have to read it, Fanny,' said Crawford. 'You would not need to act at all.'

'And I do believe she can say every word of it,' added Maria encouragingly, 'for she could put Mrs Grant right the other day in twenty places. Fanny, I am sure you know the part.'

Fanny was sweet and obliging, and although she did not like to act, she took the part so that the rehearsal might go ahead. I knew what it had cost her, and I thanked her for it warmly, and then it was time to begin.

Maria had got her lines by heart and needed no prompting. Crawford, too, knew his part well, and imbued it with a great deal of feeling, his voice carrying around the room. We had just got to the part where he seized Maria's hand when the door was thrown open and we all turned towards it in surprise.

Julia stood there, with a face all aghast, exclaiming, 'My father is come! He is in the hall at this moment.'

We looked at each other in stunned amazement! Our father? But he was not due back for another month! Then Tom, Maria, Julia and I, recovering ourselves, went to pay our respects to him in the drawing-room. And there he was, looking thinner, and burned by the sun, and tired after his journey, but pleased to be home.

We had hardly all greeted each other when he said, 'But where is Fanny? Why do not I see my little Fanny?' in such a kindly way that I loved him all the more. His stateliness had sometimes frightened her in the past, but his mood was so affectionate that I knew his notice would delight her.

Fanny stepped forward, and he embraced her, saying how much she had grown, and taking her over to the light so that he might see her better.

'I have no need to ask after your health, for I have never seen you more blooming,' he said. 'And how are your family?'

'Well, sir, I thank you.'

'And how is William?'

'He is well, sir.'

'Has he been made Captain?' he asked her with a smile.

'No, sir,' she said, adding, 'not yet.'

He laughed, glad to see her so bold, for she did not have the courage to say two words to him before he went away.

He bade us all sit by the fire and then told us of his adventures: his perils on the voyage, with storms and calms, and his business in Antigua, which had at last prospered. He broke off now and then to say how lucky he was to find us all at home.

'You must have something to eat, Sir

Thomas,' said my aunt. 'I will ring for some dinner at once.'

'No, no, I do not want to eat. I will wait for the tea to be brought in.'

'And how was your passage to England, sir?' asked Tom.

'Ah, now that was not such plain sailing,' he said. 'We had any number of storms, but worse was to come. We saw a sail on the horizon, and suddenly the ship sprang into action, for she was a French privateer. As she drew closer —'

'Sure, my dear Sir Thomas, a basin of soup would be a much better thing for you than tea,' broke in my aunt. 'Do have a basin of soup.'

'Still the same anxiety for everybody's comfort, my dear Mrs Norris,' said my father indulgently. 'But indeed I would rather have nothing but tea.'

Mama rang for tea directly, and my father continued with his tale.

'We could see her colours, and it looked for a moment as though we might not outrun her, but then the wind filled our sails and off we sped, leaving her behind us.'

'But how are you with us so soon?' Mama asked.

'I came directly from Liverpool. I had an opportunity of sailing in a private vessel, rather than waiting for the packet, for I saw one of my old friends in Liverpool who offered me passage on his yacht — and what a remarkable piece of good fortune it was to find you all here!' he said again, smiling at us all.

'It could not be too soon for me,' said Mama, watching him with love.

He looked around. 'How glad I am to find you all here, for I have come among you unexpectedly, and much sooner than looked for. And how lucky to find you here, too, Rushworth,' he said, for he did not forget Maria's fiancé.

'How do you think the young people have been amusing themselves lately, Sir Thomas?' said Mama. 'They have been acting. We have been all alive with acting.'

'Indeed! and what have you been acting?'

'Oh! They will tell you all about it.'

'The *all* will soon be told,' cried Tom hastily, and with affected unconcern; 'but it is not worthwhile to bore my father with it now. You will hear enough of it tomorrow, sir. We have just been trying, by way of doing something, and amusing my mother, just within the last week, to get up a few scenes, a mere trifle. We have had such incessant rains almost since October began, that we have been nearly confined to the house for days together. I have hardly taken out a gun since the third. Tolerable sport the first three days, but there has been no attempting anything since.'

Tea was brought in, but afterwards, my father would not be still, and said he would just go on a tour of the house. As soon as he left the room I knew something must be done. Tom went after Yates and I imagined my father's face when he found his own room was no longer recognizable, with an air of confusion in the furniture, the removal of the bookcase, and the door leading through to the theatre. And what a theatre! Not the discreet affair I had hoped to encourage, but, under Tom's fresh orders, an extravagant construction of timber, with stage and wings and scenery, complete with festooned curtains in yards of green baize.

It was not long before my father, Tom and Yates returned to the drawing-room. My father's good breeding prevented him from saying anything very much, though I could tell he was put out. Yates, entirely misjudging my father's silence, would not let the matter go, however, and rattled on about the play in a most ill-conceived manner. As he spelt out the history of the affair, I felt my father's eyes on me, as if to say, 'On your good sense, Edmund, I depended; what have you been about?'

I felt anew all the impropriety of having spent his money and used his house in such a way in his absence.

The conversation turned to the Crawfords and Tom pronounced Henry to be a most pleasant, gentlemanlike man, with Mary being a sweet, pretty, elegant, lively girl.

'I do not say he is not gentlemanlike, considering,' burst out Rushworth, surprising us all; 'but you should tell your father he is not above five feet eight, or he will be expecting a well-looking man. If I must say what I think, in my opinion it is very disagreeable to be always rehearsing. It is having too much of a good thing. I am not so fond of acting as I was at first. I think we are a great deal better employed, sitting comfortably here among ourselves, and doing nothing.'

It seemed he had noticed Maria and Crawford's behaviour after all, though why he had not said something at the time I could not imagine.

'I am happy to find our sentiments on this subject so much the same,' said my father.

After which, mercifully, the evening came to an end.

I was glad to return to my room, my mind in a whirl with the events of the day. Mary

— what did her looks, her smiles, mean, as she spoke to me of love and marriage?

My father — what must he think of me for using his house so ill in his absence?

I could not sleep — I still can not. First thing in the morning I must go to my father and explain the whole, for until I have apologized I will not be easy.

Friday 14 October

I am relieved that it is over, and that I have told my father how sorry I am for letting things get so out of hand. He was forbearing and shook hands with me, and I thought how lucky I was to have such a father. He gave instructions for Christopher Jackson to dismantle the theatre this morning, and he dismissed the scene painter. When the latter had gone we discovered how careless he had been, for he had spilt quantities of paint and had spoilt the floor. My father looked grave, but said only that he would see to its restoration, and that, all in all, he was lucky it was no worse.

This afternoon proved happier than the morning. Having seen his steward and his bailiff, and having walked in the gardens and nearest plantations, my father called me to him and congratulated me on what I had done. 'It has all been well cared for. I could not have wished the estate in better hands,' he said.

Rushworth returned to Sotherton first thing, leaving Maria restless, and at last the house is beginning to return to normal.

Wednesday 19 October
The Crawfords were once more with us today, and I could not help thinking how different our meeting was from the last one. Maria blanched when Crawford announced his intention of leaving the neighbourhood, but I thought it no bad thing as, perhaps, he and Maria had become rather too friendly of late.

Thursday 20 October
Yates left this morning. My father walked him to the door and wished him a pleasant journey. I believe he was glad to see him go, for Yates is just the trifling, silly sort of fellow my father does not like. Indeed, I believe Julia is the only one of our party who will miss him, for she spent a great deal of time with him when he was here; perhaps more than was wise, considering that my father would never welcome him as a suitor. But she is young, and she will soon forget him.

My aunt soon followed Yates out of the

door, carrying a parcel.

'I will not inconvenience you by making you dispose of the green baize curtains,' she said to my father. 'I will dispose of them somehow; indeed I believe I could use a pair of green baize curtains in my own home.'

Friday 21 October

The house seemed quiet today, for with Yates and Crawford gone, and the Grants excluded — my father not wishing to meet new people just at the moment — we were reduced only to ourselves. I did not regret Yates, but I regretted the Grants, and with them the Crawfords. I said as much to Fanny as we went outside for our stargazing.

'The Grants have a claim. They seem to belong to us; they seem to be part of ourselves. I am afraid they may feel themselves neglected. But the truth is, that my father hardly knows them. If he knew them better, he would value their society as it deserves; for they are in fact exactly the sort of people he would like. We are sometimes a little in want of animation among ourselves.'

'It does not appear to me that we are more serious than we used to be — I mean before my uncle went abroad. As well as I can recollect, it was always much the same.'

'I believe you are right, Fanny. The novelty was in our being lively. Yet, how strong the impression that only a few weeks will give! I have been feeling as if we had never lived so before.'

'Do you not think the house is better for being quieter?' asked Fanny.

I brought my thoughts back from their pleasant paths.

'It is certainly a relief to have Yates and Rushworth gone. Miss Crawford we must always miss. She has been so kind to you, Fanny, that it grieves me to be without her company, but I am sure my father will want more society once he has accustomed himself to being at home.'

Fanny looked dismayed, and I asked her if she were warm enough, for the night was cold, and once I was assured she was comfortable we turned our attention to the night sky. The peace and tranquillity of it were balm to my spirit, and Fanny's spirit blossomed, too. Together we traced the constellations and did not leave off until a cold wind sprang up and drove us indoors.

Once back in my room, my thoughts returned again to Mary. When I think of her, and all the light and liveliness she has brought me, I feel admiration swelling up inside me, for she has shown me a side of life I never knew existed.

I am serious, too serious, I know it. My responsibilities have made me that way. But when I listen to her . . . watch her . . . talk to her . . . my responsibilities melt away and I feel young, as I ought to.

Monday 24 October

I happened to go past the Parsonage today and encountered Miss Crawford and Mrs Grant just setting out for a walk. I begged leave to accompany them and before long the three of us were walking along together.

'What a pity the play came to nothing, after you had all worked so hard on it,' said Mrs Grant.

'We must not be surprised that Sir Thomas wanted his house to himself,' said Miss Crawford. 'It was not to be supposed that he would welcome intrusion after his return from such a long absence.'

'No, indeed. But it is a pity, all the same. I found myself enjoying it and I was looking forward to playing the role of Cottager's Wife. She was a woman of good sense if not many lines.' She turned to me. 'And was your father pleased to be home? It must be a very big change to him, after his year in the Indies.'

'Yes, indeed, but he is very glad to be back

with us, particularly as his business was successfully concluded, for he missed Mansfield and his family.'

'He found you all in health and looks, which was a blessing,' said Miss Crawford.

'Yes. He commented particularly on Fanny's improved appearance. He was very glad to find her looking so well.'

'She is at an age when improvements are generally to be found. I hope she did not mind him telling her so, for she seems almost as fearful of notice and praise as other women are of neglect.'

I smiled at this, for it was true, and when I spoke to Fanny later, I noticed that she blushed again when I referred to my father's remarks.

'You must really begin to harden yourself to the idea of being worth looking at. You must try not to mind growing up into a pretty woman,' I told her.

She looked at the floor in confusion, for she seems to have no idea of it, and yet Fanny is one of the prettiest young women of my acquaintance. Were it not for Miss Crawford, indeed, I believe she would be the prettiest.

Tuesday 25 October
We dined at Sotherton today, and a dull

time we had of it. Rushworth talked of his dogs and his sport, Maria seemed out of sorts, and spoke barely two words to anyone. She took no notice of Rushworth and I wondered again if she should be marrying him.

I cannot make her out. Sometimes she seems pleased with him, or to miss him, but sometimes she seems as though she wishes herself far removed from him.

My aunt and Mrs Rushworth were the only people who seemed to enjoy the evening, and I was glad when it was over.

Wednesday 26 October

I could contain myself no longer. I spoke to my father about Maria's engagement this morning, telling him of my concerns, but he reassured me by saying he had already spoken to her about it.

'She assures me that she has no desire of breaking the engagement, that she has the highest esteem for Mr Rushworth's character and disposition, and she has no doubt of her happiness with him,' he said.

I looked my doubts.

'Love is not the only reason for marriage, Edmund,' he said to me seriously, 'in fact it is sometimes better if a woman is not blinded by love for then she goes into the marriage with a clear mind, and has no unpleasant surprises. Rushworth will never be a leading character, but he has no vices. Besides, a young woman who does not marry for love is in general more attached to her own home, and Mansfield Park being such an easy distance from Sotherton, it means only that we will see more of Maria here than we would otherwise.'

I was not comforted by this interview as much as I had expected to be, but if my father is satisfied that Maria will be happy, and if she herself is still in favour of the match, then I believe the marriage will go ahead.

Monday 31 October
Mrs Rushworth has moved out of Sotherton, in preparation for Maria's wedding, and has gone, with her maid and her footman, to Bath.

NOVEMBER

Friday 11 November

And so it has happened at last. This morning Maria was married. The wedding went well, with Maria being in good looks and elegantly dressed, attended by Fanny and Julia.

Mama stood with her salts in her hand all the time, whilst my father looked dignified. Dr Grant performed the ceremony with feeling and then it was done.

'I knew how it would be as soon as I saw her with him for the first time last year,' said Aunt Norris this evening. ' "What a thing it would be for our Maria to marry Mr Rushworth", I said, and now, you see, with a little contriving, it has come to pass. How happy Maria looked this morning! And no wonder. The mistress of Sotherton, with a house in London, and the added felicity of a few weeks in Brighton to enjoy. How lucky she is, to be going to Brighton!

And it is just as lovely at this time of year as it is in the summer.'

'Just so,' said my father.

'And how lucky Julia is, to be going with her, for she is sure to enjoy the amusements as much as Maria. And when they have exhausted the novelty of Brighton, they will have London to look forward to.'

She continued in similar vein until at last she had talked herself to a standstill. A silence fell. There was no Maria at the pianoforte or Julia wandering around the room; no Tom, for he has gone to town, and no Crawford, for he has returned to his estate.

'How quiet we are without them,' Mama observed sadly after dinner. She turned to Fanny, who was sewing quietly, her needle flashing as her small white fingers did their work. 'Fanny, my dear, put your work aside and come and sit next to me on the sofa.'

Fanny did as she was bid and was soon sitting with Mama, who gave her Pug to hold as a mark of the highest approbation.

Monday 21 November

If my sisters' departure has done one thing, it has given Fanny more chance of coming forward, and for this I am very glad.

She went into the village this morning on

an errand and as it happened to come on to rain when she passed the Parsonage she was asked inside. Miss Crawford provided her with dry clothes and then entertained her until the rain ceased. It was just like Mary to be so considerate and I am sure Fanny enjoyed herself immensely.

I have seen little of Mary since the play. Perhaps it is a good thing, as the rehearsal brought forth feelings that should have been left buried, for I have nothing to offer an heiress and it would be folly for me to think of her except as a dear friend.

And yet . . . and yet . . . once I am ordained I will have a house and an income, and I cannot help remembering her face as she said to me, *'I'll marry.'*

'I am very glad the rain stopped before too long,' said Fanny, 'for Dr Grant threatened to send me home in the carriage otherwise.'

I smiled at her use of the word threatened. Anyone else would have said *promised.*

'And why should he not, Fanny? It is only what any gentleman would do for a neighbour. You must learn to think more of yourself, for I assure you, we all think very highly of you. And so Miss Crawford played the harp for you, did she?'

'Yes, she did.'

'And did you not think her a most superior performer?' I asked.

At which Fanny agreed that Miss Crawford was indeed a superior performer, and before very long we had agreed that she was a superior young woman in every way.

Monday 28 November

Fanny's intimacy at the Parsonage continues and this afternoon, my mother wanting her, I walked to the Parsonage to find her. Mrs Grant took me out into the shrubbery, where Fanny and Mary were sitting. Their being together was exactly what I wished to see, for they will do each other good, Fanny by losing some of her shyness, and Miss Crawford by having a friend of sense and intelligence.

'Well,' said Miss Crawford brightly when she saw me, 'and do you not scold us for our imprudence in sitting out of doors so late in the year?'

'I have been too busy with the housekeeping to be alarmed by anything else,' said Mrs Grant with a sigh.

Miss Crawford laughed, declaring she would never have any such grievances.

'There is no escaping these little vexations, Mary, live where we may,' said her sister. 'And when you are settled in town and I come to see you, I dare say I shall find you with your vexations, just as I have them in the country.'

'I mean to be too rich to lament or to feel anything of the sort,' said Mary. 'A large income is the best recipe for happiness I ever heard of.'

'You intend to be very rich?' I asked.

'To be sure. Do not you? Do not we all?' she asked.

'I cannot intend anything which it must be so completely beyond my power to command. Miss Crawford may choose her degree of wealth. She has only to fix on her number of thousands a year, and there can be no doubt of their coming,' I said, my spirits sinking, for she could win the heart of any man she had a mind to, I was sure. 'My intentions are only not to be poor.'

'By moderation and economy, and bringing down your wants to your income, and all that,' she said lightly. 'I understand you — and a very proper plan it is for a person at your time of life, with such limited means and indifferent connexions. What can *you* want but a decent maintenance? You have not much time before you; and your relations are in no situation to do anything for you, or to mortify you by the contrast of their own wealth and consequence,' she went on satirically. 'Be honest and poor, by all means, but I shall not envy you; I do not much think I shall even respect you.' She gave an arch smile. 'I have a much greater respect for those that are honest and rich.'

'Your degree of respect for honesty, rich or poor, is precisely what I have no manner of concern with,' I said, answering her in a similarly lighthearted tone. 'I do not mean to be poor. Poverty is exactly what I have determined against. Honesty, in the something between, in the middle state of worldly circumstances, is all that I am anxious for your not looking down on.'

'But I do look down upon it, if it might have been higher. I must look down upon anything contented with obscurity when it might rise to distinction.'

'But how may it rise?' I asked her. 'How may my honesty at least rise to any distinction?'

She thought. 'You ought to be in parliament, or you should have gone into the army ten years ago.'

'*That* is not much to the purpose now; and as to my being in parliament, I believe I must wait till there is an especial assembly for the representation of younger sons who have little to live on. No, Miss Crawford,' I went on more seriously, for she was looking very pretty and I thought that any man who could win her would be fortunate indeed, 'there *are* distinctions which I should be miserable if I thought myself without any chance — absolutely without chance or possibility of obtaining — but they are of a different character.'

She laughed at me, but it was a laugh of friendship and not derision, so that, despite her words, I felt there was hope. Satisfied, I recollected that I had come to collect Fanny, and we made our adieus.

On the way out we were met by Dr Grant, who invited us to dinner tomorrow, and, being grateful to the Grants for taking notice of Fanny, I accepted for both of us. Then Fanny and I walked home together.

Wednesday 30 November

'I am very glad the Grants thought of inviting you,' I said to Fanny, when, at twenty past four this afternoon, we went down to the Parsonage in the carriage. 'I knew how it would be. Now that my sisters are away, our neighbours are starting to realize that you are not a girl any longer, but a young woman, and I am sure more invitations will follow this one. I must look at you, Fanny, and tell you how I like you. As well as I can tell by this light, you look very nicely indeed. What have you got on?' I asked her, for indeed the winter twilight was so dim I could scarcely tell.

'The new dress that my uncle was so good as to give me on my cousin's marriage. I hope it is not too fine; but I thought I ought to wear it as soon as I could, and that I might not have such another opportunity all winter.'

'A woman can never be too fine while she is all in white. Besides, it is your first dinner invitation, and so it is a special occasion.'

As we passed the stable yard I saw a carriage.

'Who have they got to meet us?' I said. I let down the side-glass to have a better look. 'It is Crawford's barouche. This is quite a surprise, Fanny. I shall be very glad to see him.'

Fanny was distinguished as we went in, and she was fussed over in a way that, whilst it confounded her, delighted me. I will be happy indeed when she can take these little attentions as a matter of course, for then my little Fanny will have truly grown up and taken her natural place in the world.

Conversation flowed easily, and Crawford entertained us all with tales of his stay in Bath.

'I am glad to have you back, Henry, my

boy,' said Dr Grant, wiping tears of laughter from his eyes after one of Crawford's anecdotes. 'You must stay awhile.'

'But I have to return to my own estate,' said Crawford.

'Nonsense! It can manage without you a little longer. What do you say, Mary?'

'Yes, Henry, do stay,' Mary urged, with the most pleasing sisterly affection.

'I have nothing here . . .' said Crawford.

'What does that signify?' said Dr Grant. 'You can send for your hunters.'

'Nothing would be easier,' I said, thinking how lucky we would be to have another gentleman for company over the winter, especially one as well informed, and agreeable to the ladies, as Crawford.

'And what say you, Miss Price?' asked Crawford, turning to Fanny.

I blessed him for bringing her forward, for she was inclined to be silent, overawed by so much company.

She flushed and said nothing.

'Do you think this weather will last?' he persevered.

'I cannot say,' she returned in confusion.

'Should I send for my hunters?'

'I really do not think I can give an opinion,' she said.

'Well, then,' said Crawford, continuing

with the breeding and kindness of a true gentleman, 'do you think I should stay?'

'It is not for me to say.'

'But you would not dislike it?'

'No,' she said, when pressed. 'I should not dislike it.'

'Then it is settled.'

He smiled at her, and Fanny managed a small smile in return, and though it was no more than civility demanded I was glad she had managed so much.

My sisters were, of course, mentioned. After dinner, Crawford spoke of Maria's marriage, saying, 'Rushworth and his fair bride are at Brighton, I understand?'

Mary drew Fanny into the conversation with quite as much kindness as her brother, saying, 'Yes, they have been there about a fortnight, Miss Price, have they not? And Julia is with them.'

'How we miss them. You were Mr Rushworth's best friend,' he said to Fanny. 'Your kindness and patience can never be forgotten, your indefatigable patience in trying to make it possible for him to learn his part. *He* might not have sense enough to estimate your kindness, but I may venture to say that it had honour from all the rest of the party.'

I smiled to see her so well entertained, and by such an agreeable man.

I was about to speak to Mary when Dr Grant claimed my attention.

'About your living, Edmund,' he said. 'You will be ordained at Christmas, I believe?'

'Yes, that is so. I will be going to stay with my friend Owen and we will be ordained together.'

'And you will then come into the living. Well, it is not a bad living, the one at Thornton Lacey . . . ?'

'Seven hundred pounds a year.'

'Just so. Not a bad living. But it could be improved.'

He gave me the benefit of his advice, and once we had finished our discussion, Crawford said, 'I shall make a point of coming to Mansfield to hear you preach your first sermon. I shall come on purpose to encourage a young beginner. When is it to be? Miss Price, will not you join me in encouraging your cousin? Will not you engage to attend with your eyes steadily fixed on him the whole time — as I shall do — not to lose a word; or only looking off just to note down any sentence preeminently beautiful? We will provide ourselves with tablets and a pencil. When will it be? You must preach at Mansfield, you know,' he said to me, 'that Sir Thomas and Lady Bertram may hear you.'

'I shall keep clear of you, Crawford, as long as I can,' I said with a wry smile, for he would be sure to disconcert me.

The party broke up, and I am persuaded Fanny enjoyed her evening in company, and will have many more such evenings to come.

December

Friday 2 December

Business taking me up to town, I called in to the jewellers and ordered a gold chain for Fanny. Now that she is going out and about she will need some adornment, and it will give me great pleasure to give her such a gift. I looked at a variety but in the end I chose a simple chain so that she will be able to wear it on any occasion. I asked for it to be shortened as it was rather long for her and I was told it would not be ready until I had left town. When I called on Tom, I asked him if he would collect it for me. He promised to do so, and to send it on to me at Mansfield.

He was in good spirits. He asked me if I had proposed to Mary yet, and when I shook my head he said I was making slow work of it.

'I want to find you all married the next time I come home: you, Fanny, Julia — and

226

Aunt Norris!'

I could not get a serious word out of him, but it was good to see him again, all the same.

Monday 5 December
Fanny and I dined at the Parsonage again this evening, and on Fanny happening to mention her brother, Crawford continued to draw her out by asking her all about him.

'William is on the *Antwerp,* you say?' he asked, drawing his chair closer to hers.

'Yes,' said Fanny.

'And you are longing to see him again, no doubt,' he said with a smile. 'You have been parted for a very long time.'

'Oh, I have. I would like to see him again above anything. I wish I knew when he was coming home.'

'I will ask my uncle. Admiral Crawford will know, or if he does not, then some of his connections at the Admiralty will be able to find it out. The *Antwerp* is in the Mediterranean, you say?'

'Yes, or at least it was, the last time I heard.'

'Well, it is not so very far from there to here. I am sure he will be home again soon. Will you see him when he is?'

'I hope so.'

'And so do I, for I can tell how much you miss him.'

They continued in similar vein, and I thought how very good it was of Crawford to take such an interest in William, for if there was anything guaranteed to please Fanny, it was someone's taking an interest in her brother.

I said as much to Mary, who remarked satirically, 'Oh yes, Henry is always able to please young ladies.'

'And I . . .' I caught myself, as she looked at me expectantly, and I realized I had almost asked if I could please them, too . . . 'will be very glad to see William, too.'

'Ah, yes, I am sure you must be longing for a visit from him quite as much as Fanny,' she said, laughing at me.

I was bewitched, and wondered again if I had any chance of being accepted by her. If her smiles were anything to the point, then yes. But if her professions of a desire to be rich were to be taken seriously, then no.

I was no closer to understanding her when the evening came to an end.

Tuesday 6 December

As sometimes happens in life, talking about a thing has brought it on, for Fanny had a letter from William this morning.

'Well, Fanny, are you not going to tell us your news?' I asked her, as I saw her bright eyes, and knew it must be good. 'Do not keep us in suspense!'

'The *Antwerp* has returned. William is home!'

'I wondered why the letter was so short!' I said with a smile.

She smiled back at me, for William's letters are usually exceedingly long.

'He had time for no more than a few lines, written as he was coming up the Channel. He sent the letter in to Portsmouth with the first boat that left the *Antwerp* when she lay at anchor.'

'The first boat? I would expect nothing less!'

'That is very good news,' said my father kindly. 'You will like to see him, I am sure. There will be no difficulty in his obtaining a leave of absence.'

'No, none at all. It is one of the advantages of being a midshipman,' she agreed.

'Then we must invite him here. Fanny, you must write to him. I will dictate the letter myself.'

Fanny furnished herself with pen and paper, and I could not help remembering the first letter she had written to William, blotted with tears, and strangely spelt. As I watched her even hand flow over the paper, I thought how much she had grown, not just in stature but in person, and how graceful she had become over the years.

She was in the middle of the letter when Crawford strolled up from the Parsonage, carrying a newspaper.

'My dear Miss Price, what do you think? As I turned to the ship news this morning, I saw that the *Antwerp* had docked, so I came at once to give you the news.'

'I know,' she replied, looking up from her letter. 'I have had a letter from William this morning.'

'Ah! I had hoped to be the first to tell you. But I cannot be sorry you have had it already, when I see how much pleasure it brings you. I have never seen you looking happier.'

'You are too kind. And it was very thoughtful of you to bring me the paper,' she said, 'for if I did not already know, it would have delighted me beyond anything.'

'Then I am rewarded for my small trouble,' he replied with a bow.

The letter was finished, and Crawford suggested we go out for a ride. I asked if Miss Crawford might like to come with us, but she was indisposed, and so the three of us went out together. When we had done,

Fanny and I returned to the Parsonage with Crawford, and I asked after Miss Crawford. She was better, but her head still ached, Mrs Grant said.

I sent her my good wishes, and after lunch I repaired to the study where my father and I talked over estate business until dinner.

The table seemed lifeless without Mary. I have come to depend on her presence, and the liveliness of her company; a liveliness I am increasingly unwilling to live without.

Friday 9 December

Fanny could not settle to anything all day, so busy was she watching for William's arrival. I came across her in the lobby, in the hall and on the stairs, her eyes looking out of the window, and her ears straining for the first sound of a carriage. At last she repaired to the drawing-room and took up her needlework, though I believe very few stitches were laid, for every time a step came on the gravel she jumped up, and if she heard a horse whinny she ran to the window.

'He cannot be here before dinner,' I told her.

'If he has a good journey he could be here by four o'clock,' she said.

'You have measured the distance?' I asked her teasingly.

She said with a smile, 'I have been looking at the map.'

She sat down again, and picked up her needlework.

'What a lucky boy William is, to be sure, to have had so much help from Sir Thomas,' said my aunt, as Fanny's eyes went every few minutes out of the window. 'I hope he is properly grateful for all the help he has received, for without it he would not have done half so well.'

'I did very little,' said my father kindly. 'He has worked hard and made the most of his advantages. I gave him his start, perhaps, but he has progressed on his own merits.'

My aunt continued in a similar vein until, hearing the carriage, she said, 'There he is! What a day this is, to be sure! How happy he will be to be here, in the house of his benefactor. I must go and welcome him at once.'

'Pray, do not stir yourself,' said my father, as Fanny ran out of the room, 'for I am sure there is no need.'

'But Sir Thomas, there is every need in the world,' she said, eager to be doing something.

'It is cold in the hall, you had much better remain by the fire,' I said to her, for I was determined to give Fanny some time alone with William before she had to share him with others.

'I have never been one to worry about a little cold, when there is a duty to perform,' said my aunt. 'Indeed, where would we all be if we allowed such trifles to prevent us from doing what we knew to be right?'

As she stood up, my father spoke, and I realized we had the same idea.

'Mrs Norris, I need your advice,' he said. 'Do you think I should have the fire built up? It is, as Edmund so rightly says, cold today. Do you think we should have more coal on the fire, or will we grow too hot?'

She looked surprised at being consulted on such a trifling matter but the ruse served, for it gave Fanny a few minutes alone with William. By the time the fire had been thoroughly discussed, Fanny and William had joined us, faces aglow, evidently delighted in each other's company.

William proved to be a young man of open, pleasing countenance, and frank but respectful manners, a credit to my father, the Navy, and himself.

My father welcomed him cordially, and though she sprinkled her conversation with, 'I am sure you will be grateful to your uncle' . . . 'benefactor' . . . 'stirred himself on your behalf' . . . my aunt made William welcome, too.

Mama showed him Pug, and before long we were all being entertained by stories of life at sea.

Fanny watched William avidly, tracing in his manly face the likeness of the boy she had known. I saw her emotions change from elation at being with him, to perplexity at seeing the changes time had wrought in him, to a welcome recognition of certain expressions and features, and then a more happy, settled joy at being with her beloved William again.

Saturday 10 December

William kept us entertained with stories of his exploits at sea and Fanny lived through every minute of them with him, whether he was telling of his time in the Mediterranean or in the West Indies.

'My captain sometimes took me ashore, and the places were strange at first, and so were the people. They wore —'

'I have lost my needle,' said my aunt. 'Pray, has anyone seen my needle? I cannot sew without it. Sister, have you seen it? It was here with my sewing not five minutes ago.'

We all stopped and looked for her needle. When it was found, William continued, telling us of a chase as the *Antwerp* ran down a prize.

'We were gaining on her every minute, and at last we drew alongside her, and then —'

'Now where is that button? I know I had it somewhere. Do help me to look for it, Fanny.'

'The button can wait, I am sure, until we have found out whether the *Antwerp* captured her prize,' I said. 'So, William, you boarded the ship? And what then?'

We sat enraptured as he painted the scene for us, and did it so vividly that Mama murmured, 'Dear me! How disagreeable. I wonder anybody can ever go to sea.'

'Why, sister, if no one ever went to sea, what would we do with so many men on land?' asked my aunt. She turned to William. 'I hope you are grateful for all the chances you have been given because of the beneficence of your uncle. It is not every young man who has someone to speak for him.'

'Indeed, I am very sensible of it,' said William, though he looked surprised to be reminded of it for the third time.

After lunch, I suggested that Fanny should show her brother the Park, and they set out on horseback. As I watched them go I was glad that they would have the afternoon alone with no one to interrupt them. I thought how tender Fanny's heart was, and how never a brother had been loved as well as William.

Thoughts of brothers and sisters took my own to Miss Crawford and before long I was at the Parsonage, asking after her health. It was much improved, she told me, and smiled at me as she thanked me for taking the trouble to enquire.

Tuesday 13 December

I had a letter from Tom this morning, saying that he would not be able to collect the necklace at once, but promising to send it on as soon as he could.

Wednesday 14 December

The Grants were eager to meet William, and Fanny, having had him to herself for a time, was happy to share him with others, or at least, to allow them to bask in the delight of his presence. That being so, we dined at the Parsonage this evening. Afterwards, Mary played her harp, and I took the opportunity of going to sit beside her. She finished her air, and after I had complimented her on her playing, we began to talk.

'How happy Fanny is,' she said, glancing towards the side of the room where Fanny sat, with face aglow, watching and listening to William. 'I am sure I have never looked at Henry like that.'

'But perhaps you would if you had not seen him for years, and had been parted when you were ten years old.'

'I am glad for her. She has a good heart, and she deserves her happiness.'

This could not help but warm me, and her brother warmed me more when he offered William a horse so that he could join us in our ride tomorrow.

Fanny's face was a mixture of heartfelt gratitude for such kindness to her brother, and fear that he would take a fall.

'Nonsense!' said William. 'After all the scrambling parties I have been on, the rough horses and mules I have ridden, and the falls I have escaped, you have nothing to fear.'

'Do not worry, Miss Price. I will bring him back to you in one piece,' said Crawford indulgently.

The party broke up in good humour, with an arrangement for us all to dine together tomorrow.

Thursday 15 December
We had a fine day's sport, and once Fanny saw William come home safely again she

was able to value Crawford's kindness as it should be valued, free of the taint of fear. She was so much reassured by William's return, without so much as a scratch, that she was able to smile when Crawford said, during dinner at the Parsonage, 'You must keep the horse for the duration of your visit, Mr Price.'

'I thought your brother was going to return to his estate?' I asked Mary.

'He was, but he has changed his mind. We have Fanny and William to thank for keeping him here,' she said. 'He has decided to stay indefinitely.'

Crawford looked round.

'What was that? Did someone say my name?'

'I was telling Mr Bertram that you had decided to stay with us instead of returning to your estate.'

'Yes, indeed. I find the place suits me. When I was out riding this morning, I found myself in Thornton Lacey,' he went on. 'Is not that the living you are to have, Bertram?'

'It is. And how did you like what you saw?' I asked.

'Very much indeed. You are a lucky fellow,' he said, adding satirically, 'there will be work for five summers at least before the place is liveable.'

'No, no, not so bad as that!' I protested. 'The farmyard must be moved, I grant you; but I am not aware of anything else. The house is by no means bad, and when the yard is removed, there may be a very tolerable approach to it. I think the house and premises may be made comfortable, and given the air of a gentleman's residence, without any very heavy expense, and that must suffice me.' I could not help adding, with a glance at Miss Crawford, 'And, I hope, may suffice all who care about me.'

'I have a mind to take something in the neighbourhood myself,' said Crawford. 'It would be very pleasant to have a home of my own here, for in spite of all Dr Grant's very great kindness, it is impossible for him to accommodate me and my horses without material inconvenience. Will you rent me Thornton Lacey?' he asked me.

My father replied that I would be residing there myself, which surprised Crawford, who had thought I would claim the privileges without taking on the responsibilities of the living.

'Come as a friend instead of a tenant,' I said. 'Consider the house as half your own every winter, and we will add to the stables on your own improved plan, and with all the improvements that may occur to you this spring.'

Crawford said he had half a mind to take me up on it, but the conversation progressed no further for William began talking of dancing, and it captured the interest of everyone present.

'Are you fond of dancing, Fanny?' he asked, turning towards her.

'Yes, very; only I am soon tired,' she confessed.

'I should like to go to a ball with you and see you dance. Have you never any balls at Northampton? I should like to see you dance, and I'd dance with you if you *would,* for nobody would know who I was here, and I should like to be your partner once more. We used to jump about together many a time, did not we? When the hand-organ was in the street? I am a pretty good dancer in my way, but I dare say you are a better.' And turning to my father, who was now close to them, said, 'Is not Fanny a very good dancer, sir?'

'I am sorry to say that I am unable to answer your question. I have never seen Fanny dance since she was a little girl; but I trust we shall both think she acquits herself like a gentlewoman when we do see her, which, perhaps, we may have an opportunity of doing ere long.'

'I have had the pleasure of seeing your sister dance, Mr Price,' said Crawford, leaning forward, 'and will engage to answer every inquiry which you can make on the subject, to your entire satisfaction.'

Fanny flushed to hear herself so flatteringly spoken of. Fortunately for her modesty the conversation moved on to balls my father had attended in Antigua. So engrossed were we all in listening to him that we did not hear the carriage until it was announced.

I was about to take Fanny's shawl to lay it round her shoulders when Crawford did it for me. I glanced at Mary and she smiled at me, wishing us a safe journey back to the Park.

And now, back in my room, I feel the time is coming when I must put Mary's feelings to the test, for I cannot hide my own any longer. I am in love with her, and I wish to make her my wife.

Once Christmas is over and I have been ordained, I will be in a position to know exactly what I have to offer her.

But will it be enough? When I think of all the encouragements she has given me, the smiles and playful comments, the thoughts and feelings shared, then I think yes. But when I think of her comments on the necessity of wealth and her decided preference for London life, I am sure she will say no.

Friday 16 December
This morning my father announced that he intends to give a ball in honour of Fanny and William, and I was relieved and pleased. Relieved, because it would give another turn to my thoughts, which are at present occupied by the serious considerations of my ordination and the torment of wondering whether Mary will marry me. And pleased, because Fanny has little opportunity for dancing, and I want her to be given the pleasure.

My aunt was soon busily deciding that she must take all the care from Mama's shoulders, and Mama had no objections to make.

My father suggested the twenty-second, a date my aunt declared to be impossible because of the shortness of the notice, but he was firm.

'We must hold it soon, for William has to be at Portsmouth on the twenty-fourth, so we have not much time left. But I believe we can collect enough young people to form ten or twelve couples next week, despite the shortness of the notice.'

As soon as I had a chance to speak to my father alone, I said, 'I am very happy at the idea of a ball, for it has been troubling me recently that Fanny has not yet come out.'

My father was surprised to learn of it.

'Mama felt that her health made it wise to wait until she was older.'

'Just so,' he said. 'Well, this shall be her come-out ball then.'

The invitations were sent out this afternoon, and as I happened to be going past the Parsonage, I took the Crawfords' and the Grants' invitation in person. I was pleased to see Mary's eyes sparkle, but learned it was not with thoughts of the ball. She had just then received a letter from her friends in London, and they had invited her to stay.

'I thought you were fixed here,' I said, my spirits sinking.

'And so I am, but you would not begrudge me a visit to my friends, I am sure,' she returned. 'Henry has kindly agreed to remain at Mansfield until January, so that he might convey me to them.'

And so, before January I must offer her my hand, for if I do not, I may miss my chance for many months, or, if she decides to stay in London, for ever.

Wednesday 21 December
William and I went into Northamptonshire

243

this morning and I collected Fanny's chain, which Tom had sent on for me. William was pleased to see it.

'It is exactly the sort of thing I wanted to buy for Fanny, to go with the amber cross I bought her, but as a midshipman my pay would not stretch so far.'

'Your time will come,' I reassured him. 'When you are a captain, you will be able to buy Fanny as many chains as you wish.'

Our business concluded, William and I rode back to the Park and I took the chain upstairs, thinking to find Fanny in her sitting-room, but she was out. No sooner did I sit down to write her a note, explaining that the chain was hers, and what it was for, than she entered the room. Hardly had I handed it to her when she told me that Mary had already given her a chain for that very purpose. I was heartened to hear of it, and then thought, a moment later, that I should have expected it, because Mary has always been thoughtful, particularly where Fanny is concerned. Fanny said she would return Mary's gift, but I would not allow it, for it would be mortifying to Mary.

'But it was given to her by her brother,' said Fanny. 'I tried not to take it when I knew, but she insisted, saying he gave her so many things, one more or less did not signify. But I was not comfortable with it then, and I am not comfortable with it now, the more so because it is no longer needed.'

'Miss Crawford must not suppose it not wanted, not acceptable, at least,' I said. 'I would not have the shadow of a coolness arise between the two dearest objects I have on earth. Wear hers for the ball, and keep mine for commoner occasions.'

And so it was settled, and I was heartened as I returned to my room, to know that Mary had so much generosity in her.

Thursday 22 December

It is not only Mary who has generosity in her, it is also her brother, for he has done a very kind thing. He has offered to convey William to London, whither he is bound himself, and has invited him to spend the evening at Admiral Crawford's. This is just the kind of notice that will help William in his career. To be brought to the attention of an admiral can do him nothing but good.

I went down to the Parsonage shortly afterwards, intending to thank Crawford for his kindness, and to engage his sister for the first two dances at the ball. Crawford was from home, but Mary took my thanks very prettily and invited me to sit down.

'I am here on another errand as well,' I

said. 'I have come to ask if you would stand up with me for the first two dances.'

'Certainly,' she said, adding, 'For it will be the last time I will ever dance with you.'

'But why? What is this? You are to return from London, surely? I thought you were only going to pay a visit to your friends.'

'And so I am, but when I return, you and I will never again be partners.'

I was astonished. 'How so?'

'I have never danced with a clergyman, and I never *will*.'

I could not make her out. Was she joking? If so, it was in very poor taste. If not . . .

At that moment Mrs Grant came in and I could not say any more about it, but as soon as I returned to the Park I sought out Fanny.

'I come from Dr Grant's,' I said to her. 'You may guess my errand there, Fanny. I wished to engage Miss Crawford for the two first dances.'

'And did you succeed?'

'Yes, she is engaged to me; but . . .' I forced a smile. '. . . she says it is to be the last time that she ever will dance with me. She is not serious. I think, I hope, I am sure she is not serious; but I would rather not hear it. For my own sake, I could wish there had been no ball just at — I mean not this very week, this very day; tomorrow I leave home.'

'I am very sorry that anything has occurred to distress you. This ought to be a day of pleasure. My uncle meant it so.'

'Oh yes, yes! and it will be a day of pleasure,' I said, recollecting myself, for the ball was intended for Fanny, and I did not want to spoil her enjoyment. 'It will all end right. I am only vexed for a moment. I have been pained by her manner this morning, and cannot get the better of it.'

I shook my head as I thought that Mary's former companions had encouraged her in such shallow opinions and poor taste.

Fanny thought as I did, that Mary's words were the effect of a poor education.

'Yes, education! Her uncle and aunt have much to answer for!'

Fanny hesitated.

'Excuse the liberty; but take care *how* you talk to me,' she said gently. 'Do not tell me anything now, which hereafter you may be sorry for. The time may come —'

'The time will never come, I have almost given up every serious idea of her,' I said, shaking my head, for the more I remembered her words and expression, the more I began to feel that I had been a fool to believe I could ever win her. 'But I must be a blockhead indeed, if, whatever befell me, I could think of your kindness and sympathy without the sincerest gratitude,' I said to Fanny with a smile.

We were disturbed by the housemaid and, though I would have liked to say more, this prevented further conversation.

I returned to my room to dress for the ball, and my head was full of Mary. I recalled every nuance of her voice and her expression, and by and by I began to think that I had lost heart too easily, and that things were not so very bad. It was playfulness, surely, and not rejection, for even in London there were clergymen, and she could not refuse to dance with them if they asked her. With these happier thoughts in my head I went down to dinner.

My humour was so far improved that I was fully able to appreciate Fanny's beauty and elegance of dress, and to compliment her on it.

'But what is this?' I said, seeing her cross hanging from my chain.

'Miss Crawford's chain was too big. It would not fit through the hole,' she said. 'Yours was just the right fit. I thought it only proper to wear Miss Crawford's chain also, as she had been kind enough to give it to me, and so I wore it on its own.'

I saw Mary's chain hanging beside mine.

'An excellent solution. The amber becomes you, Fanny. You are in looks tonight. You must keep two dances for me; any two that you like, except the first,' I said to her.

No sooner had the ladies withdrawn after dinner than the carriages began to arrive. Mary looked more lovely than ever, her hair arranged in the most becoming style and her dress as faultless as ever. To my delight, Crawford sought out Fanny. They made a handsome couple, and admiring eyes were turned on them. My father looked pleased, and Mama, too, smiled, as Fanny walked on to the floor.

And then I had eyes only for Mary. When she smiled upon me, I banished the last of my fears and gave myself over to an enjoyment of the evening.

'It was very kind of you to supply Fanny with a chain for her cross. It shows to advantage against her delicate neck,' she said, as I led her out on to the floor.

'No kinder than it was of you. I know she wanted to wear your chain with the cross, and was prevented only by its being the wrong size.'

The music started. I bowed, she curtsied, and the dance began.

'But she is wearing it anyway. I believe a

better girl does not exist. She seems to be enjoying herself,' she said, glancing towards the top of the set, where Fanny and Henry were dancing, adding, 'though she seems to be looking at William as often as she looks at Henry.'

'She has seen so little of him these last eight years, I believe she feels she must keep her eyes on him in case he disappears!'

'Which he will do all too soon, alas.'

'Yes. It is good of your brother to interest himself in William. My father has done all he can to help, but he has little influence in the Navy and can do no more. If your uncle would take up William's cause and help him to a commission as lieutenant, it would mean a great deal to him. We would all like to see him do well.'

'He is ambitious,' said Mary approvingly. 'He tells me that, if only he can be made a lieutenant, he means to rise through the ranks and not stop until he makes Admiral. It will be a lucky young woman who wins his heart. A handsome young man with a fortune, to say nothing of a uniform, will always be popular with the gentler sex.'

'He has many years of bachelorhood ahead of him yet. He is only nineteen, hardly more than a boy!'

'He has achieved a great deal for someone

who is hardly more than a boy,' she re-turned. 'He has had adventures many an older man might envy.'

My heart sank, as I suspected where her conversation was tending. Sure enough she began, gently at first but then with more passion, to tell me what a fine career the Navy was, and how a man might take a pride in his achievements, whereas there was no glory in being a country parson, and I was left to realize that her remarks to me this morning were not in jest, after all.

'Would you have me do something for which I am unsuited, and in which I have no interest?' I asked her, as the steps of the dance parted us.

'I would have you use your talents and abilities instead of wasting them,' she said, as we came together. 'You have it in you to make your mark on the world. There is a need for men like you in public life. Great orators —'

'I am hardly that.'

'You underestimate yourself. I have heard you reading from books with Fanny, and you have a power that other men would envy,' she said coaxingly. 'Your words could sway others and bring you renown. London would be at your feet.'

'I prefer the country,' I returned.

'But could do so much more in the town. It would give you more scope, and a greater stage for your endeavours.'

'I thank you, but I have had enough of stages. I have no taste for acting,' I returned.

'Indeed,' she said, and there was something vulnerable in her voice. 'I rather thought you liked it.'

I was reminded of the scenes we had performed together, and softened.

'As Amelia you did not seem so set against the clergy,' I said more gently.

'As Amelia I was not.'

The dance parted us, but when we came together again I tried to make her understand.

'If I could only make you see that the life you want for me would not bring me happiness,' I said. 'The noise you speak of, the bustle and importance, are only necessary because they hide an emptiness at their heart.'

'William Price does not appear to think so.'

'William's case is different. He is in the Navy, and we depend on the Navy for our freedom.'

'And do we not depend on our politicians for our freedom, too?'

'But I have no taste for politics,' I said,

'and if I did, it would have no taste for me. A younger son belongs nowhere in such an arena. This is where I belong, in the neighbourhood where my family have always lived. I am a part of it, and it is a part of me. In the parish I have a chance of making a difference; in London I can do nothing except make myself miserable.'

'You are determined to squander your talents,' she said, annoyed. 'I thought that you, of all people, would pay attention to the parables.'

I shook my head at her notion that I was hiding my light under a bushel.

'My light would soon be extinguished in London,' I said. 'And so would yours. Think again about going there.'

'So now you want me to forgo my own pleasures because they do not match your own?' she demanded.

'I would by no means rob you of any pleasure,' I said stiffly. 'But there is a price to be paid for everything, and I hope you may not find that the price you pay for the life you desire is too high.'

We relapsed into silence, whilst all around us my father's guests danced. We continued down the set, but my thoughts were not on the steps, they were on Mary and her unquenchable desire for wealth and renown.

The dance ended, and we parted with vexation on both sides. Mixed in with my anger was the dismal knowledge that she would never consent to marry a country parson; and that I could never be happy being anything else.

I wandered here and there amongst the dancers, offering my hand to the ladies who were sitting out, talking to the chaperons and making everyone feel welcome, for I could not let my personal feelings interfere with my duty. But all the time I was thinking of Mary, and feeling the loss of her like a physical pain.

At last it was time for me to claim Fanny, and I found her with relief.

'I am worn out with civility,' I confessed, as I led her on to the floor. 'I have been talking incessantly all night, and with nothing to say. But with *you,* Fanny, there may be peace. You will not want to be talked to. Let us have the luxury of silence.'

She smiled in silent sympathy, and I found it a great solace to be able to dance with her.

How different was our silence to the one that had fallen between Miss Crawford and myself, for that had been angry and not at all comfortable. But then, Fanny is one of my oldest friends, and it would be a strange day, indeed, if I should ever find myself at outs with her.

Friday 23 December

I arose in bad spirits, and glad to be going away. No good could come of my seeing Miss Crawford again, for all hope of a marriage between us had gone, and my absence, followed by her own, was the best thing for both of us.

I went down to breakfast and found Crawford just arriving. He ate with us, for his sister was fagged after the ball and had not wanted to get up so soon. Crawford and William were cheerful, but I could think of nothing to say, and so I sat silently. Fanny, too was silent. She watched William avidly as he ate his pork chop and mustard, refusing to take her eyes from him even for a minute, so unwilling was she to lose one precious moment of his company.

At last William pushed back his chair, and Crawford did likewise, then William embraced his sister robustly. But although he was sorry to leave her, it was clear he was equally eager to be gone, for he knew that on the next forty-eight hours his whole future depended.

There was all the usual bustle of departure and then the carriage pulled away. Fanny would not relinquish her post at the door until it had turned the corner and gone from sight.

'Come in Fanny, before you catch cold,' I said to her.

She allowed me to take her inside, and I plied her with eggs and tea, which she cried over very prettily. But she ate all the same, for much as she missed William, she was hungry, and besides, she wanted to please me.

After she had eaten, I suggested we go out for a walk, and the beauty of the morning revived her.

Once indoors again, I made her join me for a second breakfast, where I persuaded her to eat a little seedcake, and then I bade her and the rest of my family goodbye for a week, mounted my horse and set off for Peterborough.

Once on my way, I was free, at last, to think of my own business. The day was fine, though cold. Frost coated the bare branches, and covered the last blooms of summer that remained in sheltered hollows or in the lee of walls. I wanted Fanny with me when I saw a red rose still blooming, one hardy flower keeping its place amongst the thorns, for I was persuaded she would have liked to see the

Hoary-headed frosts
Fall in the fresh lap of the crimson rose.

I reached Lessingby and was glad to find myself going up the road to Owen's house before darkness fell, though the daylight was already fading, dwindling into a soft twilight brightened by the translucent frost.

A light shone in the window. Then the curtain was pulled back, and the candlelight flooded out in all its splendour, staining the drive gold with its brilliance. The curtain fell; I was at the door; my horse was taken, and then I was being welcomed into the house by Owen and his family. It was bright inside, so bright that I had to blink, and the heat flowed over me and wrapped itself round me like a blanket.

'Welcome,' said Owen's mother, looking every bit as elegant as she did when I first met her eight years ago. 'You must be cold. Here, sit by the fire. Beddows, a glass of wine.'

And before long, I found myself seated by the fire with a wineglass in my hand, surrounded by Owen's family.

His sisters were elegant and pretty and were much grown since my last visit. They were sitting over their needlework; which, however, they neglected so as to listen to the conversation.

After the details of my journey had been thoroughly dealt with, and enquiries had been made as to my family's health, Owen and I began to talk of our forthcoming ordination. It was a relief to be able to talk about it in sympathetic company, knowing the subject would not prompt ridicule or frustration; for with Owen's father being a clergyman himself, and Owen to be ordained with me, it was a house of clergymen.

We continued our conversation over dinner, and the three Miss Owens added their thoughts. Everyone was very pleasant, and the meal was excellent, and I found myself looking forward to the coming week.

Over the port, we discussed the subject more thoroughly and then went through to the drawing-room, where the women entertained us with singing and playing on the pianoforte.

I thought of Thomson:

An elegant sufficiency, content,
Retirement, rural quiet, friendship, books.

And thought of the three Miss Owens, and how different they were from Mary Crawford.

This has been perhaps the happiest week of my life. To have finally fulfilled my destiny and become ordained has left me feeling at peace with the world.

'We are so proud of you both,' said Mrs Owen this evening over dinner. 'You are both fine additions to the clergy.'

'Yes, indeed,' said Mr Owen. 'The church needs young people like you, forward-thinking young men with ideas and energy. Men who will lead by setting a good example to their parishioners, and who will restore the clergy to its proper respectability. There has been too much easy living of late; too much ignoring of parish duties; too many clergymen inclined to take their ease and let others do the work. They do not seem to realize that it is in the work of the church that its future lies. You young men have a chance to make a difference, to enhance your parishioners' lives with your judgement, example and understanding, and to set the tone of the country for generations to come.'

'Yes, indeed,' said Mrs Owen.

'I only hope my brother might soon have a living. You have one, I understand, Mr Bertram,' said Miss Owen who had grown very pretty.

'I have, at Thornton Lacey,' I told her.

'Thornton Lacey! What a coincidence. We passed through there on our way to Aunt Hester's in October. I remember it well. The rectory was a gentleman's residence, and the parish was a good size. Do you mean to live there?' she asked me.

'Yes, I do. I can see no point in going into my parish only to read the sermons.'

'Good, good,' said Mr Owen approvingly.

'And is the house well situated?' asked Mrs Owen.

'Oh, yes,' said Miss Owen, before I could answer. 'To be sure, the farm could perhaps be moved, but the situation is admirable. The house is very fine, quite the finest house in the neighbourhood, and the view is very pretty. There is a dear little garden, with meadows beyond, and a stream —' She realized she had said too much and relapsed into silence, blushing.

I found myself wishing that Mary could have been as well pleased with the house, but Mary was of a different kind from Miss Owen. I remembered her insulting words at the ball: *A clergyman is nothing . . . can do nothing . . . be no one . . . easily satisfied . . . no ambition . . . a real man makes his mark in the world. . . .*

I was so busy thinking of her that I did

not realize Mr Owen was speaking to me. I brought my thoughts back from their own paths in time to hear Mr Owen say, 'You have been fortunate.'

'Indeed I have.'

'And how are your friends the Crawfords?' asked Owen, as the conversation moved away from the church. 'The Crawfords are the brother and sister of Dr Grant,' he explained to his family. 'Mr Crawford has an estate in Norfolk, and Miss Crawford is an heiress. A beautiful and intelligent young woman by all accounts. Are they still at Mansfield?'

'For the present, but they will not be there for much longer. Miss Crawford is going to stay in London for an extended visit.'

'She will be staying with her uncle?' asked Owen.

'No, with her friend, a Mrs Fraser.'

There was a short pause, then Mrs Owen said, 'It seems a shame that you should have to hurry back to Mansfield tomorrow, Mr Bertram, we have seen so very little of you. Will you not do us the very great favour of staying another week?'

I thought of Mansfield and I knew that Mary would not yet have left, so that if I returned as planned I would be forced into company with her. I found I did not want to see her again. What use would it be for me to torment myself with the sight of her, when I knew she would never marry me? For she would not be satisfied until she had a house in town and a husband who was universally acclaimed.

And then I thought of Owen's house, with his welcoming family and his pretty sisters, and I said, 'You are very kind. I would like to stay above all things.'

Mrs Owen smiled.

'Then it is settled,' she said.

■ ■ ■ ■

1809

■ ■ ■ ■

January

Thursday 5 January

'Your sister Maria is newly married, I understand?' said Mrs Owen, as I walked through the village with the family this morning.

'Yes, she is, to Mr Rushworth.'

'He is a man of considerable property, I believe. Your mother must be very pleased. I would not stand in the way of my daughters if their feelings called them to such a marriage, but I confess I would rather see them married to clergymen. They would make such good clergymen's wives, all of them. They have been used to helping their father about the parish, visiting the sick and the elderly, helping with the children, sewing clothes, giving advice, and of course now they will be able to help their brother, too. Do you have anyone to help you in your parish, Mr Bertram?'

I could not misunderstand her, and let

her know, in a roundabout fashion, that I was not in a position to marry, for although I had wanted to marry Mary, I had no desire to marry any of the Miss Owens, no matter how pretty they were.

'But you will be, one day,' she said. 'I hope you may find a pretty and useful wife to support you, a young woman who will bring gladness to your life, and turn your Parsonage into a home. There is more to life than work, however noble the calling and, as I often say to my son, he must not neglect his future in the busy application of the present. But come, we have fallen behind the others, we will have to hurry if we are to catch them before they turn into the lane.'

We soon drew level with them. Owen was walking next to Miss Anne, and his father was walking next to Miss Lucy.

'Jane, dear, you look fatigued,' said Mrs Owen.

I offered Miss Owen my arm, which she took with a smile, and then I offered her mother my other arm. She took it, and thus arranged, we headed home.

I made sure to raise no expectations in Miss Owen, and this evening I paid attention to her two sisters, to make my intentions clear: having given her mother a hint that I was not ready to settle, I felt it incumbent upon me to give Miss Owen a hint likewise. But I could not help thinking that it would be a lucky man who won her, for her kind of beauty, elegance and sweet nature are seldom met with.

Tuesday 10 January

My visit came to an end this morning. The Owens sent me off with good wishes, with Mrs Owen telling me I must stay with them whenever I should find myself in the neighbourhood, and Mr Owen seconding her invitation. Owen rode with me as far as Peterborough, where he left me, and I went on alone. The weather remained fine, with a piercing blue sky and sharp shadows, but it was bitingly cold, and I was glad of the exercise to keep me warm.

As I neared Mansfield I was glad I did not have to fear meeting Miss Crawford, for her satirical comments on my new status would have been hard to bear. To be laughed at before I was a clergyman had been hard enough; to be laughed at when my ambition was accomplished would have been far worse. I had so far schooled myself to forgetting her, that when I saw her walking through the village with her brother I was astonished. I was forced to stop, and I steeled myself to her satirical words. But I was surprised to hear her saying, in the most affable manner, 'Mr Bertram! This is a welcome surprise. You have been very much missed.'

My thoughts were sent reeling. What did it mean? Had she been thinking about what I had said? Had her natural justice done what her hastiness could not, and shown her the truth of my words? And had they been strong enough to do away with her unreasonable prejudices?

The smile that accompanied her words was so radiant it gave me cause to hope. I returned her greeting, and rode on to Mansfield Park with my spirits singing. She was still at Mansfield! And she had greeted me warmly! And with such a smile! She had decided — *perhaps* she had decided — that the church was an honourable calling; and that true friendship, and more than friendship, outweighed all other considerations. But whatever the case, of one thing I could be certain: she had missed me!

There was more good news when I reached home. Once I had greeted my family, I settled myself by the fire, ready to hear all the Mansfield news. I was hoping, too, to hear why Miss Crawford and her brother were still in the neighbourhood.

'What do you think, Edmund?' asked my

aunt. 'William has been made a lieutenant.'

It was the best possible news for Fanny, and her looks spoke her happiness. I forestalled my aunt, who would have given me every particular, by asking Fanny to tell me all about it, and I soon learned that William had been helped to his good fortune by Admiral Crawford, at Henry's instigation.

'Fanny, this is a wonderful thing,' I said, delighted at her happiness.

'Oh, yes, Edmund, is it not?' she said. 'William was so worried about being passed over, but Mr Crawford took him to dine with the Admiral, and the Admiral bestirred himself, with the result that William is now second Lieutenant of HM sloop *Thrush.*'

'And never a young man deserved it more! But how good of Crawford to help him!'

Fanny blushed, but it was not until after dinner, when I sat over the port with my father, that I learned the cause of her blushes. No youthful colourings these, for in my absence Henry Crawford had proposed to her!

I could not believe it at first, but when I had grasped it, I thought it was an excellent thing, for it meant that Fanny and I would not be parted. When I married Mary — *if* I married Mary; if her smiles had told me what her heart felt — and Fanny married

Henry, then we would be united through two bonds, and would be together for ever. Mary would want to visit Henry at his own estate, and what could be more natural than that we should go for lengthy visits, when I would have not only the pleasure of gratifying Mary's wishes to see her brother, but my own wishes to see my dearest Fanny? And in return, they would come and stay with us at Thornton Lacey.

I was about to express my wholehearted delight in the engagement when my father hesitated, and said, 'There is just one thing I find it hard to comprehend. Fanny has refused him.'

'Refused him?' I asked in surprise.

'Yes. You have always understood her very well, Edmund. It would be an excellent match for her. It would provide her with an establishment, a very good establishment I might say, and a settled and secure future. It is a match I could not have presumed to hope for, as I can give Fanny very little in the way of a dowry, and Crawford is entitled to look much higher, but I am very happy to think of it. He is not only wealthy, he has no vices, and he is an agreeable young man into the bargain. The ladies all seem to like him. And yet she has still refused him. Why do you think she has done it?'

'I should imagine she was taken by surprise, and did not know what to say.'

'Perhaps. Although I cannot think why she should be surprised. I have noticed his interest in her with pleasure for some time now, and have hoped it might lead to something. Fanny's future has often troubled me. Taking her in as we did, we took on responsibility for her, and I did not want to see her dwindle into an old maid, but I confess there have been times when I have not been able to see a different future for her. She is so quiet, and we live so retired, that I knew she would have little opportunity to meet other young people. I was hoping that Maria might ask her to stay, although I also dreaded the idea, for I feared the noise and the bustle of London would not suit her. But if she marries Crawford, she will be well provided for, and I am persuaded she will be happy. And yet she has turned him down.'

'Fanny thinks so poorly of herself, and her own claims to the ordinary happinesses of life, that, until he proposed, she probably thought his attentions were nothing but kindness.'

'Then it does not surprise you?'

'Not at all, and I honour her for it. She could do nothing else. But now that she has been alerted to his preference she will have time to grow used to it and to enjoy it by and by. She deserves to have the love of a good man, one who can give her the elegancies of life, as well as his kindness, his friendship and his affection.'

'It will be a very big change for her.'

'Yes, it will. She will go from being our quiet, shy Fanny, to being the centre of attention, but I am sure she will come round. Indeed, I think it must be so. Crawford has been too precipitate, that is all. He has not given her time to attach herself. He has begun at the wrong end. But with such powers of pleasing, he must be able to win her over.'

'I am glad to hear you say so.'

'Depend upon it, it will all come right in the end.'

As soon as my father and I returned to the drawing-room for tea, I sat down next to Fanny and took her hand.

'Fanny, I have been hearing all about your proposal,' I said warmly. 'I am not surprised. You have powers of attaching a man that another woman would envy, through your goodness and your purity of spirit. Now I see why Crawford put himself out to help William. He was helping his future brother-in-law!'

'But I have refused him,' she said quietly.

'Of course, for the moment. But when you come to know him better you will see that he is just the sort of man to make you happy.'

She said no more but, feeling sure that she would soon change her mind, I let the matter drop and turned the conversation instead to William.

'William is coming to stay with us, I understand,' I said.

She brightened.

'Yes, he will be here before long. He wants to see us all and thank us for our help in his promotion.'

'Though it was all Crawford's doing,' I put in.

'He would like to show us his uniform, too, but he is not allowed to wear it except on duty.'

'Never mind. He will just have to describe it to us and we will then be able to imagine him in all his splendour.'

She talked on happily, looking forward to the day when she will see him again.

Wednesday 11 January

I was so heartened by Mary's reception of me that I went over to Thornton Lacey this morning to give instructions for the farmyard to be moved, for I wanted to make the place respectable before showing it to Mary.

'It needs to be over there, behind the copse, out of sight and downwind of the house,' I said to the men.

They began to work, and I thought how big an improvement it would make to the property. I went into the house and looked into every corner, seeing what needed doing. Over luncheon I asked my father if I could borrow some more men to help me, and he gave me leave to take anyone I wanted.

This afternoon I returned to Thornton Lacey with Christopher Jackson. He followed me in, pausing just inside the front door, then swinging it back and forth and listening to it squeak.

'This needs attention,' he said.

'See to it for me, will you, Jackson?'

He nodded, and we went through to the drawing-room.

'There are some loose floorboards over here by the window.'

'Shouldn't take too long,' he said.

As we were about to leave the room he looked at the fireplace.

'I could make you something better than that, something worth looking at,' he said. 'What this room needs is a carved chimneypiece.'

I saw at once what he meant. The grate was a good size, and it would repay framing. An ornate chimneypiece would give the room an elegant feel, and I could picture Mary sitting in front of it, playing her harp.

'A good idea. Give me something worth having.'

His eyes lingered on the chimney, and I could tell he already had some ideas in mind.

Upstairs, there were some cupboards that needed shelves, and a window frame that needed replacing. When we had been all round the house, I asked him to start work tomorrow.

I rode back to Mansfield Park and changed, just in time for dinner.

When I went downstairs I discovered that Crawford had called, and my father had invited him to stay for dinner. I wished he had brought his sister with him, but thought that, after all, perhaps it was a good thing he had not, as it would give me an opportunity to see him and Fanny together; if Mary had been present, I would have had eyes only for her.

I was hoping to see some signs of affection for him in Fanny's face and demeanour, for I was sure that liking for the brother of her friend, gratitude towards the friend of her brother, and sweet pleasure in the honourable attentions of such a man, would combine to spread a warm glow over her face. A blush, a smile, a look of consciousness — these were the things I was expecting, but I did not see any of them. I was surprised but Crawford did not seem disturbed, and he sat beside her with an ease and confidence that spoke of his expectation of being a welcome companion. As he took a seat beside her, I thought her reserve and her natural shyness must soon be worn away. But no such thing. I tried to explain it to myself as embarrassment, but I thought Crawford must be really in love to press his suit with so little encouragement.

After dinner, luckily for Crawford, things improved. When we returned to the drawing-room, Mama happened to mention that Fanny had been reading to her from Shakespeare. Crawford took up the book and asked to be allowed to finish the reading. He began, and read so well that Fanny listened with great pleasure, gradually letting her needlework fall into her lap. At last she turned her eyes on him and fixed them there until he turned towards her and closed the book, breaking the charm.

She picked up her needlework again with

a blush, but I could not wonder at Crawford for thinking he had some hope. She had certainly been enraptured by him and I thought that if he could win half so much attention from her in ordinary life he would be a fortunate man.

I admired him for persevering, for it showed that he knew Fanny's value, and knew that she was worth any extra effort he might have to make to overcome her reserve. And I could understand why he would not give her up, for as her needle flashed through her work, her gentleness was matched by her prettiness.

'That play must be a favourite with you,' I said to Crawford. 'You read as if you knew it well.'

'It will be a favourite, I believe, from this hour,' he replied. 'But I do not think I have had a volume of Shakespeare in my hand before since I was fifteen. But Shakespeare one gets acquainted with without knowing how. It is a part of an Englishman's constitution. His thoughts and beauties are so spread abroad that one touches them everywhere; one is intimate with him by instinct.'

'To know him in bits and scraps is common enough; to know him pretty thoroughly is, perhaps, not uncommon; but to read him well aloud is no everyday talent.'

'Sir, you do me honour,' said Crawford, with a bow of mock gravity.

'You have a great turn for acting, I am sure, Mr Crawford,' said Mama soon afterwards; 'and I will tell you what, I think you will have a theatre, some time or other, at your house in Norfolk. I mean when you are settled there. I do indeed. I think you will fit up a theatre at your house in Norfolk.'

'Do you, ma'am? No, no, that will never be,' Crawford assured her.

I was surprised, for if the plays were well chosen, there could be no objection to Crawford setting up a theatre. He had a good income and was entitled to do with it, and his own home, as he wished. It would certainly give him an outlet for his talents, which were of no common sort in that direction.

Fanny said nothing but I am sure she must have guessed that Crawford's avowal never to have a theatre must be a compliment to her feelings. She had made them known at the time of our disastrous theatrical affair and I was pleased that Crawford was willing to make such a sacrifice. It boded well for Fanny's future happiness that he put her own wishes above his own.

I asked Crawford where he had learnt to

read aloud so well and Fanny listened intently to our discussion. I mentioned that it was not taught as it should be, and Crawford agreed.

'In my profession it is little studied,' I said, 'but a good sermon needs a good delivery and I am glad my father made me read aloud as a boy, so that I could develop a clear and varied speaking voice.'

Crawford asked me about the service I had already performed and Fanny listened avidly. I admired Crawford, for he had found the way to her heart. She was not to be won by gallantry and wit, but by sentiment and feeling, and seriousness on serious subjects; something of which he showed himself eminently capable.

I drew away after a time, giving the two of them some time alone. I took up a newspaper, hoping that Fanny would be persuaded to talk to her lover, and I gave them my own murmurs: 'A most desirable Estate in South Wales'; 'To Parents and Guardians'; and a 'Capital season'd Hunter' to cover their own.

It did not seem to go well, from what I heard, for Fanny seemed to be berating Crawford for inconstancy, and though I tried not to listen I could not help their words reaching me.

'You think me unsteady: easily swayed by the whim of the moment, easily tempted, easily put aside,' I heard Crawford say. 'With such an opinion, no wonder that . . . But we shall see. It is not by protestations that I shall endeavour to convince you I am wronged; it is not by telling you that my affections are steady. My conduct shall speak for me; absence, distance, time shall speak for me. *They* shall prove that, as far as you can be deserved by anybody, I do deserve you. You are infinitely my superior in merit; all *that* I know. You have qualities which I had not before supposed to exist in such a degree in any human creature. You have some touches of the angel in you beyond what — not merely beyond what one sees, because one never sees anything like it — but beyond what one fancies might be. But still I am not frightened. It is not by equality of merit that you can be won. That is out of the question. It is he who sees and worships your merit the strongest, who loves you most devotedly, that has the best right to a return.'

I was surprised to hear such ardour, and was just beginning to be uncomfortable at overhearing it when Baddeley brought in the tea. Crawford was obliged to move and I returned to the group.

Fanny said no more but I felt she could not have been unmoved by Crawford's protestations. I was expecting her to speak to me when he left but she kept silent. I did not ask her about him, for I did not want to press her. But as I have always been her confidant, I hope she will turn to me when she feels she needs someone to talk to.

Thursday 12 January

As I dressed this morning, I found myself wondering what Mary thought of her brother's feelings for Fanny. I knew she was fond of Fanny, but I also knew that she had a high regard for wealth and distinction, and I thought she might feel that Henry should unite himself to both.

I rode over to Thornton Lacey and found that the work was going on apace. There was already a difference in the size of the farmyard and Jackson was at work on the door. The fine weather was helpful, and I went round to the stables to ascertain whether there would be room to keep my horses as well as a mount for Mary. There would, perhaps, be enough room but I felt it would be better to extend the stables, something which could be easily done, and I spoke to Jackson about it before leaving.

Returning to Mansfield Park, I found

myself wondering again about Mary's view on her brother's choice of bride. We were dining at the Parsonage, and I resolved to broach the subject, but in the event there was no need, for she began to speak of it herself not five minutes after I had arrived.

'Well, Mr Bertram, and what do you think of my brother and Miss Price?' she asked.

Mrs Grant laughed at her for her rapidity, saying, 'Mary, give Mr Bertram time to sit down, at least!'

'But I want to know,' she said.

'I confess I was surprised,' I returned.

'Were you? I was not. I have been seeing his attachment for some time, and seeing it with pleasure. There is not a better girl in all the world than Fanny Price. Her gentleness and gratitude are of no common stamp, and I am glad that Henry has seen it. She has nothing of ambition in her, and she is the only woman I have ever met who would not be swayed by Henry's fortune and his estate. Only love will do for Fanny Price.'

'There you are right,' I said.

'Such a beautiful girl,' said Mrs Grant. 'Henry has been full of her charms. Her face and figure, her graces of manner and goodness of heart are exhaustless themes with him. He talks of nothing else.'

'Unless it be her temper, which he has

good reason to depend on and praise. He has often seen it tried, for Mrs Norris is unstinting in her criticisms, and yet Fanny never answers her sharply,' said Mary.

'No, indeed, I have never heard her speak a word of complaint,' said Mrs Grant.

'She is sometimes too forbearing, and needs a champion,' I said.

'Oh! Henry will champion her, should there ever be a need, but why will there be, when he takes her away to her own home? There will be no aunt there to criticize her, only a husband who loves her, and a staff whose business it will be to make sure she is comfortable in every way. There is only one fault I have to find in her, and that is that she has refused Henry. For that I am very angry with her!'

But she said it with a laugh in her voice and a sparkle in her eye, so that I knew she was only teasing.

'He has taken her by surprise,' said Mrs Grant wisely. 'Such a quiet, unassuming girl, would be overwhelmed at so sudden a proposal. But let her get used to the idea, and she will soon give him the answer he deserves. Her affections, once they take hold, are strong. We have seen it with her brother.'

'Yes, she loves William as no girl has ever

loved a brother before,' said Mary with delight. 'It is sweetness itself to see them together.'

'There she owes your brother a great debt,' I said. 'It was very good of him to take William to see the Admiral.'

'He thinks nothing of it,' said Mary. 'He was glad to do everything in his power to assist William, because he knew that, by assisting William, he was pleasing the woman he loves.'

'And her understanding is so good,' said Mrs Grant.

'It is beyond everything, quick and clear,' said Mary.

I was heartened by her words, for they showed she had the goodness I had always expected her of, for how else would she be able to value Fanny's true worth?

'Such steadiness and regularity of conduct, such a high notion of honour, and such an observance of decorum —'

'Any man might depend on her faith and integrity. He will be able to absolutely confide in her,' said Mary.

'It was a happy day, indeed, when he met her,' said Mrs Grant.

'They will do each other good. Fanny can not fail to do Henry good, and he will give her the consequence she deserves. She will feel it every day, every hour, in the way people approach her and speak to her. And he will make her happy. There is no woman Henry cannot fail to please, if he sets his mind to it, and he is certain to set his mind to pleasing the woman he loves. He has already done it. Fanny's happiness is his only thought.'

'Ay, so much so that he talks of renting a house round here, so that he need not take her from everything she knows,' said Mrs Grant. 'He means to let Everingham and rent a place in this neighbourhood — perhaps Stanwix Lodge.'

'Settle in Northamptonshire?' I asked, much pleased. 'That will be a very good idea.'

'Yes, is it not pleasant?' said Mary. 'Then we shall all be together.'

The look she gave me with this encouraged me more than I can say. *We shall all be together.* My heart leapt at the thought that she wanted us all to be together as much as I did.

Henry and Fanny, and Mary and I.

As I returned home at last, I resolved to put my hopes to the test. As soon as Thornton Lacey is ready to receive a mistress, and as soon as I have settled my affairs so that I know exactly what I am able to offer her, I will ask her to be my wife.

Friday 13 January
I was at Thornton Lacey early this morning, and rode round the grounds, reining in
my horse at the southern edge and looking
over the adjacent fields. If I can persuade
Robert Ingles to sell them to me I can
improve the living and increase my income.
Having examined them, I returned to Mansfield Park and talked over the idea with my
father.

'An excellent notion,' he said. 'Thornton
Lacey is capable of a good deal of improvement in the right hands, and I will help you
in any way I can.'

He hesitated, and I said, 'You wish to talk
to me about something? About Fanny?'

He nodded.

'I wish you would have a word with her,
Edmund. Crawford talks of constancy, but
he is going away in a few days' time, and I
think it is best not to try him too far.'

'If he knows Fanny's true worth — and I
think that he does — he will not forget her,'
I reassured him, for I did not feel it was in
Crawford's feelings that the obstacle lay.

'Well, it may be as you say, but I would
like some indication of her present feelings.
I cannot advise or guide her if I do not know

her mind or her heart.'

'I have been thinking the same thing. I will take the first opportunity of speaking to her alone. The time has come for me to find out what she truly thinks and feels.'

'Good. She is walking through the shrubbery at the moment. I saw her from the window not five minutes ago.'

'Then I will join her.'

I donned my coat and a very few minutes took me outside.

'I am come to walk with you, Fanny,' I said. I drew her arm through mine companionably, but I was disturbed to find that she did not lean against me, as was her custom. 'It is a long while since we have had a comfortable walk together, you and I.'

She agreed to this by look rather than word and I could tell by her silence that her spirits were low. My heart felt for her.

'I know you have something on your mind,' I said gently. 'Am I to hear of it from everybody but Fanny herself?'

She sounded dejected. 'If you hear of it from everybody, cousin, there can be nothing for me to tell.'

'Not of facts, perhaps; but of feelings, Fanny. No one but you can tell me them. I do not mean to press you. If it is not what you wish yourself, I have done,' I said, adding only, by way of encouragement, 'I had thought it might be a relief.'

'I am afraid we think too differently for me to find any relief in talking of what I feel,' she said quietly.

'Do you suppose that we think differently?' I asked in surprise. 'I dare say, that on a comparison of our opinions, they would be found as much alike as they had been used to be. I consider Crawford's proposals as most advantageous and desirable, if you could return his affection. I consider it as most natural that all your family should wish you *could* return it; but that, as you cannot, you have done exactly as you ought in refusing him. Can there be any disagreement between us here?'

'Oh no!' she cried in relief. 'But I thought you blamed me! I thought you were against me. This is such a comfort!'

I pulled her arm further through mine and was relieved and reassured to feel her lean on me.

'How could you possibly suppose me against you?' I asked her softly.

'My uncle thought me wrong, and I knew he had been talking to you.'

'As far as you have gone, Fanny, I think you perfectly right. Can it admit of a question? It is disgraceful to us if it does. If you did not love Crawford, nothing could have justified your accepting him.'

She gave a sigh, and as I heard all her worries rushing out of her I was glad I had brought her such comfort. How unhappy she must have been, thinking we were all against her.

But once she was more comfortable I felt I must show her the advantages of Crawford's offer, for I did not want her to grow old regretting the chance she had thrown away in her youth. Crawford was offering her love and affection; her own establishment; and all the joys of a rich and varied life.

'Crawford's is no common attachment,' I said gently, as we walked on together, feeling the sun on our faces and crunching the frost beneath our feet. 'He perseveres with the hope of creating that regard which had not been created before. This, we know, must be a work of time. But let him succeed at last, Fanny,' I said, for I felt sure she only needed a little encouragement to welcome his attentions, and that, as Mrs Crawford, she would be a happy woman.

I was astonished when she burst out, 'Oh! never, never, never! he never will succeed with me.'

'Never, Fanny?' I asked, surprised into

adding, 'This is not like yourself, your rational self.'

'I mean, that I *think* I never shall,' she said, controlling her passion. 'As far as the future can be answered for; I think I never shall return his regard.'

I could not understand why she was so set against him, of leaving the home of her uncle for one of her own — and then all was made clear to me. Fanny's tender nature had given her a strong attachment to early things, and made her dislike the thought of change or separation. One of the things I had thought of as being in Crawford's favour was in fact against him, for in gaining a home of her own, she would have to leave behind the home she knew. I wished again that he had taken things more slowly, attaching her to him before speaking of marriage, so that she would have been prepared for his declarations and even wanting them; and, wanting them, she would have been able to face the thought of leaving the securities and pleasures of childhood with composure.

'I must hope that time, proving him (as I firmly believe it will) to deserve you by his steady affection, will give him his reward,' I said.

But she did not enter into my hopes. Quite

the reverse.

'We are so totally unlike,' she said, 'we are so very, very different in all our inclinations and ways, that I consider it as quite impossible we should ever be tolerably happy together, even if I *could* like him. There never were two people more dissimilar. We have not one taste in common. We should be miserable.'

This was bleak indeed. So bleak that I felt fancy was at work, rather than reason.

'You have both warm hearts and benevolent feelings,' I pointed out. 'And, Fanny, who that heard him read, and saw you listen to Shakespeare the other night, will think you unfitted as companions? There is a decided difference in your tempers, I allow. He is lively, you are serious; but so much the better: his spirits will support yours.'

She hesitated, and then said reluctantly, 'I cannot approve his character. I have not thought well of him from the time of the play. I then saw him behaving so improperly by poor Mr Rushworth, not seeming to care how he exposed or hurt him, and paying attentions to my cousin Maria, which — in short, at the time of the play, I received an impression which will never be got over.'

I protested at this, but she said, 'As a bystander, perhaps I saw more than you did;

and I do think that Mr Rushworth was sometimes very jealous. And before the play, I am much mistaken if *Julia* did not think Mr Crawford was paying her attentions.'

'To be sure, the play did none of us credit, but Fanny, you have lived so retired that you have made too much of Crawford's lively nature, and my sisters' desire to be admired. To condemn the behaviour of that time is right and just; but to let it destroy your future happiness is folly. He will make you happy, Fanny; I know he will make you happy, and you will make him happy,' I re-assured her.

She looked tired. I did not want to press her further, so I turned the conversation to other things, talking of my time with the Owens.

'You spent your time pleasantly there?' asked Fanny, reviving once the subject of Crawford was dropped. 'The Miss Owens — you liked them, did not you?'

'Yes, very well. Pleasant, good-humoured, unaffected girls. But I am spoilt, Fanny, for common female society. Good-humoured, unaffected girls will not do for a man who has been used to sensible women. They are two distinct orders of being. You and Miss Crawford have made me too nice,' I told her.

She smiled, but it was a tired smile, and I felt she had had enough conversation. So, with the kind authority of a privileged guardian, I led her back into the house.

Saturday 14 January
I spoke to my father after breakfast and told him that I thought we should make no further attempts to persuade Fanny, but that everything should be left to Crawford's addresses and the passage of time.

'She must become used to the idea of his being in love with her, and then a return of affection might not be very distant.'

'It shall be as you say, but I only hope that she might persuade herself into receiving his addresses properly, before his inclination for paying them is over.'

'He will prove himself steadfast, I am sure,' I said.

'I hope so,' was my father's only reply.

I was not a little curious to see how Fanny would receive Crawford this evening, and in the event their encounter promised well. He came and sat with us some time, and I saw a softening of Fanny's face, and a tenderness in her expression that led me to believe all would finally be well.

'It is a pity your brother has to go to town tomorrow,' I said to Mary.

She followed my eyes towards Fanny and her brother.

'Yes, it is, but he has promised to escort me to my friend's house and, having once delayed my visit, I cannot delay it again. And who knows? Absence might prove to be his friend. When she is no longer receiving his attentions, Fanny might come to miss them and welcome their return.'

I thought it only too likely.

'And tomorrow you are leaving, too,' I said to her.

'Yes, I am. You will not begrudge me a stay in town? Mrs Fraser has been my intimate friend for years.'

'I could never begrudge you anything. I have already been more fortunate than I dared hope, for you were still here when I returned after Christmas when I was expecting to find you gone.'

'I should have gone, by rights, but when it came to it I found I could not leave the neighbourhood whilst Henry was trying to fix Fanny. It would not have been fair to take him away at such a time.'

But something in her eye and voice told me that that was not her only reason for delaying her departure.

'I thought I would not see you again.'

'Did you?' she asked with a smile.

'I did. I thought you were lost to me. But now I hope we may meet often. I will be going to town myself before long. Will I see you there?'

'I rely upon it. You must come and visit me at Mrs Fraser's.'

'You may be certain of it.'

There was time for no more. The evening was drawing to an end. Crawford was taking his leave of Fanny, who seemed sorry to see him go, and I took Mary's hand and bent over it.

'Until then,' I said.

Tuesday 17 January

'Well, Edmund,' said my father, as we sat over the port, 'and do you think Fanny misses Crawford now that he has gone?'

'I hardly think three or four days' absence enough to produce such a feeling.'

'And yet she has been used to attention, to being singled out in the most flattering way. It is strange that she should not miss it. The attentions of her aunts can hardly compensate for the company of an intelligent young man.'

What puzzled me more was that Fanny did not seem to regret Miss Crawford, for Mary had been her friend and companion for far longer than Crawford had been her acknowledged lover.

'I will be going to town in less than a fortnight,' I said to Fanny, when my father and I rejoined the ladies. 'Do you have any commissions for me?'

'I cannot think of anything at the moment.'

'You must let me know if any occur to you. And if you have any letters for Miss Crawford I can take them to her.'

'You will be visiting her?' she enquired.

'Yes, indeed. I am looking forward to it. I am persuaded that she, too, is looking forward to it. She will be able to hear about you, and everyone at Mansfield.'

Fanny said nothing.

'You are very quiet, Fanny. Have you nothing to say of your friend? I thought you would be constantly talking of her. It cannot be pleasant for you to be all alone again.'

'I have my aunts, and —'

'And?'

'And . . . that is enough.'

My mother calling to me, I could say no more, but as Mama was happy to talk of Mary, I was well satisfied with my evening, and could only have enjoyed it more if Fanny had confessed to missing Crawford as much as I missed his sister.

Wednesday 18 January

I spoke to Ingles about the field and although he said he did not want to sell, and could not let it go below an exorbitant price, I believe he was only bargaining and will let me have it in the end.

Monday 23 January

Fanny's indifference to Crawford's and Mary's absence has been made clear: she is too excited at William's visit to have room in her mind and heart for anything else. He is to join us on Friday, and I hope that seeing him, newly promoted, will make Fanny think more kindly of Crawford, whose good offices brought the promotion about.

Friday 27 January

William arrived, looking bright and handsome, and was full of his new honour. He lamented the fact that he could not show his uniform to us, but he described it in enough detail to please even Fanny. I wished she could see it, but I fear that, by the time she does, it will no longer be a source of such joy to William. A lieutenant's rank will satisfy him for now, but before long he will want further promotion; his uniform will seem like a badge of disgrace when all his friends have been made commanders. I only hope that by then, Fanny will be safely married to Crawford, and that the Admiral will be disposed to help William again. That would be a happy occasion indeed, if we could see William in a captain's uniform. I said as much to Fanny, and she smiled, and said she was sure his merits would lift him to the highest rank. It transpired that Fanny will settle for nothing less than seeing him an admiral!

Saturday 28 January

Crawford left a horse for William to ride and we went out together this morning. We had not gone far before he had a fall. Having ridden mules, donkeys and scrawny horses he was not adept at handling a highly bred animal, and came to grief whilst jumping a fence. The horse was none the worse, which was a mercy, or Crawford would have paid a heavy price for his kindness. William was unhurt, but he bruised his side and his coat was covered in mud.

'Say nothing of this to Fanny,' he begged me. 'She worries about me; though if she could see the scrapes I have survived she would know I could survive anything! On my first ship I was swept overboard and was only able to climb back again by grabbling hold of a piece of torn sail that had washed overboard with me. By luck it was still attached to the rest of the sail, and I used it as a rope to haul myself in.'

The stories became more gruesome; far worse than the ones he had told in the drawing-room; and I was glad he had spared Fanny the details of his hardships and deprivations, and the rigours of Navy life. I admired him all the more for being so considerate, as well as for being a brave man.

'We can go to Thornton Lacey,' I said. 'You can wash there and brush your coat when the mud has dried. I can lend you a shirt,' I added, noticing his own was ripped, for luckily I had begun to move some of my things over to the rectory.

We were soon there and I took him into the kitchen so that he could wash. As he stripped off his shirt I saw there were a number of scars on his back and arms and he told me about each one; how a Frenchman had got in a lucky thrust as he boarded a foreign vessel; how he had been outnumbered and had had to fight his way out of a corner with his sword in his left hand; how he had been down, with a sword at his throat, when his friend had run his adversary through, and he had taken a cut when his adversary fell. And tales of a better sort:

the deep scar on his right arm had come from his standing between his captain and injury; and the scar on his shoulder was from protecting the cabin boy, a young lad on his first voyage, who, because of William's prompt action, had survived to make a second one.

I gave him a clean shirt and once the mud had dried he was able to brush it from his coat before we returned to the Park. We found Fanny in the drawing-room, sketching.

'I am glad to see you have taken Mary's advice,' I said, when I saw the fruit of her labours; explaining to William, 'Fanny's friend, Miss Crawford, advised her to have a picture of you to keep by her when you are away.'

'Now that I have my promotion, it is perhaps worth having,' he acknowledged.

'It was always worth having, to me,' said Fanny.

'You should draw a likeness of Edmund,' said William. 'Your sketching is really very good. Is it not?' he asked me.

'Yes, excellent. Well, Fanny? Will you draw me?'

'If you will still for as long as it takes, and not be off on parish business.'

'I believe it can spare me for the rest of

the day.'

William stood by Fanny's shoulder as she drew, saying, 'A little more length here,' or 'a little more shading there,' until it was done.

'Very creditable,' I said. 'I will have it framed, I believe, the next time I go into town.'

'And perhaps, the next time I see you, you can sketch me in my new uniform as well,' said William.

Monday 30 January

My father was impressed with Fanny's drawings, and he has thought of a scheme to help her see William in his new uniform.

'I am planning on sending her back to Portsmouth with him, to spend a little time with her family,' he said to me. 'What do you think of the idea, Edmund?'

'I think it an excellent one. I know she will welcome it.'

'Good. Then send her to me and I will tell her of it,' he said.

When Fanny heard of it she was in raptures. Though she did not make the noise my sisters would have done at such delight, her shining face told me her feelings, and her swelling heart soon gave them voice.

'I can never thank my uncle enough for

being so kind,' she said to William and me. 'To go home again! And to be with you, William, until your very last hour on land. And then to stay with my family for two months, perhaps three. Oh! never was anyone luckier than I.' Then her face fell and she said to me, 'But will your mother be able to manage without me?'

'Of course she will,' I said. 'She will have Aunt Norris.'

'But Aunt Norris will not fetch and carry for her as I do.'

'Then I will do it for her.'

'But you will not be here.' She coloured. 'You will soon be going to town, and you will have other demands on your time, other people . . .'

I thought of Mary, and I was sure her thoughts had gone to Mary's brother, for why else should she fall silent? I reassured her that Mama would manage without her, but she was still perturbed, and it was not until my father reassured her after dinner that she was content.

It is so like Fanny to be always thinking of others. It will do her good to go to Portsmouth, where she can think more of herself. And if she marries Crawford — *when* she marries Crawford — she will be able to consult her own inclination on almost everything. She will have servants to run her errands, instead of having to run them for others, and everything in the house will be organized as she wishes. She will be a very happy woman before the year is out.

Tuesday 31 January

Having told Fanny Mama could manage without her, I was surprised to find that Mama saw it in a different light.

'Why should she see her family?' she asked, when Fanny was out riding. 'She has done very well without her family for eight or nine years. Why can she not do without them again?'

'My dear,' said my father, 'it is only right and proper that Fanny should visit them from time to time.'

'I do not see why,' said Mama, picking Pug up and stroking him. 'I am sure she does not want to go. Ask her, Sir Thomas. I am sure she would much rather stay here.'

'She has a duty to her family,' said my father, trying again.

'And she has a duty here,' returned Mama.

'It will be a sacrifice for you, I know,' said my father, 'but Lady Bertram has always been capable of sacrifice for the good of others, and I know she will be so again.'

This courtesy did little to soften Mama's

unhappiness. 'I see that you think she must go, and if you think it, Sir Thomas, then she must, but for myself I can see no reason for it. I need her so very much here.'

At this my aunt joined in the conversation.

'Nonsense, my dear Lady Bertram. Fanny can very well be spared. I am ready to give up all my time to your pleasure, and Fanny will not be wanted or missed.'

'That may be, sister. I dare say you are very right; but I am sure I shall miss her very much,' said Mama.

Knowing that my father would have his way and Fanny would go to Portsmouth, I blessed Mama for her words; it was good to know that Fanny would be so missed by someone other than myself, for I fear she is often taken for granted.

FEBRUARY

Wednesday 1 February
Fanny has written to her mother, suggesting the visit, and now she waits for a reply.

Friday 3 February
The reply arrived, a few simple lines expressing so natural and motherly a joy in the prospect of seeing Fanny again as to confirm all Fanny's views of happiness in being with her. She was brimming over with spirits as we walked in the park, making the most of a dry spell that has left the ground as hard as iron and the air as heady as wine.

'I will be much more useful to her than when I left, and now that she is no longer occupied by the incessant demands of a house full of little children, there will be leisure and inclination for every comfort, and we should soon be what mother and daughter ought to be to each other,' she said.

William was almost as happy as Fanny.

'It will be the greatest pleasure to have you there to the last moment before I sail, and perhaps find you there still when I come in from my first cruise. And besides, I want you so very much to see the *Thrush* before she goes out of harbour. She is the finest sloop in the service, and there are several improvements in the dockyard, too, which I long to show you.

'It will be good for all the family to see you,' he went on. 'I do not know how it is, but we seem to want some of your nice ways and orderliness at my father's. The house is always in confusion. You will set things going in a better way, I am sure. You will tell my mother how it all ought to be, and you will be so useful to Susan, and you will teach Betsey, and make the boys love and mind you. How right and comfortable it will all be!'

Saturday 4 February

My aunt was horrified when she heard that Fanny and William will be travelling post to Portsmouth.

'My dear Sir Thomas, there is no need for it, no need for it at all. Only think of the expense. There are many cheaper ways for them to reach the coast,' she said.

My father delighted me by saying, 'They will certainly not travel any other way,' and settled the matter by giving William the fare.

'Well, if it is to be, then it is to be. But surely,' said my aunt, suddenly struck with an idea to her own advantage, 'there will be room for a third in the carriage. Do you know I think I will go with them. I am longing to see my poor dear sister Price. I have not seen her for an age. I must say that I have more than half a mind to go with the young people; it would be such an indulgence to me; I have not seen her for more than twenty years; and it would be a help to the young people in their journey to have my older head to manage for them. I cannot help thinking my poor dear sister Price would feel it very unkind of me not to come by such an opportunity.'

Fanny's face fell, and William's look of horror was comical. I could not blame him for his reaction. To be forced into such close company with my aunt, for such a period of time, would daunt even the strongest of hearts. Fanny retired, and fortunately my aunt changed her mind, so I followed Fanny from the room to tell her of her reprieve. I found her in the library.

'Aunt Norris has decided that she is needed here. She will not be going with you,' I said. 'Though I suspect that her real reason was a realization that she would have to pay her own expenses back again.'

Fanny's look of relief lit up her face.

'My aunt is a very good woman, but. . . .'

'Exactly. *But!*'

We both smiled.

'Come, Fanny, walk with me outside. I do not seem to have seen anything of you recently. You are always closeted with William. Your old friends have had to do without you.'

'No!' she said in consternation, then saw that I was teasing her. 'I see so little of William, I have to make the most of every minute when I see him.'

'I will let you go back to him soon, but I am selfishly claiming you for the next hour. I have no one sensible to talk to when you are elsewhere, unless it is about business, and I am tired of business. Tell me what you have been reading, and what you have been thinking, and what you have been feeling.'

And so we talked, and I kept her with me well past the hour, for we had so much to talk about.

Sunday 5 February

Mama was so downcast at the thought of

my leaving: 'You are all leaving me; Fanny, William and you', that I have promised to stay another week or two. I was rewarded by a return of her comfort, and I told Fanny of my decision as we sat in the drawing-room, having returned from church.

'I am not entirely displeased at the delay. The shops and parties in London will have all the delight of novelty for Mary in the first few weeks, but I want her to have a chance to be reminded of how empty a constant round of pleasure is before I propose.'

Fanny said nothing, for she had reached a difficult part of her work and needed to pay it close attention.

'This is very companionable, is it not, Fanny?' I said, watching the dancing fire paint a warm glow on to her winter complexion, and on to her white hands, which worked diligently with her needle. 'The two of us sitting here and talking together like this. Perhaps it will be the last time we can talk together so freely. Who knows what changes will have come about the next time we meet?'

The coming change was in the air all through the house. After dinner, Mama said, 'How sad it is to lose friends. You will be gone from here tomorrow. You must write to me soon and often, Fanny, and I will write to you.'

'And *I* shall write to you, Fanny, when I have anything worth writing about, anything to say that I think you will like to hear, and that you will not hear so soon from any other quarter,' I added, thinking that, if all went well, I would be able to tell her of my engagement.

I gave her an affectionate farewell, and she went upstairs, retiring early so as to get a good night's sleep before her early departure tomorrow.

Monday 6 February

And so, Fanny and William are now well on their way to Portsmouth, and I have put my day to good use. The farmyard has been moved, Jackson has finished the repairs and he has begun work on the chimneypiece. It is already taking shape, and I do not believe there will be a better one in the neighbourhood. The approach is now much improved, and I have given instructions for some new planting to shut out the view of the blacksmith's shop. I hope it will please Mary when it is done, for on her acceptance of my hand my happiness now depends.

Saturday 11 February

We had a letter from Fanny this morning, and it drew a vivid picture of family life. I am certain it is not what she was expecting, for between her protestations of happiness she revealed that William had had to leave sooner than planned; that her mother had little time for her; that Susan's free and easy manner with their mother was surprising; that her father's oaths were alarming; that Tom and Charles were wild, and were forever running about and slamming doors; and that the house was very small, so that everyone was always falling over one another, increasing all the arguments and chaos of a large family.

My poor Fanny! How I felt for her. But my father was very pleased when he read it.

'It will do her good to be back with them again,' he said. 'It will show her that the pleasures of a gentleman's residence are not to be overlooked, and that, as Mrs Crawford, she will suffer none of the ills her mother endures. No small house or thin walls; no troublesome servants; no curses; no lack of order.'

'So that is the direction your thoughts are taking,' I mused.

'Yes, they are. I would like to see her provided for, comfortably settled, and with a secure future; for to remain here as a companion to her aunts is no life for a young girl. She is timid, and needs encouragement, and I mean to do all in my power to try and promote her happiness by helping her to overcome her shyness, and to fully realize the advantages of the life she is being offered. Have you heard anything from Crawford?'

'Yes, he sent me a letter. He is in Norfolk at present, having some business there. He is as constant as ever, and though he said little about Fanny, what he said was to the point.'

'Good, good. I was afraid he might cry off. With so little encouragement, it would not be surprising. But it seems he means to have her, and if he will wait a little longer, I feel all will be well. Did he see your sisters in town?'

'No, but Maria has sent him a card for her party on the twenty-eighth, when she opens her house in Wimpole Street. His sister means to go with him.'

'That is all to the good. A connection between the two families will help his case.'

I did not say that I hoped for an even closer connection between the two families ere long, but I thought it.

'Will you be attending your sister's party?'

'If I am in London in time.'

We returned to the drawing-room, and I was struck by how empty it was without Fanny. I thought it strange that someone so quiet could make such an impression on the house, and that I noticed her absence more than that of my sisters, who were twice as noisy.

Saturday 25 February

Tom echoed my father's question, asking if I would be going to Maria's party when I met him in London today. He invited me to dine with him and his friends and I arrived at his rooms this evening to find all his usual cronies there. The atmosphere was jovial and the wine was flowing freely.

I said that I was, and asked if he would be there.

'I suppose I will have to look in, but I do not intend to stay for long. I have better things to do.'

'Better things in the shape of a sweet little actress,' said Langley, drawing her shape with his hands in the air, and they all laughed.

'Whilst your better things come in the shape of an opera dancer,' returned Tom.

'Have you a mistress, Bertram?' asked Hargate.

When I said no, he said, 'We must find you one.'

'Edmund has no taste for mistresses,' said Tom with a sly glance at me. 'He is more interested in horse flesh. There is a certain little filly that has caught his eye.'

'Have you put a bet on her?' asked Langley curiously.

Before I could reply, Tom said, 'No, but I have put a bet on him. I think brother Edmund will be lucky, and if he is, the filly in question will bring him twenty thousand pounds.'

'Twenty thousand? What sort of odds must you have to get . . . Oh! Well said, Bertram. A fine filly indeed!'

I tried to get Tom to be serious but it was not to be, and the evening was spent in similar vein. The conversation turned to an outing on the river they were planning and Tom said, 'Come with us.'

He would not take no for an answer, and I have promised to join him on Tuesday.

Monday 27 February

I went to see the solicitors this morning and had a long consultation with them. I feel I am better prepared to take the step of matrimony, if Mary will have me.

Tuesday 28 February

The day was unusually mild and we spent a riotous afternoon on the river. When it was time to turn for home there was a good deal of confusion and one of the boats overturned. Tom fell in, I went with him, and the result was that we missed Maria's party.

'The weather is too fine to stay in town. I have never seen such fine weather in February, it is hot enough to be May! We are all going out of town for the races next week. You should come with us, Edmund,' he said, as we changed our clothes in his rooms. 'It will do you good to have some fun for a change. You need not worry about Mary missing you. By all accounts, she is enjoying herself in London, with a constant round of parties and friends, and she will not even notice you have gone.'

That was not what I wanted to hear, and I said, 'I thought you had done with gambling.'

'Always my conscience, Edmund? You may rest easy, I am not going to bet on a horse, I am going to ride one. Let other people bet on me,' he said, as he stripped off his wet shirt.

'And do you think you have a chance of winning?' I asked him, not sure whether I liked this new turn of events, for although

Tom was a good rider, some of the races were brutal.

'As good a chance as anyone else. I have an excellent mount, Imperial Caesar. You have never seen such an animal. Langley is lending him to me.'

'Have you seen him race before?'

'No, but Langley assures me the animal is a winner.'

'And is Langley betting on him or against him?'

'Stop worrying, little brother!' he said with a laugh.

He tried to tempt me to go with him, but I refused, and after arguing the matter back and forth for some time, at last he accepted defeat.

'If you change your mind, you know where I am. I will be here until Saturday,' he said. 'After that, I will not be in town for several weeks.'

When I returned, I found an invitation from the Frasers waiting for me, asking me to dine on Friday. So on Friday I will see Mary, and discover if I am to be made happy.

MARCH

And so it has been and gone, the best and worst evening of my life.

I took a hackney cab to the Frasers' house and entered it full of apprehension and hope, for although there had been no mistaking Mary's indulgence the last time I had seen her, I was afraid that in London, with her fashionable friends around her, her feelings might have changed.

My eyes ran round the room and when they alighted on her I thought she had never looked more lovely. She was flushed from conversation, and her eyes were bright. Her dress was the whitest silk, and her skin was glowing in the candlelight. I could scarcely wait to greet her, and made my way across the room to where she stood with her friend. She looked up; my heart leapt; I joined her; but as soon as I began to speak to her I felt a sense of foreboding.

'You were not at your sister's party,' she said to me, when we had greeted each other, and though there was something playful in her manner, there was also something accusing there.

'No.'

'You were converting some poor old woman in Thornton Lacey, no doubt?' she asked me in a derisory tone of voice.

Mrs Fraser positively crowed. 'See how he avoids the question! It was a *young* woman, I have no doubt.'

Mary's lips set in a tight line. She did not seem pleased, and I was no more pleased at the notion that she really believed me capable of making love to another woman in her absence, as Mrs Fraser's remark implied.

'I was with my brother,' I said.

Mrs Fraser gave her a knowing look, and I could see she did not believe me.

'It is a pity you missed the party, whatever the reason,' said Mary, 'for then you would have seen Maria in all her glory, showing us all round the house like a woman who has got her penny's worth and knows it. It is a wonderful house, is it not, Catherine?'

'It is indeed,' assented Mrs Fraser. 'It is the best house in Wimpole Street. If Fraser would only apply himself more, we might have a house like that ourselves.'

Fraser, standing at his wife's elbow, ignored this remark, and escaped into his wine.

'Have you ever been in the house, Mr Bertram?' Mary asked me, playing with her wineglass and turning glittering eyes on me.

'No, I have not.'

'I was in it two years ago, when it was Lady Lascelle's, and prefer it to almost any I know in London.'

'Lady Lascelle made a good marriage. She has moved on to even better things,' said Mrs Fraser, in an aggrieved tone of voice. 'But then, Lascelle knows how to rise in the world. He has ambition.'

'Ambition! That is what a man needs above all things. Do you not agree, Mr Bertram?' asked Mary.

The evening got no better. Every word was a barb. If not for the fact that I was sure she was being led astray by Mrs Fraser and her sister I would have left the house there and then. But I knew Mary was capable of better things. Her worldliness had dominated her worthier feelings in her early days at Mansfield Park, but since Christmas her more natural feelings had been in evidence. I knew she was not really the cold, calculating creature I was seeing before me; her true nature was warm and tender and kindhearted. Her generosity to Fanny, her warmth to me, all told their own tale. And so I swallowed her insults and hoped for better things once her friend had left us.

'And how do you like Mrs Fraser's house?' she asked me, when Mrs Fraser had moved on. 'Do you approve?'

'It is very elegant,' I said, 'but very cold.'

'Then you do not approve.'

'No, I do not.'

'A pity. I like it here.'

'You like the people?'

'Yes, I do. Do you not?'

I looked around. They were dressed in the finest clothes and wore the finest jewels, but their glitter was all on the surface.

'I do not believe there is one single happy person here,' I said. 'This is not the place for you.'

'Do you want to save me, Mr Bertram?' she asked me in a droll voice.

I replied to her seriously, 'Yes, I do.'

'But I am not one of your parishioners.'

'I rather hoped you were more than that.'

'Did you?'

'Ah, my dear Mary,' broke in a voice.

The interruption could not have come at a worse time, for beneath her drollery Mary had been warming to my words, I was sure. But the arrival of Lady Stornaway put paid to any rational conversation, and gossip — ill-natured gossip at that — took its place.

And so I came home, less hopeful than when I went, jealous of the fashionable world with all its glitter and habits of wealth, and wondering if I had the right to ask her to abandon them. She was entitled to everything she longed for. But if she married me, even with our incomes united, we would not be able to afford the luxuries she craved.

If I did not believe she had some regard for me I would go, leave London and never return. But I am convinced she is not without a decided preference, and so I accepted Mrs Fraser's invitation to dine with them again. I cannot abandon Mary to avarice and spitefulness. If she pursues her present path she will end up like her friends; wealthy, indulged and unhappy. I love her too much to leave her to that fate.

Tuesday 14 March

I am becoming a frequent visitor at the Frasers, and though I like Mrs Fraser no more than I did, I am grateful to her for inviting me to her house so often. I could not get near Mary to begin with, for she was surrounded by a crowd, but as Crawford was there I lost no time in asking him about his visit to Portsmouth, for I knew he had been there, and I was eager to hear news of Fanny.

'Ah! You have heard about that. I could not stay away,' he said. 'I meant to remain in town after my return from my estate, for I was hoping that absence might do its work, but in the end my need to see Fanny was too strong for me. I put up at the Crown, not a bad establishment, and was soon at the Prices.'

'And how did you find them?'

'Well, all well. Mrs Price was very busy, but Mr Price invited me to see the dockyard, then on Sunday we walked on the ramparts. How good it was to be with Fanny, so that we could both rejoice in the view. It was a fine day, hot for the time of year, indeed it was more like June than March, and I believe the fresh air did her good, for I will not conceal from you, Bertram, she was looking less blooming than she ought. She misses the air of Mansfield, and counts the days she is away. Her family, alas, are a sore trial to her, lacking the refinement she is used to, and although she loves them, it is not difficult to see that their ways affect her nerves. I have offered to take her home at a moment's notice, should it be inconvenient for your father to send the carriage, for I do not believe that Portsmouth agrees with her.'

'Are you in town for long?'

'No, I am going back to Norfolk. I have work to do there. I believe my manager may be trying to impose on me, and Fanny thinks, as I do, that I should make sure that everything is well.'

My sisters were also there, and Maria said, 'Fanny seems remarkably interested in Mr Crawford's concerns.'

'Naturally so,' I replied, but as she seemed out of humour I did not continue that conversation, but turned it instead, saying, 'How are you enjoying London?'

'London is wonderful!' said Julia. 'There is so much to do, I do not know how we survived at Mansfield. There are parties and balls every night, something different all the time, and the company is very superior.'

'Superior to what is met with at home?' I asked her.

She laughed, and said, 'It cannot compete with Pug, of course, but I believe it compares favourably otherwise.'

'And yet I am very angry with you,' Maria said, recovering her good humour. 'You did not come to my party. It is a pity you missed it. It was a great success. Everyone said so.

One of the parties of the year. The house was much admired, and small wonder, for it is one of the finest in town.'

She said nothing of Rushworth, until I enquired after him.

'Oh, yes, he is very well. He is somewhere about,' she said, looking round.

I followed her eyes and saw them fall on Crawford. A cold look passed between them. I felt a moment of disquiet as I remembered what Fanny had said to me, that there had been something between them at the time of the play, and I wondered if perhaps Fanny had been right, for they did not appear to meet as friends. Maria said nothing, no word of greeting, but merely gave Crawford a nod, and I saw him draw back, surprised. I was sorry for it, for if she felt she had been slighted in the past, what did it matter? She was Miss Bertram no longer; she was Mrs Rushworth now.

Crawford made her a bow and then moved away.

Maria recovered her composure and I listened to her continuing tales of triumph, interspersed by Julia's remarks, for some time longer, until, seeing a space free near Mary, I made my way over to her. She was standing in a large group with Lady Stornaway. I waited, hoping for my chance to speak to her alone, but I became more and more disgusted with the conversation, for they were talking about the chances of Miss Dunstan catching the eye of Mr Croker, a man they thought very desirable, despite his reputation for drunkenness, because he had £20,000 a year.

I was about to move away when Mary detached herself from her companions and said, 'So, you are here. How pleased I am to see you. You are enjoying yourself, I hope? No, do not tell me. I can see you are not enjoying yourself as much as you do at Mansfield. Dear Mansfield! I must confess, Mr Bertram, that I miss it. How happy we all were there over the winter. I find myself looking forward to June, when I will be there again.'

'There is no need for you to wait so long. You will be welcome at Mansfield whenever you return,' I said to her.

'But then I would have to disappoint my friends here, for I have promised to stay. An agreement, once reached, must be honoured, do you not think?'

'Indeed it must,' I said with a smile.

I was about to lead her aside and ask if I might have a private audience with her, when Lady Stornaway joined us. Raising her lorgnette, she asked, 'And who is this?'

'Mr Edmund Bertram,' said Mary.

'Indeed. You are a country parson, I understand, Mr Bertram?'

I felt Mary grow restless beside me.

'I am.'

'Well, it is not a bad beginning for a young man of your age, but no doubt you will soon be tired of it and will be seeking advancement in town.'

'I can assure your ladyship that I am very happy in the country, and have no desire to make my mark in the outside world.'

'Indeed? How very odd,' she said. 'A young man at your time of life has no business in settling for so little, when he could achieve so much. We must encourage him to enlarge his thinking, Miss Crawford.'

'Believe me, Lady Stornaway, I have been trying,' said Mary. 'But, so far, without success.'

'A young lady of your beauty, wit and intelligence will not be denied for very long. What do you say, Mr Bertram? It would be ungallant of you to resist such loveliness, would it not?'

Mary looked at me challengingly, and, feeling myself trapped and uncomfortable, I said stiffly, 'I would not deny Miss Crawford anything I could in reason give her.'

Lady Stornaway took my answer to mean

I would seek advancement, and I had nothing more to do but to extricate myself from my predicament as quickly as I could.

If only I could extricate Mary from her London friends so quickly, I would be well pleased.

Wednesday 15 March

I saw Tom in the park this morning, where we were both riding, and he hallooed me at once, riding over with his party of friends.

'Well met, little brother.'

He was looking well, and was in good spirits, having won at the races.

'So, how is the little filly?' asked Langley. 'Got her into harness yet?'

I shook my head; Tom was sympathetic; and before I knew it, I was telling him my troubles.

'Women are the very devil,' said Langley.

'Not worth it,' said Hargate.

'This one certainly isn't. Why not marry one of the Miss Owens instead?' asked Tom. 'Any one of them would make you a respectable wife.'

'Because it is Mary I want.'

Hargate nodded sagely.

'So what are you going to do?' asked Tom.

'I will be seeing her tomorrow, but if her mood is still as changeable, and if I have no chance to speak to her alone, I intend to go back to Mansfield and hope for better things once she rejoins her sister there in the summer.'

'Brother Edmund has a rocky road ahead of him,' said Tom. 'We must make sure he enjoys himself this evening, to fortify himself for what is to come.' He saw my look and said, 'Never fear, in deference to your tender years and calling, we will be as sober as judges —'

'Drunk, but not falling down drunk!' said Hargate.

'As sober as country parsons,' amended Tom.

'Which means snoring drunk,' said Langley.

'As sober as young ladies in the seminary,' reproved Tom.

'Good God! He means it,' said Danvers, pulling a tragic face which was, nevertheless, so comical I could not help but laugh.

'Much better,' said Tom.

His high spirits lifted my own, and we had a merry day of it.

Thursday 16 March
I dined with the Frasers this evening, but I had no chance to speak to Mary alone, and no desire to do so. Her conversation made

it clear that she is torn between a love of wealth and all it can bring, and a desire for something deeper and richer which money cannot buy. But instead of choosing between them, she is tormenting herself because she cannot have both. By the time she returns to Mansfield I hope she will know what she truly desires.

Saturday 18 March
And so, I am back at Mansfield Park, with all the business of the parish to think of, for which I am grateful, as there is nothing I can do now with regard to Mary but wait for her to learn her own mind.

Thursday 23 March
Realizing I had neglected Fanny shamefully, I wrote to her this morning, apologizing for my tardiness in writing and telling her that, if I could have sent a few happy lines, I would have done so straightaway.

I meant to ask her how she was and give her all the London and Mansfield news, but speaking to her, through the medium of the letter, I found myself pouring out my feelings.

I am returned to Mansfield in a less assured state than when I left it. My hopes are much weaker, for Mary's friends have been leading her astray for years. Could she be detached from them! — and sometimes I do not despair of it, for the affection appears to me principally on their side. They are very fond of her; but I am sure she does not love them as she loves you. When I think of her great attachment to you, she appears a very different creature, capable of everything noble, and I am ready to blame myself for a too harsh construction of a playful manner.

I cannot give her up, Fanny. She is the only woman in the world whom I could ever think of as a wife. If I did not believe that she had some regard for me, of course I should not say this, but I do believe it. I am convinced that she is not without a decided preference.

You have my thoughts exactly as they arise, my dear Fanny; perhaps they are sometimes contradictory, but it will not be a less faithful picture of my mind.

Were it a decided thing, an actual refusal, I hope I should know how to bear it; but till I am refused, I can never cease to try for her. This is the truth.

I have sometimes thought of going to London again after Easter, and sometimes resolved on doing nothing till she returns to Mansfield. But June is at a great distance, and I believe I shall write to her. I shall be able to write much that I could not say, and shall be giving her time for reflection before she resolves on her answer. My greatest danger would lie in her consulting Mrs Fraser, and I at a distance unable to help my own cause. I must think this matter over a little.

I laid my quill aside, wishing I had Fanny to talk to, instead of having her so far distant. As I read over what I had written, I realized I had spoken of my own concerns and nothing else. Such a letter would surely be enough to tire even Fanny's friendship, so I picked up my quill and continued with news I knew must give her pleasure.

I am more and more satisfied with all that I see and hear of Crawford. There is not a shadow of wavering. He thoroughly knows his own mind, and acts up to his resolutions: an inestimable quality.

I hoped this would make her think more kindly of him, for to remember her when all the pleasures of London were distracting him was a sign of no ordinary attachment. I told her of Maria:

> There is no appearance of unhappiness.
> I hope they get on pretty well together
> — *and Julia* — Julia seems to enjoy
> London exceedingly — *and then Mans-*
> *field* — We are not a lively party. You are
> very much wanted. I miss you more than
> I can express — *before finishing with,*
> Yours ever, my dearest Fanny.

I sealed the letter and my father franked
it, then I went over to Thornton Lacey and
saw what had been done to the house,
before attending to parish business.

Tuesday 28 March

I made up my mind to it, and this morning
I began my letter to Mary. I had scarcely
written a line, however, when something
happened which put everything else out of
my mind. My father had a letter from a
physician in Newmarket, telling us that Tom
had had a fall, and that there was worse, for
as a consequence of neglect and drink, the
fall had led to a fever. Tom was on his own,
for his friends had deserted him. I was
alarmed, and said I would go to him at
once. My father said he would write to my
sisters and let them know the news. I

travelled quickly, and now here I am in Newmarket, and not at all sanguine. Tom is much worse than I expected. He did not know me when I walked in to the room. His physician said he was not to be moved, and I agreed it must not be thought of.

I wrote to my father, but played down my fears, saying only that Tom was ill but that I thought he would soon be well enough to be brought home.

Thursday 30 March

Tom continued feverish and there was no chance of my taking him home, for he was too ill to be moved. I wished he would recognize me, but his eyes opened rarely, and when they did, I do not believe he saw anything at all.

April

Saturday 1 April

There was some improvement in Tom's condition today. The fever seemed less, and for the first time I felt there was hope, real hope, that he would recover.

Tuesday 4 April

Tom had a good night, and the physician said that, if his improvement continues, he will be well enough to make the journey to Mansfield tomorrow. I am more relieved than I can say. I want, more than anything, to have him safely home again.

Wednesday 5 April

The physician called again this morning and pronounced himself satisfied with Tom's progress. I made arrangements for the journey, and once the carriage was as comfortable and warm as I could make it, I carried him downstairs and put him inside.

He smiled weakly, and said it made a change to have me carrying him when he was ill and not drunk, and I smiled, too, but my smile was no stronger than his. I was seriously worried, for he weighed nothing at all. I wrapped him about with blankets and then we set off. The journey was good and the weather fine, but he became progressively weaker as the day went on, and he was feverish again by the time we arrived.

Mama was horrified at the sight of him, and to be sure he looked very ill when he was carried into the house, for he was white and sweating, and he was delirious. My father looked very grave and Tom was quickly got to bed whilst our own physician was sent for. He did all he could for him, and now we must trust to the fact that Tom is at home, where he can be properly cared for, to bring him about.

Monday 10 April

Julia has offered to come home if we have need of her, but there is nothing she can do, and my father thinks she is better where she is. I wrote to her directly, telling her that she need not come home at present. She has not seen Maria recently, for Maria is spending Easter with the Aylmers at Twickenham whilst Rushworth has gone down to Bath to fetch his mother. Julia has seen Mary, though, and has told her of Tom's illness. I wish I had more time to think of Mary, but with Tom so ill, I can think of nothing else. And perhaps it is a good thing, for I am worn out by asking myself if Mary will have me or not.

Wednesday 12 April

Tom is out of danger, thank God, and Mama is at last made easy. It has been a terrible week for her, seeing Tom laid so low. But the fever has subsided, and we have encouraged her to think that, now it has gone, Tom will soon be well. She smiled again for the first time since she heard of Tom's fall, and she wrote to Fanny straightaway, to tell her that he was much improved.

I do not know what she would have done without Fanny this week, for although Fanny is not here, her presence is everywhere felt. Mama has found it a comfort to write to her every day, sharing her hopes and fears, and my father is grateful for it.

But today I felt compelled to write my own letter to Fanny, to let her know the real state of affairs, for although Tom's fever has subsided there are some strong hectic symptoms which we are keeping from Mama. The physician cannot say which way things will go. They may go well, in which case Tom will make a full recovery, but if they go badly, there is a danger to his lungs.

All we can do now is watch and pray, and hope Tom's youth and vigour will see him through.

Thursday 13 April

I sat with Tom again this morning and he felt strong enough to talk, saying, 'What a fool I have been, Edmund.'

'Nonsense. Your spirits are low. You will soon be well again, and then you will think yourself a very clever fellow,' I said.

He laughed at this, but his laugh turned to a cough which tired him and so I refrained from talking to him afterwards, instead bidding him to lie quietly and conserve his strength.

I was about to leave his room when he restrained me with a feeble hand, saying, 'Stay. It does me good to have you here. My father is too loud, and my mother too tearful. You are the only one I can stand.'

And so I sat beside him again, glad to be of use.

Friday 14 April

Tom seemed a little stronger today, and I read to him.

'What? Not *The Rake's Progress*?' he asked, as I took up the book.

It was good to hear him joking, and I pray he may soon be well. If the hectic symptoms abate, then there is every chance of it. And with the better weather coming, it will be possible for him to sit in the garden and make a full recovery at his leisure.

MAY

Monday 8 May

Just as one problem is abating, another has presented itself, for my father received a letter this morning which agitated him immensely. I thought at first it must be news of more illness, but he reassured me; saying, however, that he must go to London at once. He left me in charge of the estate and told me not to leave Mansfield in case he needed me. He was just about to depart when another letter came by express. As he opened it he let out a cry and sat down. His eyes passed rapidly over the hasty scrawl and when he had finished he sat as though stunned.

'What is it?' I asked.

He did not reply, but sat staring in front of him with unseeing eyes.

'You are ill!' I said, going to him in alarm.

But he waved me away.

'No,' he said, passing a hand over his eyes.

'I have had a shock, that is all. But what a shock! Edmund, I am going to need your help. These letters are from one of my oldest friends. The first revealed that there was some gossip about Maria and Mr Crawford, and that it would be well for me to go and see her, for her husband was uneasy. I was displeased, but not unduly alarmed, for it seems that Maria and Crawford met at Twickenham; an innocent enough occurrence, as Crawford's uncle has a cottage there; and this fact, coupled with Rushworth's absence, would be enough for many an idle person to gossip about. But his second letter, come just now, is much worse. Here. You had better read it.'

He handed it to me, and I read it quickly, and with growing horror. Maria had run away, and Mr Harding, my father's correspondent, feared that there had been a very flagrant indiscretion. He was doing all in his power to persuade Maria to return to her home in Wimpole Street, but he was being obstructed in this by Rushworth's mother, who did not want her back, for it appeared the two of them had never liked each other.

My father had by this time recovered himself and strode to the door. I offered to go with him, and before long, having communicated what was necessary to the rest of the family, we set off.

We arrived in London late this evening, but Maria's flight had already been made public beyond hope of recovery. We called briefly at Wimpole Street, where Rushworth and his mother were loudly lamenting the fact, and as there was nothing to be gained by staying there, we went next to Crawford's uncle's house. Crawford had already left, as if for a journey, and there could no longer be any doubt that Maria had run off with him.

I thought of Fanny, and her idea that there had been something between Maria and Crawford. She had suspected his liking for Maria, and she had been wary of him because of it. I had told her she was wrong, but it was I who had been wrong.

Poor Fanny! As soon as I began to grow used to Maria's shame, I saw that she, too, was a sufferer in this, for Fanny had lost the man who had offered her marriage, the man to whom she had been almost engaged.

I felt the blow deeply. For us to suffer did not seem too terrible, for we were strong enough to bear it, but for Fanny to suffer cast me down, and I resolved to go to her as soon as I could.

But it could not be at once, for there was

still much to be done.

My father suggested next that we go and see Julia, who was staying with her cousins, to reassure her that we were in town, and that we were doing all we could to save her sister.

But when we reached the house, another calamity hit us, for the house was in turmoil. My father's cousin went ashen when he saw us, and invited my father into his study. My father emerged a few minutes later to tell me that Julia had eloped!

I could not take it in. It was too much. At any other time I would have felt it as a terrible blow, but by the side of the other calamities that had befallen us its pain was scarcely felt.

I rallied quickly and asked my father, 'Do we know who with?'

'Yes. With Yates.'

'Yates!'

So the legacy of the play was haunting us still.

'It seems she had another motive for wishing to visit my cousins when she did. Yates lives nearby,' said my father. 'What have I done to deserve such daughters?' he asked, in a moment of distress.

I offered him my sympathy and he quickly recovered himself.

'Julia has gone to Scotland,' he said. 'She left a note for her maid. I cannot go after her tonight. I must find Maria.'

'I will go.'

'No. They have too much of a start. You would never catch them. Besides, you are needed here. We must try and find out where Maria has gone, but we can do no more tonight. We must get what rest we can and begin again in the morning.'

And so we retired, but I cannot sleep. It has been a year of calamities. Tom desperately ill; Maria disgraced; Julia run off; and Mary . . . I cannot think of Mary.

My only consolation in all this trouble is Fanny; good, dear, sweet, Fanny, who is everything that everyone else should be, but is not.

Oh, that she should have to suffer, too! If only Maria had run off with someone else, and not Crawford. Then it would have been bad enough. But Fanny must now sustain the double blow, a disgraced cousin and a lost lover; she who has never deserved anything but love and affection in the whole of her life.

Tuesday 9 May

I rose early, unable to sleep, indeed I had not closed my eyes for more than a few

343

minutes all night. I took up the newspaper this morning, hoping for news of the war to divert my thoughts, but I saw to my horror that the story had already reached its pages. Was there ever such shame? The report could scarcely have been worse:

It is with infinite concern that this newspaper has to announce to the world a matrimonial fracas in the family of Mr R. of Wimpole Street; the beautiful Mrs R., whose name has not long been enrolled in the lists of Hymen, and who promised to become so brilliant a leader in the fashionable world, has quit her husband's roof in company with the well-known and captivating Mr C., the intimate friend and associate of Mr R. It is not known, even to the editor of this newspaper, whither they are gone.

No sooner had I put the newspaper down than a note was delivered from Lady Stornaway, begging me to call. My heart sank. The note must have been written at the behest of Mary. What feelings of shame and wretchedness she must be enduring! I could scarcely breathe for the pity of it all. Poor Mary! For her to have learned that her brother had disgraced my sister and ruined her for ever.

I went at once, in a state of mind so softened and devoted that I believe, if she had cried, I would have proposed to her there and then.

But instead she met me with a serious, even an agitated air. I could not speak, so much did I feel for her, in her state of distress. But her first words shocked me out of all tender feelings, for they were such as I could not believe any woman would utter in such circumstances.

'I heard you were in town,' said she. 'I wanted to see you. Let us talk over this sad business. What can equal the folly of our two relations?'

Folly? I thought. To call such an act nothing but folly, when it would be the ruin of Maria, was incomprehensible to me. And to blame Maria as much as Crawford. I could not answer, but I believe my looks told her what I thought.

Her face fell. With a graver look and voice she said, 'I do not mean to defend Henry at your sister's expense.' I felt relieved. For a moment I thought she had been about to do this very thing. But then she went on. 'But it was foolish of Henry to be drawn on by a woman he never cared for, particularly as it will lose him the woman he adores.

But oh!' she broke out, 'how foolish has been Maria, in sacrificing such a situation as she had, married to Mr Rushworth, protected by his name, with his fortune at her disposal and such a house! The best in Wimpole Street! To give up all that, when a little discretion could have kept the whole thing from Rushworth and his odious mother. And for her to run off with Henry, under the idea of being really loved by him, when he had long ago made his indifference clear,' she said, shaking her head.

I could not believe it. She did not feel distress at the act, merely at its discovery. And what was she suggesting? That instead of behaving as they ought, Maria and Crawford should have been more cautious, more duplicitous, and gone on with their affair regardless? And even worse, saying that her brother had never cared for my sister; that he had ruined her on nothing more than a whim; that he had cast her into a life where, disowned by her husband, she would endure shame and misery, to satisfy nothing more than his vanity and selfish desire?

I was horrified. For the woman I loved to speak in such a way, regarding the whole thing as nothing more than an indiscretion, and lamenting, not Maria's reputation, but her house in Wimpole Street! I began to wonder who this woman was, standing in front of me. I thought I knew her, but standing there, looking at her, I realized I did not know her at all.

I was so shocked I could not speak. But Mary had no such difficulty, each word making me more and more horrified at her callousness. There was no reluctance to speak of it, no shame, only worldliness and vice.

'If anyone is to blame, it is Rushworth,' she said. 'His want of common discretion, of caution: his going down to Richmond for the whole time of Maria's being at Twickenham. And then Maria! Putting herself in the power of a servant by leaving a lover's note where it could be seen! Foolish, foolish girl. Without that, they might never have been detected. It was only this that brought things to extremity, and obliged Henry to give up every dearer plan in order to fly with Maria.'

I was like a man stunned, but worse was to come. She began to talk of Fanny, regretting, as well she might, the loss of such a friend and sister.

'He has thrown away such a woman as he will never see again. She would have fixed him; she would have made him happy for ever,' she said. 'Fanny, with all her sweetness and goodness, and all her quiet charm.'

There at least she spoke wisely, and I was almost relenting towards her when she broke the spell for ever by bursting out, 'Why would not she have him? It is all her fault. Simple girl! I shall never forgive her. Had she accepted him as she ought, they might now have been on the point of marriage, and Henry would have been too happy and too busy to want any other object. He would have taken no pains to be on terms with Mrs Rushworth again. It would have all ended in a regular standing flirtation, in yearly meetings at Sotherton and Everingham.'

I could not believe it. How could she say such things? To say, to even think, that it was Fanny's fault! Fanny, who had no faults, unless it was an inability to appreciate her own worth. Fanny, whose goodness was a shining light that brightened the lives of all who met her. And to say, further, that Crawford should have had a standing flirtation with Maria, and this when he was married to Fanny! How could anyone think of using Fanny so ill? Fanny, who had a right to the greatest happiness the world could offer? Whose tender heart could never stand such ill treatment?

The charm was broken. My eyes were opened, and I had only to regret what a fool I had been.

'I cannot believe what I am hearing,' I said. 'I knew you to have been corrupted by your uncle's influence, and by the influence of those around you here in town, but this . . . Perhaps it is better for me that you have spoken in this way, since it leaves me so little to regret; though I wish I did not have to think of you as being like this, corrupted and vitiated, lost to all sense and reason save that of expediency.'

She did not listen. She was too busy following her own thoughts.

'We must persuade Henry to marry her,' said she; 'and what with honour, and the certainty of having shut himself out for ever from Fanny, I do not despair of it. Fanny he must give up. I do not think that even *he* could now hope to succeed with one of her stamp, and therefore I hope we may find no insuperable difficulty. My influence, which is not small, shall all go that way; and when once married, and properly supported by her own family, people of respectability as they are, she may recover her footing in society to a certain degree. In some circles, we know, she will never be admitted, but with good dinners, and large parties, there will always be those who will be glad of her acquaintance; and there is, undoubtedly, more liberality and candour on those points than formerly. What I advise is, that your father be quiet. Do not let him injure his own cause by interference. Persuade him to let things take their course. If, by any officious exertions of his, she is induced to leave Henry's protection, there will be much less chance of his marrying her than if she remain with him. I know how he is likely to be influenced. Let Sir Thomas trust to his honour and compassion, and it may all end well; but if he gets his daughter away, it will be destroying the chief hold.'

When at last I could command my voice, I said, 'I had not supposed it possible, coming in such a state of mind into this house as I have done, that anything could occur to make me suffer more, but you have been inflicting deeper wounds on me in almost every sentence.'

She looked surprised.

'I have often been aware of some differences in our opinions, but I never suspected something like this, that you would make light of your brother's crime — for crime I call it to seduce a woman and take her away from her home — and all the time with no feelings for her. And to make light of wounding one of the gentlest creatures on earth. And then to suggest we promote a marriage that would lead to nothing but misery, for I would not ever want to see my sister married to such a man as your brother — the man I now know him to be. Inconstant, deceitful, immoral, everything that a man should not be. I see now that I have never understood you; that I have loved an image of you, and not you yourself.'

She did not know how to look. At first she was astonished, then she turned red, and I saw a mixture of many feelings, chief amongst them anger. I saw a great, though short struggle, half a wish of yielding to truths, half a sense of shame, but habit, habit carried it. She would have laughed if she could.

'A pretty good lecture, upon my word. Was it part of your last sermon?' she said sarcastically. 'At this rate you will soon reform everybody at Mansfield and Thornton Lacey; and when I hear of you next, it may be as a celebrated preacher in some great society of Methodists, or as a missionary into foreign parts.'

But her words could no longer wound me. I only said in reply, that from my heart I wished her well, and earnestly hoped that she might soon learn to think more justly, and not owe the most valuable knowledge we could any of us acquire, the knowledge of ourselves, to the lessons of affliction. And then I left the room.

I had gone a few steps when I heard the door open behind me.

'Mr Bertram,' said she. I looked back. 'Mr Bertram,' said she, with a smile; but it was a smile ill-suited to the conversation that had passed, a saucy playful smile, seeming to invite me in order to subdue me. I resisted; it was easy; and I walked on.

As I walked out of the house, I was shocked to see that our interview had lasted only twenty-five minutes. Such a short time to change so much!

I met my father soon afterwards, and though I did not tell him of everything that had passed he guessed it had not been good, for he suggested to me that I should write to Fanny and tell her to ready herself, then go to Portsmouth and take her home.

My gloom began to lift at the thought of seeing Fanny again, but I worried about leaving my father. He reassured me that he could manage alone, and so I sent my letter, telling Fanny I would be in Portsmouth tomorrow for the purpose of taking her back to Mansfield Park. I said also, at my father's request, that she should invite her sister

Susan for a few months, for he was sure Fanny would like to have some young person with her, someone who could help counteract her sorrow at the blow that had befallen her.

Wednesday 10 May
I arrived in Portsmouth early, by the mail, too worried to be tired by my lack of sleep, and by eight o'clock I was in Fanny's house. I was shown into the parlour, and then Mrs Price left me in order to attend to her household affairs whilst the servant called Fanny down. She came in, and I strode across the room, reaching her in two strides and taking her hands in mine, scarcely able to speak for happiness and relief at being with her again.

'My Fanny — my only comfort now,' I said, momentarily overcome.

I collected myself, for what were my griefs compared to hers?

I asked if she had had breakfast, and when she would be ready. She told me that half an hour would do it, so I ordered the carriage and then took a walk round the ramparts. As I felt the stiff sea breeze, I thought of the moment I had taken Fanny's hands, and I wondered at the strangeness of it, that her fingers were so tiny and yet they could put such strength into my own; for I had felt it flowing into me, strength and courage, when I had touched her, sustaining me in my misery, and I hoped that my touch had strengthened her, too.

I was not long on the ramparts and was soon back at the house. The carriage arrived, and we were off.

I longed to talk to Fanny, but her sister's presence kept me silent. The things I had to say were not for the ears of a fourteen-year-old girl. I tried to talk of indifferent subjects, but I could not make the effort for long, and soon fell into silence again.

And now we have stopped at an inn in Oxford for the night, but I am chafing at the delay. I want to get home, to Mansfield Park. I want to take Fanny to my mother.

Thursday 11 May

I had a chance to speak to Fanny a little this morning, for as we were standing by the fire waiting for the carriage, Susan went over to the window to watch a large family leaving the inn. Fanny looked so pale and drawn that I took her hand and said, 'No wonder — you must feel it — you must suffer. How a man who had once loved, could desert you!' I could not believe Crawford could have been so vicious. But then my own pains rose up inside me, and I longed for the soothing comfort of Fanny's voice, and the softness of her words. 'But *yours* — your regard was new compared with — Fanny, think of *me!*' I burst out.

She found words for me, even in her own troubles, and then our journey began. I tried to set Susan at ease, and comfort Fanny, but my own anxieties were too much for me and after awhile, sunk in gloom, I closed my eyes, unable to bear the sight of bur- geoning summer, which contrasted so heart- breakingly with the winter in my mind.

We reached Mansfield Park in good time, well before dinner, and my mother ran from the drawing-room to meet us. Falling on Fanny's neck, she said, 'Dear Fanny! Now I shall be comfortable.'

And so it is. Fanny brings comfort with her wherever she goes.

We went inside. My aunt, sitting in the drawing-room, did not look up. The recent events had stupefied her. I soon discovered that she felt it more than all of us, for she had always been very attached to Maria and Maria's marriage had been of her making. For her to find it had ended in such a way had hit her very hard.

Tom was sitting on the sofa, looking less ill than previously, but still far from well.

He had had a setback when he had learnt about Maria and Julia, but he had rallied and was gaining strength again.

Susan was remembered at last, and received by my mother with a kiss and quiet kindness. Susan, good soul, was so grown up for fourteen, and provided of such a store of her own happiness, that she took no notice of my aunt's repulsive looks, for my aunt saw her as an intruder at such a time, and returned Mama's greetings with sense and good cheer.

We ate dinner in silence, and we were all of us glad, I think, to plead tiredness, and so go early to bed.

Friday 12 May
A letter has come from my father. He has not yet been able to find Maria, but he has reason to believe that Julia is now married. His letter was full of his feelings: that, under any circumstances it would have been an unwelcome alliance; but to have it so clandestinely formed, and such a period chosen for its completion, placed Julia's feelings in a most unfavourable light. He called it a bad thing, done in the worst manner, and at the worst time; and though he said that Julia was more pardonable than Maria, for folly was more pardonable than vice, he

thought the step she had taken would, in all probability, lead to a conclusion like Maria's: a marriage conducted in haste, with a man as unprincipled as Yates, was likely to lead to disaster; particularly as he believed Yates belonged to a wild set.

I comforted my mother as best I could, and Fanny joined me in the task.

I drew Fanny aside this evening, and gave her an opportunity to talk of her feelings but her heart was too full. She said nothing of Crawford, but only that she hoped he and Maria would soon be found, and that Yates might turn out to be less wild than we feared, and that Julia and he might be happy.

Sunday 14 May

A wet Sunday. The weather brought out all the gloom of my thoughts and this evening, unable to bear it any longer, I confided everything in Fanny. I had hoped to spare her; to say no more than she already knew, that there had been a break between Mary and myself; but I was drawn on by her kindness. I told her of the disastrous interview with Mary; that I had at last realized Mary's true nature; that I had been foolish to be so blind.

'If only she could have met with better

357

people,' I said. 'The Frasers did her no good.'

'She met with you,' said Fanny quietly. 'She had an example before her, if she chose to see it.'

'You are such a comfort to me,' I said, squeezing her small fingers gratefully in my own. 'But I can still not believe she was so very bad. If she had fallen into good hands earlier . . . Perhaps if I had tried harder . . .'

She said nothing, but she soon left me, appearing again a few minutes later, bringing something with her. She put it into my hands. It was a letter to her from Mary.

'I cannot read this,' I said. 'It is addressed to you.'

'I cannot watch you blaming yourself any longer, and so I give you leave to read it,' she said. 'Indeed, I think you must.'

My eyes went to it almost against my will. It was dated some time before, shortly after Tom fell ill, and as I read it I felt a coldness creeping over me, chilling me to the bone.

From what I hear, poor Mr Bertram has a bad chance of ultimate recovery. I thought little of his illness at first. I looked upon him as the sort of person to be made a fuss with, and to make a fuss himself in any trifling disorder, and was chiefly concerned for those who had to nurse him; but now it is confidently asserted that he is really in a decline, that the symptoms are most alarming, and that part of the family, at least, are aware of it. If it be so, I am sure you must be included in that part, that discerning part, and therefore entreat you to let me know how far I have been rightly informed. I need not say how rejoiced I shall be to hear there has been any mistake, but the report is so prevalent that I confess I cannot help trembling. To have such a fine young man cut off in the flower of his days is most melancholy. Poor Sir Thomas will feel it dreadfully. I really am quite agitated on the subject. Fanny, Fanny, I see you smile and look cunning, but, upon my honour, I never bribed a physician in my life. Poor young man! If he is to die, there will be two poor young men less in the world; and with a fearless face and bold voice would I say to any one, that wealth and consequence could fall into no hands more deserving of them. It was a foolish precipitation last Christmas, but the evil of a few days may be blotted out in part. Varnish and gilding hide many stains. It will be but the loss of the

Esquire after his name. With real affection, Fanny, like mine, more might be overlooked. Write to me by return of post, judge of my anxiety, and do not trifle with it. Tell me the real truth, as you have it from the fountainhead. And now, do not trouble yourself to be ashamed of either my feelings or your own. Believe me, they are not only natural, they are philanthropic and virtuous. I put it to your conscience, whether 'Sir Edmund' would not do more good with all the Bertram property than any other possible 'Sir.'

I felt sick. To hear Mary speak of my ordination as a foolish precipitation, a stain that could be hidden with varnish and gilding, instead of seeing it as my calling, an inalienable part of me, and one that needed no excusing was abhorrent to me. And what was this varnish and gilding to be? A baronetcy. A baronetcy I was to gain by the death of my brother; by the death of Tom. Tom, who had been a part of my life always; Tom, who had ridden beside me, wrestled with me, swum with me; Tom who had laughed at me, plagued me and teased me. And Mary wished him dead.

Not only that, but she said Fanny wished

it, too; that Fanny was smiling and looking cunning at the idea of it. Fanny, who could not look cunning if she tried; Fanny, who would be incapable of wishing evil on anyone; Fanny, who loved my brother for all the kindnesses he had shown her.

I handed Fanny back the letter, feeling as though all life had been sucked out of me.

'If not for you, Fanny, I do not know how I would bear it. And yet you, yourself, are suffering. Crawford played you false.'

'No, I am not suffering,' she said softly, folding the letter and letting it rest on her lap, where her goodness seemed to undo its malice, rendering it harmless.

I looked at her in confusion, wondering what she meant, for it must hurt her to know that her lover had betrayed her.

'I never loved him, and I never wanted him to love me,' she said. 'Indeed, I do not believe he did. I saw his behaviour towards Maria last year, and I suspected there was still an attachment between them. That is why I could not marry him. That, and —'

She stopped, and I did not press her. I knew her heart was too full to speak.

'But is this true, Fanny? Is this really true?' I asked her. 'Has he not hurt you?'

'No.'

'Then it takes a great weight from my

mind,' I said in relief, feeling that here, at last, was something to smile about, some cheer to brighten the gloom. 'You saw more than I did, Fanny. I was blinded in more than one way at the time. It is a funny thing, I used to be the teacher and you my pupil, but it seems that our roles have been reversed.'

She gave me a look of understanding, and I thought: Fanny has grown up.

My mother rousing herself at that moment, for she had been asleep in front of the fire, our conversation came to an end.

Monday 22 May

Fanny and I went riding this morning. We rode in silence to begin with, for I was thinking about Mary and how I had taught her to ride. I remembered her enjoyment, and her saying that she was growing to love the country. But although my feelings were, to begin with, wistful, they began to change as I watched Fanny, who was riding beside me. Her face showed pleasure in the exercise and her enjoyment in the countryside. Hers was not the bright-eyed pleasure of novelty, it was the deep-seated pleasure of long acquaintance and genuine love. Her eyes sought out the new buds springing to life and the changes taking place around her.

She would ride thus in ten years, twenty years, time, as I would, never growing restless or dissatisfied, because she belonged at Mansfield Park. I was reminded of my ride with Tom when we were boys, and the way his eyes had always looked beyond Mansfield. Mary's eyes had looked beyond Mansfield, too. But Fanny's never did. At Mansfield, she was at home.

'I am beginning to think it is a good thing we are alone again,' I said. 'I missed going for rides with you, Fanny, when Mary was here.' She looked at me anxiously, and I said, 'There is no need to worry. I can speak her name without pain. I was hurt, it is true, but the countryside, and friends, can heal anything in time. *If I am not deceived, the sable cloud has turned forth her silver lining on the night.*'

She smiled.

'Milton would forgive you your deviation, glad that you have seen the truth of his words, as your friends must be,' she said.

We passed Robert Pinker and bade him good morning. We had just passed him when he called out, 'Mr Bertram!'

We reined in our horses and he approached.

'I wonder if I could call on you this afternoon, at Thornton Lacey?' he said.

'By all means. Was there something particular you wished to see me about?'

He went red and stammered that Miss Colton had been good enough to accept his offer of marriage.

'This is splendid news,' I said, and Fanny added her heartfelt good wishes.

'We would like to be married at the end of June,' he said. 'I have a house, there is nothing to wait for.'

'Then call on me at three o'clock and we will discuss it.'

He thanked me and we set off.

'That will be a happy marriage,' I said.

'Yes, indeed,' said Fanny. 'I have been hoping for it for some time.'

'You knew it was likely to take place?'

'I visited Mrs Colton when her mother was ill, and Mr Pinker was there. Miss Colton looked at the floor and blushed a great deal.'

'It is a puzzlement to me how women can behave so differently when they are in love. Mary was bold and confident — though perhaps she was not in love.'

'I think she was, as much as she was capable of being,' said Fanny.

'Yes. Her nature perhaps admitted of no more. But Miss Colton was not bold, she blushed and looked at the floor. And yet when you did the same it meant quite the opposite, that you did not want Mr Crawford's attentions. I will never understand the fairer sex.'

'Perhaps you will, in time,' said Fanny, looking at me.

'Perhaps.'

We turned for home.

'I have had a letter from Julia,' said my father, when we joined him and Mama in the drawing-room. 'She has begged my forgiveness and she now asks for the indulgence of my notice. I would like your advice, Edmund; and yours, too, Fanny. You have seen more clearly in this business than any of us.'

'It seems to me to be a good sign,' I said.

'Yes,' said Fanny. 'If they wish to be forgiven, then I think you should notice them.'

She coloured slightly for speaking so boldly but my father thanked her for her opinion.

'What do you think, Lady Bertram?' he asked.

'I would like to see Julia again,' she said wistfully, 'and so would Pug.'

'Then I will write and invite them to Mansfield Park. Perhaps something might be salvaged from the disasters that have befallen us over the last few weeks after all.'

'Mr Yates was frivolous but he was constant,' said Fanny. 'I believe he liked Julia from the first.'

'Well, we shall see,' said my father.

After luncheon, Fanny and I set out for Thornton Lacey, I to see Robert Pinker and Fanny to call on Mrs Green, who has a new baby.

'So that is the meaning of the dress you have been sewing,' I said.

'A new mother can never have too much linen,' she replied.

We reached Thornton Lacey in good time and together we looked over the house.

'Moving the farmyard has changed it completely,' she said.

'Yes, has it not?'

'The approach is now one any gentleman might admire, and the prospect is much improved.'

'And what do you think of the chimneypiece?'

'I think it is excellent,' she said, running her hand across it. 'It adds a great deal of beauty to the room. This is a good house, Edmund, and may be made more beautiful still if you wish.'

'I am committed to improving it as much as I might.'

We went upstairs and she gave me the benefit of her advice on the cupboards before she left to see Mrs Green. I soon received Robert Pinker, who told me of Miss Colton's many virtues. I wished him happy and we arranged for the banns to be read. He left me in good spirits, and Fanny returned soon after, smiling brightly.

'Mrs Green was well?'

'She was, and the baby was thriving.'

The world seemed a better place as we rode home together. Julia repentant, Tom improving, and Fanny growing in beauty and confidence daily.

I only hope it may continue.

Tuesday 30 May

Julia and Yates arrived this morning. There was some little awkwardness, but Julia was so humble and so wishing to be forgiven, and Yates was so much better than we had thought him, for he was truly desirous of being received into the family, that soon things became quite comfortable. My mother was delighted to have Julia restored to her, and the day ended more pleasantly than anyone could have rightfully expected.

JUNE

Thursday 1 June

'This marriage of Julia's is not so bad as I first feared,' said my father to me this morning. 'Yates is not very solid, but from a number of conversations I have had with him, I think there is every hope of him becoming less trifling as he grows older. His estate is more, and his debts less than I feared.'

Saturday 10 June

Our good news continues. Tom is now out of danger, and this morning he was able to take a short walk out of doors. The weather was fine, and the exercise did him good. I believe we will have him well again by the end of the summer, and none the worse for his fall.

Thursday 15 June

At last Maria and Crawford have been

discovered. Maria refuses to leave Crawford, saying she is sure they will be married in time. Rushworth is determined to divorce her. It is a scandal, but we must endure it, for there is nothing else to be done.

Thursday 29 June
Fanny and I have grown into the habit of wandering outside in the evening, enjoying the balmy air, and sitting under trees talking of books and poetry. It is like the old days, before the Crawfords came to Mansfield Park, and yet with this change, that Fanny is no longer my protégée, she is my equal. She argues with me over the authors' and poets' intentions, and her arguments are well reasoned and compelling. She makes me rethink my position, and in so doing gives me a deeper understanding of the books and poems I so love. And when we have talked our fill, we watch the sun sinking over the meadows, and take as much pleasure from the sight of it as those in London society take in a necklace of rubies.

Wednesday 12 July

Maria and Crawford's situation grows daily worse. They are now so disenchanted with each other that they fairly hate each other and a voluntary separation looks set to take place any day. My aunt wishes my father to receive her here, but he will not hear of it.

'This is all your doing,' said my aunt to Fanny, as I entered the drawing-room this afternoon. 'If you had married Mr Crawford when he asked you, then none of this would have happened.'

I rescued Fanny from my aunt's spite by suggesting a walk in the garden, where we continued our discussion of Thomson, and from thence, sparked by our joy of the soft summer air, Fanny progressed to Cowper, saying:

God made the country, and man made the
  town.

'You were not happy in Portsmouth?' I said.

'No. It grieves me to say it, but I was not. I missed Mansfield, not just the countryside, but the people. I had thought, before I went, that I would feel at home there, with my family, but their ways are so different to ours — in truth, I was often horrified. My father . . .'

'You may say anything to me, Fanny. If you want to ease your heart, I am at your disposal.'

'It seems wrong to speak disrespectfully of my parents.'

'There is no disrespect in turning to a friend for comfort and guidance,' I said.

'You do me good, Edmund. You always do me good.'

'Except . . .' I thought of the time I had tried to persuade her to marry Henry Crawford. I had been blinded by my own concerns. I had not been a friend to her there. But I put such thoughts aside and continued, 'Your family were not what you were expecting them to be?'

'No. My father cursed a great deal, and my mother seemed content to proceed without any order. I confess, I learnt the lesson that I believe Sir Thomas had been endeavouring to teach me, that wealth and position bring with them many advantages, and that poverty brings with it many hardships that cannot be overlooked.'

'And yet you did not succumb to the lure of riches that was being held out to you.'

'No. I would rather live in an attic at Mansfield Park than in a manor house where I did not love.'

'I too. One evening spent walking by the river with you, talking of things that matter, is of far more value to me than a year in London, talking of nothing and attending the most glittering parties.'

The light began to fade and we went indoors, to continue our conversation in the library, away from Aunt Norris.

Wednesday 19 July

Tom went out riding for the first time since his fall, and though he was wary to begin with he soon regained his confidence and came home looking as well as he did before his illness.

Thursday 27 July

Our evening walks have become a settled thing, and not a day goes by without Fanny and I strolling through the grounds. As we walked by the river this evening I stopped to survey the water, whose surface was sparkling in the sunlight. I thought that it was like Mary, dazzling on the surface, but with mud beneath. Further on, there was no sparkle, but the water was clear and deep, and I thought of Fanny, whose goodness ran down to the depths of her being. I turned to face her and thought how lucky I was to have her, for she had safeguarded my faith in women when Mary would have shattered it.

As long as I have Fanny, I will always know that goodness exists, because I will have it right in front of me.

August

Tuesday 1 August

My father is so pleased with Julia and Yates, who improve daily, that he has decided to acknowledge them with a ball in their honour. The invitations have gone out and my father's recognition of their marriage will ensure they are accepted in society.

Wednesday 2 August

I asked Tom if he wanted to go into town with me this morning but he said he was too busy seeing to the improvements on the home farm. He has changed since his illness. He has recovered his health and spirits but he has had a shock, and says he does not want to spend all his life racing and drinking.

'And that is what it almost was, Edmund. *All* my life,' he said to me.

Instead, he has started to take an interest in his inheritance, as well as an interest in pleasure.

I left him setting out to look over the home farm and went into town alone, where I ordered a string of pearls for Fanny.

Thursday 3 August

I asked Fanny if I might secure her as my partner for the first two dances of Julia's ball and she agreed. As I did so, I remembered the ball at which I danced the first two dances with Mary, but it seemed almost as though it had happened to another person and not to me.

To my surprise, it no longer hurts me, or angers me, or even interests me to think of Mary. She seems of no consequence at all.

Thursday 10 August

As soon as I had dressed for the ball I took the pearls to Fanny's sitting-room, where I found her. She was watering her geraniums. She was already dressed for the ball and I felt as though I was seeing her, for the first time, as a desirable young woman. Her dress was new and its whiteness set off the soft gold of her arms and face. Her hair was piled on top of her head, showing the gracefulness of her neck, and I could not understand why it had taken me so long to see the truth: I was in love with Fanny. It was Fanny who shared my thoughts and feelings; Fanny who was like me; Fanny who was part of me.

She turned round and saw me.

'I have brought you something,' I said. I noticed she was wearing my gold chain round her neck, and William's amber cross. 'Would you wear these for me tonight instead?'

She smiled her acquiescence and, unfastening her chain, she turned round so that I could put the pearls round her neck. As she bent forward I was suddenly nervous. I fastened the necklace, telling myself that I had performed the same office for her many times before, but this time was different, for as I closed the clasp I felt my hand tremble.

She straightened her head and looked at the pearls in the mirror, thanking me for them with her sweetest smile, then I gave her my arm and led her downstairs.

All through dinner, I had eyes only for Fanny, and even when the guests began to arrive I could not take my eyes away. She greeted them all with a mixture of sweetness and intelligence, no longer tongue-tied in company, but setting everyone at their ease by talking to them of their own concerns and replying with the same ease to their questions about her own.

As I watched her, I found myself wondering how it had happened, how long she had been like this. Had she suddenly blossomed? Or had I simply not noticed the moment at which she had turned from a hesitant girl into an assured woman.

The musicians began to play, and Julia and Yates took their places, ready to open the dancing. I saw my father watching them approvingly, whilst Mama looked on and smiled. I claimed Fanny's hand with pleasure and led her on to the floor. I could not take my eyes from her.

'You are quiet tonight,' she said to me, as the steps of the dance brought us together.

I roused myself.

'I am not doing my duty. I am a poor partner.'

'No,' she said, 'You are the perfect partner.'

And as she smiled, I knew. Fanny loved me! I returned her smile, and there were no two happier people in the room.

The first two dances came to an end, but I could not go to Fanny as I wanted, for I was committed to dancing with Julia. I could not pay attention to my sister, however, for I could not take my eyes from Fanny.

Julia followed my longing gaze and gave

an arch smile.

'Fanny is looking well tonight,' she said.

'Yes, she is,' I said, for the candlelight was behind her, giving her a radiance that made her shine.

'It was an evil day for us when Crawford ran off with Maria, but it was a good day for Fanny. It will not be long before she attracts another offer of marriage, and one from a man of far more worth.'

'I hope so,' was all I could manage.

After Julia, I was engaged to dance with several other young ladies, but just before supper I was free to reclaim Fanny.

'You are tired,' I said.

'Too tired for dancing, but not otherwise fatigued,' she returned.

'Then will you take a walk with me along the terrace?'

She agreed readily, and we went outside.

'Fanny . . .'

'Yes, Edmund?'

'Fanny, I have been a fool,' I said ruefully. 'Can you ever forgive me?'

'There is nothing to forgive.'

'Then will you do me the honour, the very great honour of accepting my hand in marriage?'

Her smile lit the night.

'Yes, Edmund, I will.'

'How long have you loved me?' I could not resist asking her, as we walked on together.

'I hardly know, but certainly before the Crawfords moved into the neighbourhood,' she said.

'So long ago? I knew you worshipped me as a child, but I never, until this evening, knew that your feelings had turned to love.'

'I did not notice the change myself, it was so gradual. But when the Crawfords came to Mansfield Park I came to know myself, for I envied Mary Crawford your attentions. I am ashamed to say it, but it was so. I could not bear to see you throw all your love away on someone who was not worthy of you. I tried to tell myself that, if she had been everything that was wise and good, I would not have minded, that I would have been happy for you, but I knew it was not so. I would have envied anyone who had your love.'

I thought of the events of the past year and knew how painful they must have been for her, and how lucky I was that, through them all, she had loved me. She had seen me with all my faults and failings and her feelings were unchanged. I did not need to make myself someone I was not in order to please Fanny; she loved me as I was. I had done with dazzle and sparkle, and had fallen in love with goodness, intelligence, beauty and true worth.

'I would never have talked to you about Mary had I known,' I said. I thought of the way I had gone to Fanny's room, asking her to help me with the play, expecting her to prompt Mary and me as we spoke words of love to one another under the guise of drama.

'That was not the hardest part,' she said.

'No?'

'No. The hardest part was when you urged me to marry Mr Crawford.'

'I shudder to think of it. I cannot believe I was so blind. You would have been trapped with a vicious, shallow man, and I would have been left to rue the day I urged my Fanny to marry him.'

'Not if Miss Crawford had accepted you.'

'Yes, even then, for the scales must have fallen from my eyes eventually, and then I would have bitterly repented my blindness, and bitterly repented my loss of you. But let us not speak of such things. We have been saved from disaster, and now we can look ahead. We will be very happy, will we not?'

'We will,' she said.

'You have been right about everything else, Fanny, and I know you will be right about this as well.'

We were disturbed by a sound from indoors, and Fanny said, 'We had better go in to supper.'

'If we must. I would rather stay out here talking to you, but duty must be done.'

We sat together at supper and, Fanny pleading fatigue afterwards and partners being plentiful, I spent the rest of the evening sitting by her side.

Friday 11 August

As soon as I had broken my fast I went into the drawing-room, hoping to find my father and ask him if I could have a private word with him, but the only person there was Aunt Norris.

'I saw you,' she said to me accusingly, as I was about to go. 'With her, that interloper, last night. We have nursed a viper in our bosom. When I think what we have done for that girl, taking her in and raising her here at our expense, and this is how she repays us: first, by ruining Maria because of her own stubborn stupidity, and then by artfully throwing herself at you — hoping, no doubt, that your brother would die, and she would find herself the mistress of Mansfield Park.'

I did not even deign to reply, but my aunt

had not finished.

'Sir Thomas saw how it would be, even before she came here. He knew it would be difficult to preserve the difference in rank between Fanny and his daughters, but I told him nothing could be easier than making sure the distinction was preserved. And I am sure I have played my part, not allowing her to sink into idleness but giving her errands to run, making sure she did not expect to have the carriage ordered for her, seeing to it that her clothes did not match those of dear Maria and Julia, and ensuring she never had a fire in her room. I reminded her of how fortunate she was, to be taken in by her wealthy relatives —'

'That is certainly true,' I said, as she paused for breath. 'You never let her forget it.'

She was still ranting when I left the room.

I found my father in his study, and felt a momentary qualm as he told me he was at my disposal. Maria and Julia had disappointed him, and I was afraid I was about to do the same, for I knew there had been some truth in my aunt's words, and that he hoped I would marry a wealthier woman than Fanny.

But when I told him that I loved Fanny, and that I would like his permission to marry her, his response was everything I could have wished for.

'To think I once feared this outcome!' he said. 'My feelings are now so very different that I give you my permission willingly, even happily. That is, if Fanny accepts you.'

'I have already asked her and yes, she does.'

'Then I will also add my blessing. I used to want something very different for you, but I am sick of ambitious and mercenary connections, and I am glad you never wanted them. I have been watching the two of you with pleasure for some weeks now, and hoping you would find your natural consolation in each other for all that has passed. Events of recent months have made me prize the sterling good of principle and temper, and there is no one with better principles or a better temper than Fanny.'

I found Fanny in the garden and told her of my father's consent. She smiled happily, and as we walked together down the avenue, under the shade of the arching trees, with the warm air playing about us, I said, 'I have been thinking about Thornton Lacey. I think we will enlarge the garden, then you can grow your geraniums there.'

'Oh, yes, Edmund, I would like that.'

We walked and talked as the sun climbed

in the sky, and had not exhausted our conversation by dinner-time.

After dinner, I told Mama the happy news. There was a moment of alarm when she first heard it, for she said, 'What! Take Fanny from me? Oh, no, I cannot do without Fanny.'

'But she must go with Edmund to Thornton Lacey when they are married,' said my father.

'But what will I do without her?' asked Mama.

'You must ask Susan to stay,' said my father.

Susan's face was glowing. She, too, had found it hard to live at Portsmouth, where there was no order or discipline, and delighted in being at Mansfield Park.

'Oh, yes, Sir Thomas, you are such a comfort to me, you always know what to do,' said Mama. 'Susan, my dear, you will stay with us, will you not? For I do not know what I would do without you.'

Susan said she would be delighted to stay, and by her attentions to Mama after dinner, made herself so indispensable that it seemed as though she had always been with us.

DECEMBER

Sunday 31 December

How much has changed since last year's end. Maria has left her husband and is now living in retirement with Aunt Norris, whilst Rushworth is suing her for divorce; Julia has married, and after an unpromising start, seems to be happy with Yates; Tom has been seriously ill and recovered, and no longer lives only for pleasure but is taking an interest in the estate; Dr Grant has died, so that I have acquired the Mansfield living; and Fanny and I are married.

We are the same, Fanny and I. As I watch her tending the flowers in her garden, or comforting one of our parishioners, or dancing at a ball, or sitting opposite me at dinner, I bless the day she came to Mansfield Park.

ABOUT THE AUTHOR

Amanda Grange lives in Cheshire. She has published many novels, including *Lord Deverill's Secret, Mr. Knightley's Diary, Captain Wentworth's Diary,* and *Harstairs House.* Visit her website at www.amandagrange.com.

We hope you have enjoyed this Large Print book. Other Thorndike, Wheeler, Kennebec, and Chivers Press Large Print books are available at your library or directly from the publishers.

For information about current and upcoming titles, please call or write, without obligation, to:

Publisher
Thorndike Press
295 Kennedy Memorial Drive
Waterville, ME 04901
Tel. (800) 223-1244

or visit our Web site at:

http://gale.cengage.com/thorndike

OR

Chivers Large Print
published by BBC Audiobooks Ltd
St James House, The Square
Lower Bristol Road
Bath BA2 3SB
England
Tel. +44(0) 800 136919
email: bbcaudiobooks@bbc.co.uk
www.bbcaudiobooks.co.uk

All our Large Print titles are designed for easy reading, and all our books are made to last.